THE LAST GIRL

by

Nick Twist

Acknowledgments

This book would not have been possible without the love and support from my readers. Thank you for your patience and being friends more than fans in my journey. I'd also like to thank Holly Gannaway and Faith M. Baldwin for editing this book with their heart and soul in it. Last but not least, thanks to my supporting beta readers who treated this book as one of their own (many more have read it but I missed some names): Greetje Wijnstok, Mel Heeney, Angie Portell Paule, Marlene Ann Paul, Debilee Angel, Shylee Wilde, Dawn House, Claire Louise Michelle Beck and Lauren Kuker for our repeated discussions about characters like the protagonist in my story.

Preface

Some of the events in the book are inspired by actual facts. However, they are used in the spirit of entertainment. Certain details have been altered to fit the story. Please check the afterword for references.

We need stories, not only for entertainment, but for survival.

—Brook Ward

Beginning

Chapter 1

A loud blare in my ears brings me back from the dead. My eyelids stay glued shut in spite of my desire to open them and see where I am. When I finally win the battle, I find myself staring at an inexplicable, murky shade of blue. I watch it morph into a translucent surface with a piercing beam of orange slithering through from above. I have no idea where I am or what I'm looking at. All I know is that I can't breathe.

I want to scream, but salty water fills my lungs. I try to cough but end up choking. Tiny bubbles of air float before my eyes.

My instinct is to swim up toward the orange light. That must be the sun, right? I try to kick for the surface but something is pulling me down, deeper into the abyss below.

I'm not sure I can survive without breathing any longer, and I don't remember how long I've been here. Did I black out? A great darkness drapes upon me, like the curtain at the end of a theatrical play.

No!

I toss and turn in place, wondering why I can't move. Then I realize I'm strapped to something. A seat. It's pulling me under.

My hand reaches behind me, feeling for a seatbelt release. I find it, but I can't unlatch it for some reason.

Panic attacks me when I see a row of sinking seats nearby. It has dead passengers with bulging eyes and open mouths strapped to it.

I see a woman. Old but still alive. Our eyes meet for a fraction of a second. Bubbles pop out of her nostrils as she mouths something to me...

"The girl!"

I watch her sink lower into the abyss.

In fight-or-flight mode, I manage to unstrap myself from my seat. I swim up toward the light, hoping I can reach it before I faint. I paddle past sinking metal parts from above. My left arm is weak. I have to compensate with my right.

The blaring in my ears grows louder. *How can I hear the sound underwater?*

It's a miracle that I find myself splashing my arms out of the water, waiting for life to welcome me back.

My first breath of polluted air feels like a shot of cocaine, jolting me back to existence. I don't know why this is my choice of comparison, but it feels right. My lungs struggle to take the air in and then exhale it in a steady rhythm. My breaths are ragged and my throat is burning from the flames surrounding me. I cough as the intense dose of oxygen almost blinds me. Life is so precious. A wonder like no other.

The image of the world around me seeps in through my eyes. I begin to understand what is going on.

The sky above me is a mist of eternal grey. My neck hurts when I look up, but I need to locate the source of the orange light. It's not the sun. It is fire.

It's all around me, feeding on chunks of metal, rows of seats with burning people strapped to them, feeding on flesh and resulting in a nauseating smell in the air. The image is ominous enough that I feel my arms and legs start to give in; I could easily sink back into the abyss.

I struggle to wrap my arms around the nearest chunk of metal to hang on to. I snap away from the heat it produces. It takes me a while to swim to a log of some sort. I get on it, not sure what it is exactly. A terrible pain hits me in my abdomen, but I am too weak to check it out. I think I have survived a plane crash, but I can't quite remember.

Chapter 2

I keep looking for survivors. I see none.

Lying with my stomach flat on the log, I paddle with weary arms and legs, trying to evade the suffocating smoke all around me. The pain in my lower abdomen is still real. Something is pressing hard against it, but I'm still too weak to twist around and look.

All around me, dead passengers float upon the water. Faces down, arms out to the side, as if this is some kind of a ritual. I shudder, feeling guilty to have survived this. How did I trick such a dreadful fate?

It takes effort to scream for help. My ribcage hurts. My jaw is tense, and my own voice is a stranger to me.

The only reply I get is the fluttering of a few birds in the sky.

My second attempt to call for help is consumed by the loud crackling of fire all around.

I crane my neck, hoping to glimpse something beyond the plane wreck. Thick layers of fog imprison me in all directions, building a wall between me and what is beyond.

My lower lip quivers. "Breathe. Just breathe."

The blaring in my ears returns. It's intolerable, and I'm too weak to cover them with my hands. I wonder if the loud blare is a water pressure issue in my ears. A peculiar emotion overwhelms me whenever it *toots*. A mixture of déjà vu and a premonition of sorts.

My gut feeling urges me to leave this place. I feel like I'm late for something. An imaginary clock is ticking in my head. I shouldn't be here, dealing with the aftermath of a plane crash. I should be...

My head aches. Fear snakes through my veins like slow poison. The panic returns. I want to swim through the fog, to the other side. I want to know what's there.

I start paddling away again. My left arm is almost of no use now. My legs are heavy with pain and exhaustion. I doubt my strength is going to get me past the fog.

Just before I faint, I realize it's not just the plane crash I don't remember. I have no recollection of who I am or what my name is.

Chapter 3

I wake up lying on my back. Sand shapes my spine underneath me. It's cold and uneven. None of my pain has subsided. It's gotten worse, so much I can barely move.

I gaze above at feeble sun rays weakened by a cloudy sky. A breeze tickles my face and passes the sound of ocean waves on the sand to my ears. I'm on a shore?

I lie back a little longer and listen to the steady rhythm of my heart. The hope of my memories coming back too is false. All I know is that I'm grateful beyond words. Surviving a plane crash and being swept to some shore is the kind of thing that only happens in movies. I can't believe it.

Another whiff of air swirls through my salt-stiffened hair. The smell of pine trees, I suppose. I think it is coming from behind.

Slowly, I prop myself up on my elbows and stare at the ocean ahead, doing my best to disregard the pain in my back. I see the raging tides that had spat me here. My left arm feels slightly better now.

The log I used earlier is floating in the shallower water in front of me. I'm only a couple of strides away from the water's edge.

The wreckage isn't visible now, probably hidden behind the fog that looks like thousands of ghosts on the afternoon ocean. It has built a wall between me now and where I had once been. Between my past and present.

Did I swim this far?

My neck aches when I tilt it to peek behind me. I see a fortress pines and palm trees. They stretch forever on both sides. I can't see beyond them. Only the white sands stretching across the distance.

No one else is visible on this shore.

"Help!" I cry out, staring at the clouds. My voice is stronger and clearer, but another swirling breeze whisks my words away.

I feel worse than before.

It's one thing to lose one's memory, and a totally different thing to add loneliness to it. It makes me wonder why the universe helped me survive all of this. Definitely not to end up alone on what looks like a deserted island.

The weight of my fears throws my head back again and forces my eyes to close. I sink deeper into my own abyss of loneliness and lose consciousness for the second time. The blaring horns in my ears won't leave me alone, not even in my dreams.

Chapter 4

It's almost sunset when I wake up again.

This time my mind feels clearer, and I am able to stand up, even if I can hardly keep my balance. I stare at the floating fog one last time. It feels nearer to the shore now, as if it's chasing me. The weather is worsening and colors are dimming all around. Nighttime is coming.

I give it one last shot, trying to remember anything about the plane. My flight's destination. Where I departed. Why I was on it. Where I was going.

Nothing comes to mind. I'm a blank slate.

If I want to survive, I'll have to eat. I'll have to find people. I have to chance the walk through the pines and hope there is a world beyond it. An inhabited place whose residents can help me contact the outside world, so I can remember who I am and what really happened. A safe, inhabited world beyond the trees.

A shattered laugh escapes me before I walk to the forest. I'm laughing at myself. And at my foolishness. Why haven't I checked my pockets for an ID yet?

Frantically, I go from one pocket to another. My jeans are empty. I didn't even realize I was wearing them. Who travels with empty pockets? It feels strange to be curious about oneself.

A few pockets later, and the pain in my lower abdomen strikes again. I realize I've hit something around my waist. It's been pressing against me. I am wearing a fanny pack.

So that's the pain I felt in my abdomen?

Hoping and praying, I reach for my bag to unzip it. Whatever is inside must have been the source of my pain. My hands stop halfway, though. This overwhelming feeling strikes again. *I shouldn't be here. I should be somewhere else, doing something very important.*

My hands are trembling, disobeying my wish to open the fanny pack. So many questions come to mind. Do I have a family? A boyfriend? A husband? Parents? Kids? What do I do for a living? Even scarier, what do I even look like?

What's happening to me? I should be eager to open the bag and know the answers. If I'm lucky, I might find a cell phone. Luckier, I might have reception.

Why am I so reluctant?

I slow my frantic breathing and unzip the bag, but the zipper is stuck against some seaweed. A thin line of water streams out. I stay with it until it gives in. The bag fully unzips.

There is no ID inside. No driver's license. No gym membership card. Neither can I find a picture of me and my family, nor is there a cell phone.

The thing my hands come up with is an e-reader. Kindle, to be precise.

What?

I raise it to eye level and stare as water dribbles from it. A black Kindle with a cracked screen. Part of the plastic is sticking out, so it must be what was pushing against my stomach. Not a clue to who I am. I push its buttons. Of course, it doesn't work.

I'm disappointed, but realize the bag is still heavy. Something else is inside. I reach for it, almost knowing what it is. It's made of metal and it's cold. The kind of thing that raises more questions about who I am. The kind of thing that explains my reluctance and fears to open the bag. The kind of thing no ordinary person carries on a plane.

In my fanny pack, I carry a gun.

Chapter 5

"Breathe," I remind myself. "Whoever you are, just breathe."

I pull out the gun and glare at it, as if it's offending me. My instinct tells me I know how to use it. Funny how I can remember that but not who I am. The way I grip it in my right hand confirms my fears.

How did I manage to get a gun onto a plane?

A surge of anger runs through my veins. I can taste revenge on my dry lips. I have a feeling that the gun will eventually help me remember. The overwhelming feeling returns. A clock is ticking in my head.

Who am I?

I slide my hand into the bottom of the fanny pack, hoping for something definite about my identity, but that's it. Nothing else is inside.

A gun and a Kindle. What an unusual combination.

The sight of the gun is nauseating. I switch my gaze to the Kindle again, trying to get a feeling from it. Do I love reading? If it still worked, I could find out what kind of books interest me. I am betting on nonfiction. Calculating and factual books. Even better, I could have discovered my username or email. A billing address, maybe?

I have to wait to see if this thing still works after the water inside dries out.

I flip the device in my hand again. Still no stickers or—

Wait. There is something on the back. Someone has scratched the back with a sharp instrument.

Zigzags.

No, letters.

Words, actually. Messy and hard to read.

Two words? I tilt my head.

The second one is easier to read. A strange word: *toot.*

The Ts are angled. The second T could be the number 1.

But it's the first word that can't be mistaken. A word that worries me about my past more and even more.

The first word is *kill.*

Chapter 6

Kill Toot?

Oh, that is so helpful. Thank you very much.

So the words on the back of the Kindle are as threatening as the gun itself. Who said words can't kill?

I decide to tuck the Kindle back in and pretend I didn't read the word *kill* on its back. Then I return my gaze to the gun in the other hand.

It's not a heavy gun, I notice. It's smaller than what I'd expect a gun to be. I need to know if it's loaded, and I have no doubt I know how to do that. But something about it distracts me from that thought. I tilt it in my hand and inspect the outside. It's not hard to notice it has the same zigzag on one side, from the same trembling hand, like that of a scared child.

I bring it closer to my eyes, almost afraid to bend over toward it. The same words appear: *kill toot*. They're much smaller here. Much more cramped, with no space to finish the letters properly.

My heart starts racing. I don't resist it. Let it express how fucked up and confused I am.

Did I say fucked up? Is that the kind of language I normally use?

It occurs to me that my grip has tightened on the gun. My knuckles are white, and my lower lip is curved with tension. My jaw aches from grinding my teeth. Anger and revenge coat the interiors of my soul.

I loosen up, as much as possible, tuck the gun next to the Kindle, and zip the bag. My hands are mechanical. My mind is absent. My eyes are fixated on the darkness veiling the forest ahead. Suddenly, I don't care about the plane crash so much. The unsure feelings stirred by the words on both the gun and the Kindle have possessed my every bone.

The sound of crashing waves behind me grows louder as the sun says its last goodbyes. Staring at the pines ahead, I am stuck between two strangers: the past of an angry and misty ocean behind me, and the future of a nameless girl with a gun and a Kindle.

Girl?

I still don't know what I look like. My hands are pale and the parts I can see from my hair are brunette. I don't feel like a *girl*, though. I am definitely an older girl. Late twenties, maybe. I've seen shit in this life. I'm sure of that.

And I could be hallucinating. No better time for a girl to lose her mind than when no one's around.

This is going nowhere. I step forward toward the pines. I have to find someone. Anyone. Closer to the trees, I reach to rub my aching neck and relieve some of the pain. There is something wrapped around it. A necklace.

It's a short one. I take it off and look at it. Silver. Ordinary. Nothing special at all, but...

Finally, I think I know what my name is.

June.

The design is simple and carved, not scratched or zigzagged. It's cheap but done professionally. Custom-made. It doesn't strike me as something you can purchase in a store.

"June?" My name is a stranger to me.

I keep staring at the necklace for a while, then grip it and tuck it in my back pocket. I tiptoe with caution into the forest until darkness surrounds me in every direction. I am not here for the darkness; I am here for the light beyond.

I delve deeper and mentally pat myself on the shoulder. *Come on, June. We can do this.*

Chapter 7

Inside the forest, I feel like an actress, role-playing an identity I'm not quite familiar with. I wonder if a woman with a gun should be as intimidated by the darkness as I am. The canopy of curving trees shadows my existence as my heart drums with every step into the muddy grounds.

The forest is buried six feet deep in silence. I can't hear animals. No scurrying squirrels or singing birds. No woodpeckers in the trees. Everything is consumed by the scent of abandonment. I don't know why, but I think I have been a friend of such a scent for years.

Plain nothingness stirs heavily in the air. It stirs layers of loneliness upon me, more than an amnesiac can handle. All I want is to meet another human being. Isolation and solitude with a gun in my hand strikes me as suicidal—again, something I might know about?

I hear something. A companion? Not an enemy, but not what I expected either. I hear a baby's cries.

"Focus, June," I whisper to myself. "You could be imagining this."

The cries are faint and veiled by recurring breezes from the sea. Something about the cries reminds me of the woman I saw underwater.

I change my route, following the invisible footprints of baby's tears. It's hard to discern direction among the entangled tree branches. I realize that it's not all silence. I can actually hear the faint waves of the ocean splashing in the distance. It reminds me that I can't go back. My only hope for survival is holding on to my sanity for as long as I can.

I keep following the baby cries, but then a louder sound takes over. An engine. A vehicle. I hear the clear blare of a horn. Instantly, I change routes and start running in its direction.

Panting, I follow the new sound. Even better—this isn't just sound. I glimpse pools of light, cutting through the dense trees.

Closer, the beams of light thicken. Hope is welcoming in its arms.

"Come on, June," I tell myself. "We can do this."

After reaching the edge of the forest, I stop. Dozens of men are talking outside. Only men. More sounds of engines, too. Panting, I carefully take a peek out, watching from behind a thick tree. The scene takes a few seconds to sink in. I am looking at a vast habitat of trailer-like houses with military men walking all around.

Parting branches, I now see the vehicles. Not just one. The place is swarming with Jeeps driven by soldiers. A military base.

One soldier frantically radios his superiors in English. In the Jeep closest to the forest, soldiers are talking about some rescue mission. I can't make out the details of their conversation, but I come to understand that not all of them are Americans. There is a notable diversity of ethnicities. Their uniform isn't of the American military. It's a dull shade of grey with no insignia. I can't even see an American flag anywhere.

I wonder if I have been trained to think this way. Normally, a girl would cry for help and show herself, right?

But I need help. I need to drink and eat and get medical care. I need a connection to the outside world to learn about my plane crash and who I am. Fuck it. I part a few more branches and step forward, about to call for help.

But then my feet stiffen. They disobey me, as if they know something that I don't. Something in me doesn't want the soldiers to see the fanny pack. Come to think of it, I wouldn't know how to explain it.

My speculations are interrupted by a Jeep driving my way. Light blinds my eyes. They have spotted me while I'm still holding the bag.

Chapter 8

"We found one!" The soldier next to the driver points in my direction. "There, right behind the pines."

I am not sure whether it's instinct or planning, but I gently drop the gun and bag behind me then step forward with my hands up. The Jeep screeches to a halt. Soldiers hop out as rain suddenly pours down on me.

"Are you all right, ma'am?" a soldier asks. He looks concerned. He can't be the enemy. I look silly with my hands up, like I've done something wrong. "She's shivering. Bring me a blanket!"

I didn't know I was shivering. In fact, my teeth are chattering. I lower my hands, and the soldiers wrap me up in a blanket. I close my eyes and enjoy its warmth for a moment, realizing how much I'd kill for sleep right now.

"Did you survive the plane crash, ma'am?" the young soldier asks, rubbing his hand over my blanket.

"What?" I grimace.

"The plane." He points up. "We saw it crash into the ocean but couldn't get to it due to the bad weather."

I nod. I prefer not to talk much now, not sure of myself or how I'd be treated if my true identity were revealed—whoever I turn out to be. I wish I'd buried the bag, not just dropped it behind me.

"Are there others?" the soldier asks, lowering his head, trying to look me in the eyes.

I shy away. Eyes are windows to the soul. What if his stare reaches too deep and exposes me?

"Others?" I shrug. "I think I heard a baby crying in the forest."

"That's impossible. She's in shock," another soldier says. "We should get her to Ward Nine. Interrogate her later."

"Did you see the baby yourself?" the kinder soldier says.

"I—I'm not sure."

"I told you she's in shock!"

"It's okay." The soldier pats me on the shoulder. "You're a brave girl." He guides me to his Jeep. "Boys! We have a survivor."

"How did she survive?" the skeptical one asks. He has a diagonal scar across his right cheek. "Did she swim in such a raging ocean? She's a woman, for God's sake."

"Shut up, Hecker," the other soldier says, helping me sit. "I know women who could kick your armored butt so hard you'd need to visit a proctologist for the rest of your life."

The other soldiers laugh.

I sit in the back of the Jeep. Hecker asks the soldier if he should drive. It turns out his name is Ryan. Two other soldiers squeeze me like a sandwich in the back seat. The Jeep staggers up a hill toward wherever this Ward Nine is. Hecker's driving is reckless. I feel like I am going to vomit.

"You have a name, miss?" Ryan turns back to me from the passenger seat.

"June." I spit the name out instantly. I pull out my necklace and show it to him, as if I need proof my name is June. Something tells me I shouldn't tell them about my amnesia.

"She doesn't look like a June to me." Hecker glares at me in the mirror. My heart sinks into my feet, but he ends up pointing at the cloudy sky above. I want to ask what time of year it is, but it would expose my situation.

I look up as rain starts to pour heavily. For a moment, I'm afraid I will drown in it, as if death isn't done with me, as if it's going to hunt me down until it kills me, like everyone else on the plane.

Chapter 9

"Hang on, June," Ryan shouts, hanging tight to the Jeep's door. "I'll take care of you."

I mouth a silent thank you and nod in appreciation. With the two silent soldiers on both sides, and the heavy rain, it's impossible to take another look around.

"You're American?" Hecker asks, gripping the wheel.

"Yes." I am not sure, but my accent and instinct suggest it.

Hecker's skeptical face changes. He squints in the mirror, taking another look at me. I remind myself that I haven't seen a single flag on the island. Is Hecker uncomfortable with my being American, or does he not believe me?

I lower my head and pull the blanket tighter over my shoulders.

"Stop asking her questions," Ryan says. "We agreed to get her to the ward first."

"Major Red will want to know a lot about her," Hecker retorts.

"Leave the major to me. I will handle him."

"Yeah? How are you going to explain us driving her up the hill without covering her eyes?"

Ryan frowns then rubs his chin. "June," he says. "Could I ask you a favor?"

I nod.

"Whatever happens, don't look west until we reach Ward Nine," Ryan says. "West would be your left side. Understood?"

"I won't," I say, wondering what kind of request that is. "I just need to rest and sleep."

"Good girl," Ryan says.

Now that we made a deal, I am curious about the west side. Should I care? This is a military base. It makes sense if they have secrets.

When we reach the ward, I see it looks like a military compound. Hecker halts the car and Ryan helps me down. There is a big sign hung above a double steel door with heavy bolts. It reads *W9*. The door and sign look old. I mean, like fifty-year-old construction or something.

Ryan says his goodbyes and assures me that they will take care of me inside. I'm escorted by the other two soldiers into a long hallway, crowded with busy soldiers. Same as the outside, the interior is old, like from a 1950s movie or something.

Further in, one of the soldiers guides me toward a doorless room. Apparently this is where I will be staying.

"A nurse will arrive and help you out," he explains.

The feeling of comfort and safety relaxes me. It's hard to believe that I made it here. I plan to sit on the bed and wait for the nurse, but the pillow tempts me. I rest my weary head on it, my body curled into a fetal position.

I see the nurse entering the room. Though it's not a nurse. It's a male soldier in a blue coat and Crocs. My eyes twitch as I realize I haven't seen a single woman so far. Slowly I find myself passing out.

Chapter 10

The loud blaring jolts me up and awake again.

I sit straight up on my bed. How long have I been asleep? I run my trembling hand over my sweating face and look around. It takes me a moment to collect my recent memories. A plane crash. Survival. The shore. The bag. The Kindle. The gun. The forest and the baby's cries. The soldiers picking me up and bringing me to Ward Nine to this room without a door.

A blanket covering the opening of my room does give me a little privacy, but does not keep out the voices of the soldiers outside. I let out a long sigh and realize someone has changed me into cleaner clothes.

It's a lime-green outfit, like a hospital gown. I don't feel good about it, though. The thought of a male nurse changing my clothes while I was asleep does not make me comfortable.

I can still glimpse soldiers' shadows from beneath the blanket.

I stretch my arms, and every part of my body aches. I also notice an IV is connected to my right arm. Food and drink are set on the metallic tray on a wheeled table nearby. Like Ryan promised, they are taking care of me.

I guess I shouldn't panic about being the only girl in a kingdom of males after all. Their intention seems honest and genuine. It's me who is paranoid about things I can't even remember. All my worries might end up being figments of my imagination.

My feet feel a bit numb when I get off the bed and touch the floor. A few images attack my vision. I can't make them out. They're blurry and distant, and none of them are of a plane crash. I am hoping it's a good sign. Maybe it'll all come back to me soon.

"Just breathe, June," I find myself saying. Why do I keep saying this?

Maybe there is a logical explanation for everything. Something tells me this isn't true. I think the soldiers on this island aren't supposed to know who I am. If I can only discover who that someone inside me is...

Which reminds me—I haven't taken a look at myself yet.

I rip the IV out, not caring about any blood or wounds, then semi-limp to the only real door in my room. A bathroom.

Inside, I close the door behind me and enjoy the privacy. The place is narrow and small, but clean. A bathtub, a toilet, and a mirror over a sink. Just what I am looking for. I rest my hands on the edges of the sink and stare at myself in the mirror.

I have black, disheveled, short hair with undercut sides. One side is slightly shorter. Super blunt lines and jagged edges. A bold cut. It comes across as a rebellious statement more than a haircut. I wear no earrings, but my ears are drilled with holes. My shoulders are narrow. I'm fairly short. Five feet five, I'm guessing. Pale white skin sucks the color from the small yellow light bulb overhead. My eyes are also pale. Blue, but pale. Some faint freckles on my face. Not many, though. Without the haircut, I'd look like my ancestors are Irish. Maybe Germans. Nothing special about me, really. If I were in a movie, I wouldn't survive a plane crash. I'd be that helpless girl sitting next to the main door. The unlucky girl that would take a kick in the butt and then get thrown out in the air and die.

Yet my left bandaged arm does make me look badass—in a bad way. Looking at it reminds me how much it hurts, like thousands of needles and pins hurting at once. I can't quite remember if it'd been bandaged before the soldiers found me and brought me to Ward Nine. Everything is so blurry to me.

I was also right about my age. Late twenties. Give or take.

I lean forward, looking into the mirror, wondering if a closer look would tell me the truth about myself.

"Seriously, June," I say to my reflection, "what is the gun for? And who the heck is this *toot* you want to kill?"

Chapter 11

I walk back into my room and dismiss the food on the tray. There is a window next to my bed. I am curious if I can get a better look at the island from here. The window is foggy and shows condensation on the inside. I wipe it with the back of my hand but can't see clearly due to the heavy mist outside.

But I can make out a few things.

I can see the forest from here. Parts of it. It's dense and huge enough that it blocks the view of the sea. Before it, I see the military base where the soldiers picked me up. The base looks like what you'd see in action movies, except that it's on an island. Nothing special.

I wonder where on the island Ward Nine is. It puzzles me why I was asked not to look west. I guess I keep forgetting it's none of my business. The west side is obscured by the angle, anyway.

"Miss June?"

I turn and look. It's the nurse from earlier.

"I see you haven't eaten." He points at the tray on the table.

"I was about to," I say. "Thank you."

"You're welcome." He is probably in his twenties and looks a bit shy. "The weather is horrible outside."

"I noticed. How long have I slept?"

"Six hours. Three of them were good sleep."

"Oh? How can you tell?"

"You stopped saying 'toot,'" he says. "At first, I thought you were saying 'food.' Then I realized it was 'toot,' whatever that means."

"I said that one word—nothing else?"

The soldier shrugs. "You also said something else. 'Kill.'"

"Ah." I run my hand through my hair and let out an awkward laugh. "'Kill toot.'"

He is neither angry nor sympathetic. Suspicious, but in a polite and considering way. Why did my damn mouth expose me in my dreams?

"So where can I find Ryan?" I ask.

"Sergeant Ryan?"

"Yes."

"He won't be here for a while."

"I need to talk to him. He said he would take care of me. I need to find a way back home."

"Oh, that," he says. "I'm sorry to inform you, ma'am, that it's unlikely."

"What is unlikely?"

"We can't even fly our own choppers out in this weather." He points at the window. "So you will not be able to leave the island for a while."

"But you can contact land, right?"

"Not even that. The weather interferes with outside communication."

"That's not possible. You must have a radio or something." I have no idea how this works, but I can't imagine the soldiers are unable to contact their families all over the world, at any time and under every circumstance. "There must be a way—"

"Major Red can explain these matters to you when you meet him," he cuts in. "He understands your situation, that you must have lost your passport in the crash. Otherwise, we never allow strangers to enter the island."

"Major Red will help me?"

"Certainly. He will do his best to get you back home when the weather gets better."

I let out a sigh, realizing how tense I was. "That's a relief. Thank you. So when do I get to meet him?"

"First, you will have to fill out this form." The soldier hands me a file with papers clipped together.

"What is that?" I grimace.

"Just formalities. Please write down your full name, where you live, occupation, address, and so forth."

Chapter 12

The shy soldier respects my wish when I ask him to give me a few minutes alone to fill out the form. I am left sitting with a pen in my hand, gripping it tightly, as if I am about to stab someone.

What am I supposed to write? Would it be better to confess my amnesia now? Still, my damn inner voice disagrees. If I tell them everything, will I include the gun?

I gaze out the window again, reminding myself that this island has its own secrets. I have no idea who they work for or why they don't wear a specific insignia—let alone their request not to look west. Maybe it's better for each of us to keep our own secrets.

On the other hand, what if my wish comes true and we can establish outside communications? What if my identity causes more conflicts?

Who are you, June? Why are you so paranoid?

I take the form with me to the bathroom. It's as if I can't think straight in the room, knowing it's not completely private. I lock the door behind me and sit on the edge of the bathtub.

"Think, June. Think." I bury my head in my hands.

Taking my time, I decide that my instincts aren't helping. If I forge this form and they later discover I am lying, things will get complicated. I doubt military folk tolerate lies. Never mind this feeling I have about not telling them—confessing my amnesia will at least show my good intentions in a place where I might be the only female present.

I think I am losing my mind. What if I'm not as dangerous as I think? What if I just escaped an asylum or something? But how would I have been on a plane if that were true?

I stand up, stretch my arms, and take another look at my reflection in the mirror. I feel as if my reflection is talking to me. The June in the mirror looks more collected than my perception of myself.

"I have to fake an excuse not to fill out the form and meet with this Major Red and see how he can help me go home," I tell the mirror.

My reflection doesn't reply, but a sudden noise outside does.

Soldiers seem to be pounding away from my room, shouting and cursing. I pull the door open and carefully walk toward the blanket. Just when I am about to pull it back to look outside, I glimpse something on the floor. A white envelope.

Seeing it makes me forget about the noises in the corridors.

I kneel down and pick it up. I wonder if it's a good idea to open it. Why do I think it's for me? Did some soldier drop it while spying on me?

I realize that I've already opened the envelope while thinking. It reeks of some kind of oil. A black, greasy oil that slowly seeps through my fingers. I reach inside the envelope and come out with a note.

Words are written in the same black oil. It looks like someone has dipped a quill in oil instead of ink to write it. It's a short sentence. One I can't comprehend at first. When I do, I stand there frozen for a moment.

I dash outside. Most of the corridor is empty, except for a few soldiers gathered in the far end.

Advancing with careful steps, a soldier stops me.

"Please go back into your room," the soldier requests. "We had a car accident. It's nothing, really."

I nod and retreat without turning around. Whatever the accident, I have a feeling it's the work of the person who sent me the note, to keep the soldiers busy while they entered my room.

Who could it be? How is it possible he knows about the things he mentioned in the note? I go back and sit on my bed, staring at the writing. It reads:

Kill Manfred Toot. Trust no one.

Chapter 13

When the nurse returns, I am back in the bathroom again, ripping the note into pieces. I flush it down the toilet, feeling like a spy burning a letter after reading.

"Miss June," he calls out. "Are you ready?"

"For what?" I fake a vomiting sound.

"Major Red wants to see you. Are you all right?"

"Yes. Just a sec."

"Of course. I'll be waiting."

I take a minute, trying to remember if the name Manfred Toot means anything to me. Manfred Toot. Such an unforgettable name, it seems. And who sent me this note? Does that mean there is someone on this island who knows who I am? How can I find them?

I grip the door handle, not sure what my next move is. "I'm ready. Shall we?" I say when I step out.

"Have you filled out the form?"

"I did," I lie.

"Could you pass it over, please?"

"I'd prefer to show it to Major Red myself."

The soldier hesitates for a second. "Why not? Please put this raincoat on, and wear those boots. It's messy outside."

I do as he instructs me, and we leave the room.

The corridor is bustling with soldiers again. I inspect each and every one carefully, wishing I could figure out the note's sender. Then I prefer not to make eye contact at all. It's obvious that I am not welcome here. Only the nurse and Ryan don't mind my presence. It would make sense if the soldiers' stares were out of lust in an all-male facility. That's not the case, though. I have the feeling they want me to fuck off and leave this island.

"So Major Red is in charge of the island?" I ask as we leave the building.

"Yes, ma'am."

"May I ask what is happening on the island?"

"Can't say, ma'am. It's above my pay grade. Please step inside."

He shows me into another Jeep, and I climb in.

"I'm sure you've been told not to look west, ma'am. Right?"

"Yes." I sit in the back, squashed between two other soldiers, like before.

This time the ride is short, right between clusters of L-shaped tents, barely visible in the mist. I still haven't seen one woman anywhere.

The Jeep stops.

The soldier ushers me into Ward Six, a larger building among the others. It's still old, but with a more exquisite style. I follow him into a clean corridor. He shows me into a large meeting room, and instructs me to wait for Major Red.

Chapter 14

The room is huge. It's exquisitely furnished, air conditioned, with an oval meeting table at one end. Not only is the furniture impressive, but it's also Victorian—or at least an imitation of the style.

Hands behind my back, I catch a row of framed certificates on the wall. I'm surprised they are medical certificates, not related to the military. All acquired by Major John Red. When I near the wall for a better look, a voice from behind stops me.

"Miss June." A deep voice resonates in the room. The authoritative voice of someone who is not used to opposition.

I turn and gaze at the massive figure of Major Red. He has a broad chest and big hands. His face is rugged, his wrinkles stiff lines of hardened, sunburned flesh. He wears a slightly different version of the grey uniform everyone wears on the island. No insignia.

"Yes," I say, feeling the need to tiptoe around like a little girl.

The major doesn't show interest or empathy. He strolls toward his desk, hands behind his back, then sits. He peeks at a few documents in front of him as if I am not in the room. An uncomfortable moment later, he raises his icy blue eyes to look at me.

His gaze is sharp and penetrating. He sizes me up from top to bottom. Then he suddenly stands up again and walks around me to a window. I watch him violently pull the shutters down. A deep breath fills his nostrils. Then he closes his eyes to calm himself down.

I watch him return to his desk. It occurs to me that perhaps the window was looking west, but I can't be sure. Major Red doesn't feel the need to explain himself.

Another silent minute passes before he speaks again. "I assume you've been told we've lost all communication with the outside world."

"Yes, but—"

"Which means we'll have you on the island for a few more days."

"I thought military bases have ways to contact—"

"We don't. We're not an ordinary...military base, as you put it. So don't call us that."

"I didn't mean to—"

"I'm not fond about having you here, Miss June." He taps his fingers on the desk. "A woman among my soldiers is quite a challenge. But the tides of the Atlantic Ocean have sent you over."

At least I know my plane crashed into the Atlantic Ocean. Was I maybe flying from New York to London? Does this mean the island is in the middle of the Atlantic?

"So I have a few questions—" I begin.

"I have only one." His gaze sharpens. "Have you filled out the form?"

I am hesitant to answer, having not decided what to tell him yet. I thought we'd be discussing if we can contact the outside world first.

"I thought so." He pulls open a drawer next to him.

"Thought so?" I tilt my head.

"I knew you would not be able to fill out the form." His gaze is so tense. My heartbeat quickens. I have a feeling he knows more about me than I do. Is it possible he knows about the oil-stained message? "You have a lot of explaining to do, Miss June."

"Explaining? Like what?"

"How is it possible you're the sole survivor of the crashed plane? When we saw it fall over the island with an engine in flames, we were sure there'd be no survivors."

"I don't know how. I guess I am lucky." I'm trying to imagine the scene of the soldiers watching the plane crash from the beginning.

"Not lucky. It sounds like a miracle to me. Tell me what you remember."

The hardest question of all. I try to summarize it: "I woke up underwater, strapped to my seat. Somehow, I managed to break free and swim up and hang on to a log, probably a broken piece of the plane. It was a horrifying experience. I don't really want to talk about it."

“Are you expecting me to believe that?”

“Why wouldn’t you? I’m standing here in front of you.”

“But I have no proof you were on the plane.”

“Major Red, why would I lie about this? How do you think I arrived here?”

“Never mind. Tell me what happened next.”

“I passed out on the log and woke up on shore.”

“That simple, eh?” He taps the desk again, glancing at the drawer.

“It’s a miracle, like you said.” I nod. “I feel like Robinson Crusoe.”

“You know what the odds are, you surviving the plane crash and the tides spitting you out on shore?”

“Slim to none, but it’s the truth.”

“Do you know how far the island is from the plane crash? It’s impossible that you’ve made it this far.”

“Major Red, what do you want me to say?”

“The truth.”

“I just did.”

“Try once more.”

“What is that supposed to mean?” I ask.

“This is what it’s supposed to mean.” He points at the drawer next to him. Slowly, he pulls out my gun and Kindle and throws them on the desk before me.

Chapter 15

I realize I can't take my eyes off the gun on the major's desk. It's as if I am hoping a longer stare will refresh my memory. I think it's time to tell him all that happened—in detail.

"Did someone send you to spy on the island?" he says.

I grimace. Not only did I not expect that, but it complicates my inner conflict. Am I actually some kind of spy or assassin sent to kill Manfred Toot?

"No one sent me, Major Red." I fist a hand behind my back. "I survived a plane crash."

"Always fly with a gun on board?" His laugh comes out like a bark. It's not just mockery. I feel disdain—hatred? "Who are you? Tell the truth."

"The truth is..." Am I being paranoid about the vibe he is giving me? I make sure he sees me staring back. "I don't remember."

"Wow." He clamps one hand over the other. His hands are thick. "And yet another lie."

"It's the truth." My voice pitches up. "I woke up underwater and couldn't remember who I am or what happened to me. I don't even know what my destination was or what month it is. Certainly not why I carry a gun."

"Oh?" He leans forward on the desk and grunts. "Then how do you know your name is June?"

I show him the necklace, which I had wrapped around my wrist. My steps are reluctant when I approach the desk. "I was wearing this when I woke up on shore."

Major Red flips it in his hand. Closer to him, I notice a foul smell of sweat. He takes his time to inspect it. Front and back. He weighs it upon his palm. Shakes it. Lifts it up near his ear and listens to it. Then he runs his dirty hands upon it, wipes it with the back of his hand, grimaces and squints, and pulls out a magnifier to check out the name.

My breathing slows as he takes his time. The thorough examination will prove nothing is wrong with the necklace. He should believe me now.

Major Red smiles bitterly, showing his uneven teeth. "On shore, you say?"

"Yes." I nod.

"Were you wearing it at the crash site?"

I shrug. "I think so."

"And you had no ID in your pockets? No ticket or passport? No documents about where you were flying?"

I shake my head.

"Only a Kindle and a gun?"

"And the necklace." I point at it.

His gaze darts back to the Kindle. "We fixed it."

"You did?"

"One of my soldiers is a tech geek. He brought it back to life. Only it's locked with a password." He taps it with his thumb. "You know the password?"

I glare at him. "I. Don't. Remember." I sigh. "Look, I can still try. Maybe I'll remember."

He doesn't respond immediately. He rubs his chin, not taking his eyes off me, checking me out from top to bottom again. I feel stripped and naked. "Are you telling me you have no idea where we are?"

I can't understand how this man thinks. The order of questions doesn't make sense. "Somewhere in the Atlantic Ocean," I say. "You just told me—and I remember now that one of the soldiers said something about the ocean."

"That's it? You have no idea what this island is?"

Chapter 16

"What?" I say. "I am not sure what you mean."

"Never mind. What about the gun?" He holds it up.

"I told you, I don't know anything about it."

"You don't know how to shoot it?"

My right eye twitches. "Actually, I do. But this doesn't mean—"

"Then it must be yours," he says. "But you are sure you don't know anything else about this gun?"

"Should I?" I stare at it.

"It's a Beretta." He waves it in the air. "A relatively small gun, suitable for women. Some men use it because it's light and easy to carry. Famous for having been James Bond's first choice of weapon before they stopped him using it. A great weapon to smuggle on a plane."

I don't have the logic to defend myself at the moment. I fold my arms in front of me and listen.

"Did you read the scratched message on its side?" Major Red says.

"Message?" I squint at the gun, pretending I know nothing about it.

Major Red smirks. He makes no effort to angle the gun and show me the message. "Don't pretend you don't know, Miss June."

"Know what?" I straighten up.

He almost whispers, "Maybe you shouldn't speak in your dreams. It's a bad habit."

I purse my lips. Of course the shy soldier told him. *What a fucking stupid move, June.* The Manfred Toot message that I flushed down the toilet made me so paranoid. Now I'm deep in shit.

"Don't worry," Major Red says. "I didn't expect you to tell the truth. You've been lying since you've arrived."

I am Pinocchio's long and exposed nose. I have no truth to tell, and the lies I do tell are all the truth I have.

"However, I'm not sure you knew about this sign on the gun." This time, he angles the gun to show me.

I look. First I don't see it, but then I do. It's too small. I'm not sure it's intentional. It's an inverted red cross.

"I hadn't noticed it," I say. "What about it?"

"It makes this gun one of only a hundred of the same type."

"It does?"

"Manufactured in the eighties but by a secret society of soldiers."

My left cheek numbs. I wonder if it's a nervous tic I have. It's followed by a shot of pain in my bandaged left arm. "What kind of soldiers?"

"The most evil in the world," he evades my question. "They've never been caught. The guns disappeared, until fourteen years ago."

I blink. "Fourteen years?"

"When they reappeared again in small American towns."

"So they *are* American?"

"On passport, yes. It's complicated. They were men who knew no mercy."

The numbing spreads to my other cheek. I have nothing to say—do I see a suppressed smirk on Major Red's sealed lips?

"It's a disgraceful old story," he says. "It being old is the only reason I don't expect you to know the gun's significance."

"That's a start," The numbing subsides slowly.

"It doesn't mean I believe you. Whoever gave it to you and persuaded you to infiltrate my island, didn't tell you about it."

Back to square one. "Did they have a name?"

"Not that I know of," Major Red continues. "There were rumors they called themselves the SS or SSS.

"Secret Society of Soldiers." I speak my mind.

"Could be. The sign on the gun is their mission statement."

"Mission statement?"

"They hunted and killed certain individuals," he says matter-of-factly.

"What individuals?"

Major Red takes a deep breath. A diagonal cut across his face wrinkles and deepens as he does. "The sect had their own beliefs. You could say they hated certain ethnicities."

"Racists?"

"Worse."

I say nothing. It's hard to imagine I have anything to do with this secret society. True, I have no memory, but I don't see it. The gun isn't evidence enough. I could have bought it from anywhere.

"I'm curious, Miss June." He drops the gun with a thud on the desk. "Either you're some smart terrorist, playing games with me, or you've been dragged into a hell of a complicated story that I need to figure out."

"Believe me, I'm dying to know who I am."

"Believing is the act of speculating or assuming," he says. "I only deal with facts. Which means that, so far, I don't believe a word you've said. However, I will send you to one of our doctors to confirm your amnesia." He glares at me again. "You'd better not be lying to me."

Actually, I have nothing against the idea of seeing a doctor. Now that I don't have much to hide from Major Red—except for the Toot note from under the door—a doctor can help me remember. Whoever I turn out to be, I will have to deal with it.

"I'm looking forward to meeting your doctor," I say.

Major Red summons a soldier to usher me out. A few seconds of mutual staring precedes the soldier's arrival. It's like we want to see each other's soul. It disturbs me that I want to know about him as much as I want to know about myself. I turn around and follow the soldier.

"Miss June," Major Red calls after me. "You really don't know what month it is?"

I sigh and turn to face him again. "I told you, *I don't remember.*"

"It's the fifteenth of *June*, Miss June." Major Red hurls my necklace in the air. I am too stunned to play catch, and let it fall at my feet. That's why he was laughing at me earlier.

Chapter 17

"Could I be crazy?" I ask the young doctor with the cute face and longish blonde hair.

The soldier left after showing me to the small clinic in Ward Six. I seem to have entered and lain on the couch, trying not to think about my conversation with Major Red. I'm not really sure how I came here. It's as if there was a time lapse. I'm not sure if that is a symptom of amnesia.

"I mean, maybe I am just imagining all of this?" I say.

"First of all, call me Suffolk, Dr. Alan Suffolk." He offers a tanned and firm hand.

"Smith," I mock myself, not taking his hand. "June Smith."

Dr. Suffolk smiles. He knows my last name isn't Smith.

"In the month of January, my name is January Smith. May Smith in May."

He has a great smile. White teeth. Nothing to hide. "You're not crazy. You're a sole survivor of a plane crash. It's not an easy thing to get through. We'll figure it out."

I lie back on the couch, staring at the ceiling.

"That's better," says the doctor. "Just relax."

"You're not a soldier, are you?"

"I'm not in a position to say." He tucks his hands into the pockets of his white coat. "You must've heard that phrase a few times by now."

"'*I'm not in a position to say*' and '*this is above my pay grade,*' yes, I have. The secretive island where you're not supposed to look west." I roll my eyes.

I think the sight of Dr. Suffolk is a good prescription for a better mood. Maybe I am just too tired from all the confusion, and being inappropriately flirtatious.

"We don't usually accommodate strangers, but we'll take care of you until you go home." He pats my shoulder. "So tell me, are you famous?"

I chuckle. The back of my neck hurts. "I can't remember who I am, and you're asking if I am famous?"

"Humor me."

"Is this a trick question? You think I am lying too?"

"Absolutely not. You look familiar."

"That's a relief. I guess it means I am not invisible. Do you think you can wrack your brain and remember me? It'd be nice to know who I am."

"I can't. It's like Deja Vu. I have no idea how," he sits down beside me, taking my hand in his warm palms.

"Wow, you're insane, just like me." I chuckle.

"Like I said, you're not insane. Amnesia is a common consequence of surviving a plane crash."

"Really?"

"Of course. Think of it like a defense mechanism."

"What?"

"Your brain could have forgotten on purpose."

"Can someone do that?"

"Not you. Your brain. You and your brain aren't the same thing, especially after a traumatic experience."

"Why?"

"You have any idea what you went through in the crash?" he asks. "The deaths you saw? The horror of the plane sinking? I was told you were strapped to your seat underwater. All of this is shocking, and you could easily end up with chronic PTSD."

He continues babbling, but I can't hear him anymore. A thought blocks his voice from reaching my head. *How did I escape the seat underwater?* It seems impossible, unless there was divine intervention.

"Breathe, June." His words pull me back into reality. "Your brain might be trying to protect you by making you forget."

"Forget the events of the plane crash?"

"And the events that led to the crash."

"If my brain forgets on purpose, it has to be something bigger than just death all around me," I say. "Something on that plane. Something scarier that I wouldn't be able to live with."

Dr. Suffolk takes his time to think, then says, "You have a wild imagination."

We both laugh. It's the first time I've felt human on this godforsaken island. "So how long will I keep forgetting?" I say.

"It shouldn't be long. That's what we'll be trying to figure out. Now let me ask you a bit of a scary question. Are you ready?"

"Not sure."

"This might trouble you. I am sorry, but I have to. It might help you remember."

"If you say so..."

"Close your eyes, please."

I do, wondering why I feel safe with him. I would have never closed my eyes in Major Red's presence.

"Do you remember if you have a family, June?"

Chapter 18

Dr. Suffolk's question hits me like ice thrown from a bucket. It freezes the muscles in the back of my neck. My shoulders tense.

Do I have a family? Don't most people have one? "I have no idea."

"We'll need to work on a better answer to this question," Dr. Suffolk says.

"Don't you think it's out of my hands?"

"I can help you remember, but you have to open up to me."

"I'm trying."

"Let's try this another way."

"How?"

"Can you go back and focus on the plane crash, please? The little nuggets of memories you still have."

My body twists and turns in place. My belly hurts again. Did the gun damage this area of my body? The pain in my bandaged arm intensifies. My breathing is shallow and the blaring of a horn sounds distantly in my ears.

"I'm sorry to make you go through this," Dr. Suffolk says. "But like I said, we have to."

"Okay." I nod, ignoring the pain. "I'll do my best."

"Are you remembering?"

"A little."

"Don't tell me the details, just focus on my words."

"Which are?"

"Is your family on the plane with you?"

For a moment, I think I'm going to bite my tongue. It's a horrible thought. I can't bring myself to imagine it.

"*Any* of your family members?"

"I—"

"A husband?"

"Not sure?"

"A mother?"

"I don't think so."

"Father?"

"No."

"Child?"

For some reason, words don't come out of my mouth.

"It's okay if you don't remember," he says. "We had to try."

"Why was that important?" I'm still not sure why I haven't answered the last question.

"If you had loved ones on the plane then you must have been worried about them when the crash occurred," he says, almost whispering, hypnotizing, soothing. "Since you still remember a few things right after the crash, I was trying to ignite feelings you may have dismissed in your struggle for survival."

"I've never thought about this. In their darkest hour, do people save themselves or their loved ones first?"

"That depends," he says. "In general, a person has to save themselves first, so they can then help their loved ones. Survival is a deeply rooted instinct. Love for loved ones is a close second, unless it's a situation where you have to sacrifice yourself to save the person you love."

I sigh. "So, I had no family members on the plane, I suppose."

"I'm not sure."

"What do you mean?"

"You didn't answer about not having a child on board."

I can't remember. I am scared. I feel like I am going to vomit. I don't like this. Maybe I should be obedient to the wishes of my forgetting mind.

What if those I love died next to me on the plane? What if I shouldn't have swam away? What if it was my responsibility to stay and save them? Was I selfish?

Goddamn it! Why didn't I ask myself this question earlier?

Who the hell am I?

Tears fall, sticky and hot. I feel like they're burning my cheeks.

Chapter 19

Dr. Suffolk hands me a glass of water, and I prop myself up on the couch to drink it.

"We'll try this again later," he says. "Don't worry about the memory now. Not remembering a child doesn't prove you had one on the plane."

"Why didn't I answer, then?"

"The mind works in mysterious ways. Maybe your brain could not handle the mere possibility of having a child on the plane, so it just froze."

"You keep saying *brain*," I say. "It's as if you don't think we have a choice in our lives, driven by a brain that's almost a stranger to us."

"It sounds weird, but trust me, science shows we're not much in control of what we think."

The idea doesn't help much. I sip the water, taking in the view of the room. A window behind Dr. Suffolk catches my eye. I can't see much outside from where I sit. "What is this place?" I ask.

Dr. Suffolk smiles, as if I am a little girl trying to be clever. I smile back. He doesn't reply. But then his smile fades.

"I guess I have to hypnotize you after all," he says with a long sigh.

“Hypnotize me?”

He nods. “I tried to avoid it with the other techniques I used. But the only way to make sure you have amnesia and are not lying to me is by hypnotizing you.”

“I am not lying. I thought you believed me.”

“I do, from a personal point of view,” he says. “But I have a job to do.” He points at the door, probably hinting at Major Red’s anger if he doesn’t prove I am an amnesiac. “It should work. Don’t you want to know, June?”

“How does it work?”

“Don’t worry. It’s not painful,” he says. “In any case, I can’t risk doing it while you’re in this condition. I will need to run a few other tests first. I’d also prefer if you eat and then sleep for a few more hours.”

At the mention of sleep, I feel my heavy eyelids. My head falls back on the pillow and I feel numb. Then I stare at the glass of water. “You’re sedating me?”

He nods and helps me lay my head to rest. “It’s for your own good.”

Chapter 20

My eyes flip open...

I am on my back. I can't move. My limbs are frozen with fear. It's dark. Too dark to see anything but silhouettes of moving things. I could be imagining them. I don't know. My body is in too much pain. I wouldn't mind going numb now. The smell of blood is everywhere. Some of it runs from my forehead into my eyes. If I could only move a hand and wipe it away...

Outside I can hear ocean waves, angry and loud, thudding against walls. I try to concentrate; in case I can hear anything else. There is a faint sound, but I can't quite figure it out. It's an infrequent sound, like short squeals. I realize I can't hear it because the loud blare overwhelms all other sounds, even my attempted screams.

I try to move my back, but it cracks with a surging ache, so I stop, biting my lower lip and tasting the blood in my mouth.

I think I see a light in the ceiling. Far away. Either it's just a small light or I am deep in some kind of a hole. But I am not crazy. The opening in the ceiling exists. I can feel a cold breeze coming from it.

"Help!" I scream, not minding the blood in my throat.

My voice is too weak to reach the opening. It comes out hollow, with an unusual echo. Where am I?

The silhouettes looming over me block the opening. Whatever they are, they don't speak, but their smell is foul and sweaty. That's when I realize I can make out the other squealing sound. It's a girl's voice. A young girl. My heart stops when I hear her talking to me. None of my pain matters. None of the blood. Not even the silhouettes looming above me.

The girl says one word: "Mommy!"

Chapter 21

I snap up straight, glad I've awakened from such a horrible dream.

Or was it?

The bed I'm sitting on feels different. I've never seen it before.

Sweating, I scan the rest of the room. I definitely haven't been in here before. When I try to stand up, my legs give in and I drop to the floor. The tiles are cold underneath me. They're much cleaner than the previous room. This feels too real to be a dream. I crane my neck up, and realize I'm in a hospital. A proper one with a normal door and bed. I prop myself up on all fours.

Where am I? Why have I left Dr. Suffolk's clinic? Ah, he sedated me. Like everyone else, he played me. Could this room be an extension of his clinic?

I'm wearing a cleaner hospital gown now. Same lime-green color. I limp toward the door. It has a square window in the middle, but I can't find a handle to open it.

What the hell is this?

Am I some kind of mental patient? Did I imagine all of this, the plane crash and the island?

I knock on the door. It's metallic. I call for someone. I ask if anyone can hear me. I doubt it. The room looks like it's in a normal hospital, but it has too much security to it.

I rest my ear on the door, hoping I can hear outside. All I get back is a low hum of machinery, as if there's a loud laundry nearby. This is insane. I turn my back to the door and let my body slide down to the floor.

I hear a few beeps, like someone is entering a code. The door vibrates. I crawl away, eyes on the door as I watch it open slowly. Someone walks in.

It's not a soldier. Not a nurse soldier. Not Major Red or Dr. Suffolk. It's actually a girl. A young nurse with a welcoming smile.

She greets me with a nod. She is beautiful. I feel safe seeing her.

"Oh, are you feeling okay?" She kneels down to help me up. "Why have you left the bed? Sorry, it's my fault. I should not have left. I wanted to go check on—"

She stops talking when I pull her closer to me and hug her tightly.

Chapter 22

The young woman doesn't mind me hugging her. I am not sure why I am so emotional about meeting her. Maybe because she is the first woman I've seen anywhere on this base. I am not sure.

"I'm Ashlyn," she says with a laugh while I'm still wrapping my arms around her. "Ashlyn Ward."

"June Smith." I pull back and stretch out a hand while I wipe tears from my cheek with the other. "Nice to meet you, Ashlyn."

"Call me Ash."

I let Ashlyn help me back to bed. She seems meticulous and caring. She wipes my sweat and tears with a towel, then makes sure I'm tucked in. She checks all kinds of charts and graphs around my bed. I notice a beeping machine in the corner of the room, but return to Ashlyn. She is super pale, with curly blonde hair. Skinnier than me, and almost the same height.

"I heard you earlier," she says. "You had a bad dream, I assume."

"I did."

"Don't worry. It's normal. All of Dr. Suffolk's patients talk under the influence of pills."

"Dr. Suffolk?"

"Of course. He sent you to us." She keeps writing on a chart. "We'll prepare you for the hypnosis session, so you can remember."

"Who is 'us'?"

"Ward Four," she says. "We have all the details about your condition. You're practically a hero, I must say. How'd you survive that plane crash?"

"So I'm still on the island?"

"You can't leave in this weather," She puts the chart aside and sighs.

"I've been told.... I think... It seems I can't focus on the things told to me."

"Don't sweat it," Ashlyn says. "The sedative Dr. Suffolk gave you—and, of course, the trauma of the plane crash—can cause a few...hallucinations as a side effect. They might last for twenty-four hours or so."

I'm not sure what this has to do with my earlier question.

"You're a brave girl. Most sole survivors suffer worse. Did you know that there's a new branch of medicine devoted to handling sole survivors of plane, train, and boat crashes?"

"I didn't," I say, noticing she likes to talk.

"I advise you to see a psychiatrist once you get home," she continues. "Just in case you go cuckoo in the head." She chuckles. "At least, they say that in the books—" She suddenly claps her hands on her mouth. "I shouldn't have told you any of this. I'm sorry. Mom says I talk too much."

"It's okay. Tell me, Ashlyn. How old are you?"

"Eighteen."

"And you're from...?" My investigative skills, if I have any, are churning.

"Long Island." She laces her hands together.

"How exactly did you end up on this island?"

Ashlyn unlaces her hands and swallows, her eyes darting sideways. "Let me show you your pills," she says. "There's quite a few, and you need to take them on time."

Chapter 23

Though she won't give away any secrets, I have a feeling I will like her. It's not reasonable to think so, but I do. Could it be because she is the only woman I've met?

She reads to me all the medications I am on, a mix of hard-to-spell names with a few undesired side effects. I'm supposed to see Dr. Suffolk tomorrow, so it's not a big deal. Ashlyn also calls me "big sister" at some point, which is sweet. I can't imagine why a girl like her works under Major Red's supervision. It is too soon to ask her about it though.

It turns out that I am physically tough. Ashlyn shows me a few graphs I don't quite understand. The short of it is that I am a bit stronger than most women. I am not sure if she is trying to cheer me up, but it's helping anyway.

"I like your name," Ashlyn says. "Very unusual."

"I'd like to tell you a great story about my mother and father spending nights and days coming up with it, but I'd be lying to you if I said I could remember."

Ashlyn laughs, cupping her mouth, as if she is embarrassed to express herself. "You're my favorite patient, by far," she says, checking her watch. "I think you need to get some sleep."

She walks to the counter and comes back with a glass of water and two more pills. I take both and raise my head, my eyes meeting hers.

"What's wrong?" she says.

"You're not sedating me like Dr. Suffolk, are you?"

"Did he not tell you before he did?"

I shake my head.

"Oh. I'm sorry. That's not like him. He's such a nice person."

"I thought so, too," I place the pill on my tongue and gulp then tell her something that puzzles me. "I trust you."

The smile on her face is a delight to watch. Her cheeks redden, even. She looks away as if embarrassed. Why do I like her so much?

She takes the glass and helps me lie down. "Everything will be all right," She kisses my forehead in such a sincere way. I don't mind it, but I wonder if she is so friendly with all her patients.

I close my eyes and listen to her typing a code, opening the door, and then leaving. Once the door closes, I hear more beeps. She is locking me in.

I toss and turn in bed, waiting for sleep. I feel like I'm reading a thriller novel that's all over the place. Should I be concerned about my past, or the mystery of the island I am trapped on? It's all blurry in this maze of unexplainable events. Maybe I should seriously worry about my mental health.

Slowly, I feel myself sink into the linens of my bed. I dream of nothing. Remember nothing. I only drown in the comfort of a temporary death, hoping for a better resolution when I am resurrected.

Then my eyes flip open again.

I sit up, not sure how much time has gone by. There are no clocks on the wall. My eyelids feel heavy, and I am not sure what awoke me. Then I remember: I think I sense someone else in the room with me.

I walk to the door. It's still locked. Could Ashlyn have come to check on me and then left? Turning around, I glimpse a trail of twilight outside my small window. I feel so disoriented. At least I am sure I am still in the same room in the clinic.

Then an unusual smell attacks my nostrils. A familiar smell. The smell of that black oil.

I immediately scan the floor. This can't be happening again, but there it is. Someone left it by the door, though this isn't the kind of door you can slip paper underneath.

There is no envelope this time. Just a crumbled, oil-stained note. The smell of oil is so familiar, but I can't place its origin. It's like the oil used for big machines in a factory or something.

I blink, wishing the note would disappear. Something tells me I can't handle its contents. It doesn't disappear.

Carefully, I scoop it up from the floor, trickles of viscous oil seeping through my fingers. I flatten the note and read it:

Manfred Toot is on the island. In the Crib. Kill him before he gets his hands on your daughter.

Chapter 24

The early hours of morning show a lighter shade of grey, scored by an eerie melody of drizzling rain in the background. An occasional faint patch of orange sunlight battles its way through, but loses to the imprisoning mist outside my window. I've been staring at this gloomy painting for hours now. My arms are wrapped around my bent knees. My body arches forward, as if I'm trying to hug myself. I need to find my daughter, whom I don't remember and know nothing about.

My soul is a surrealist painting of disturbingly confused emotions. It's not quite love. Not quite regret. Not precisely anger. Only one word sticks out for me: *protectiveness*.

I have a child I need to save, or my whole existence as a human being has no meaning. It doesn't matter that I don't know anything about her. It doesn't matter who Toot is and why he wants to kill her. It doesn't matter who I am. Fuck this island, and fuck my worries. I should have listened to my gut earlier. It told me I have to be somewhere to do something. I've wasted so much time not looking for my daughter.

What if I am too late?

I spent half the night rapping on and shouting at the door, but, of course, no one listened. Ashlyn must have thought I was asleep. She said she would check on me in the morning.

How come there is no emergency call button?

Later, I went to the bathroom, slapped my face with anger, and cursed at my reflection in the mirror.

"Fuck you, June," I said. "How could you let this happen?"

"I couldn't remember," my reflection told me.

"How the fuck can you forget your daughter?" I slammed my hand against the glass, trying to punish her—punish myself. "How can anyone forget their daughter?"

Part of the night was spent on the bathroom floor, crying and praying. I felt like Jonah in the belly of the whale, imprisoned by regret and asking for forgiveness. How does one expect divine intervention on this godforsaken island? This must be hell, with soldiers in grey outfits belonging to no country in particular.

Millions of thoughts swirl in my head, but none of the answers matter. This isn't about figuring out who I am anymore. This is about saving a precious soul. This is about being a mother.

It's weird how I can relate to the feeling of motherhood when I can't remember whose mother I am.

"Goddammit." I hit my head against my palms. "What's my daughter's name?"

How does this work? Is it an instinct? How can I know I am a mother when I don't remember I am a mother? I have no idea.

I stand up again and ram my body against the door, knowing that it won't open. I'm punishing myself for being bad. I am trying to kill my pain.

It all explains my reluctance to answer Dr. Suffolk's question. It explains my worry and need to be somewhere. It explains the imaginary baby cries—probably my daughter looking for me. It explains my dream. She called me "Mommy." Does it explain the woman in the sinking seat telling me about "the girl"? It could.

How old is she? What does she look like? What is she like?

She is a stranger to me, a dearly departed stranger I would die for. I am not even sure how old she is. Was she on the plane with me? No, I don't think so. I think she was here on the island. Someone has taken her from me, and I should be looking for her. If so, how could I have expected the plane to crash here? How would I know I'd survive it?

Reasons and facts don't matter at all now. I need to find her, or I will go insane. The guilt is eating me up. I have to find *a place called the Crib.*

Chapter 25

The door to my room hums. Someone is coming. I've been waiting for this all night.

It's a nurse, not Ashlyn. She greets me with a nod and then sets a tray of breakfast on the table next to my bed.

"Where is Ashlyn?"

"She had to do something," the nurse says. "But she'll be with you in half an hour."

I watch the nurse leave. It occurs to me to escape this room and look for my daughter. It doesn't seem like much of a plan, though. If I want to find my daughter, I need to be smart. The island is swarming with soldiers who will easily catch me. I need Ashlyn. She is the only one I feel I want to trust. I think she will understand.

The door clicks to a close, and my whole system turns into survival mode. I start preparing for my mission.

Yesterday I didn't care for food, but today I need the energy to begin my search for the Crib. I finish every bit of it and end up licking the sauce on the plate. I gulp the orange juice and half a liter of water, and I feel the glucose rush into my brain. The food tastes bitter, but it's just a means to an end.

I pull a chair close to the window, so I can stick my head out as far as I can. I need to have a bird's-eye view of the island. I need to find the Crib.

The cold outside bites at my face as I set one foot on the windowsill. I grip the window frame with my hand for balance and stick my head out. There is still nothing I can see through the mist. I only glimpse Ward Four from outside. Such an ugly, Gothic-looking old building.

I turn and squint harder. I see the bushy expanse of grey silhouettes. I wait for my eyes to adjust to the murkiness, then see the forest in the distance. The camps are in the middle. Some Jeeps and soldiers are scattered all around. Narrow concrete pathways lead to Ward Four.

Still, there is no way to see the other side of the island from here. The west side? Something tells me the Crib is part of that region. If I'm here to kill a man named Manfred Toot—for whatever reason—and Major Red thinks I am a spy, I don't think it's far-fetched to assume Toot works in the Crib.

But if so, why did they let me live?

Every interpretation will sound far-fetched at the moment. There is no point in trying to connect the dots. It is still a good idea to try to figure out the sender of the notes. Is it a prisoner on this island? An infiltrator? One of the soldiers? Could it be Ashlyn? She strikes me as too naive to be so sneaky.

As I am about to pull my head inside, a terrible laugh sounds below by the building's entrance. It's Major Red.

Chapter 26

I see him get out of the Jeep on the pathway leading to Ward Four. It's not hard to spot him, with his immense figure. His heavy feet hit hard on the muddy ground. He is shouting at someone in his gruff voice, as if he has a perpetual cold.

Whoever he is shouting at, I can't see them from this angle. I risk my mortality by leaning further out of the window. The window's ledge is slippery. I might slip and fall if I am not careful. I grip the window's edges until I gain balance—*some* balance. It's like hanging to an airplane's door while up in the sky.

My eyes are still fixed on Major Red. Strange how I haven't lost sight of him with all these acrobatics I'm performing. I'm dizzy from looking down for so long. I blink my lightheadedness away, unreasonably curious about who Major Red is shouting at. Maybe not that unreasonable, since any clue might help in finding my daughter.

I almost slip when I see who he is shouting at. A nurse.

Major Red violently twists her arm as the sky cracks with thunder. He taunts her with words full of spit. I can't make out the words. Neither can I see her face.

Then he slaps her hard.

What the fuck?

The poor girl sways to the left, unable to hold on to something, then spirals down to the ground. She is pretty light. Small. That doesn't stop him from yelling over her. He is so pissed off.

Did I see him just kick her and spit on her?

I am not sure. They're both now a mesh of silhouettes in the heavy rain. She pleads for forgiveness. I still can't make out the words. But I can tell.

I'm dizzying more. I have to get back in or I'm going to fall. I pull myself back in and fall on the bed.

Chapter 27

I wait by the door for half an hour. Partially afraid for Ashlyn's safety, but mostly worried she won't come and I will not get help leaving this room.

Minutes later, Ashlyn enters without saying a word. She only nods with a slight sniff, trying her best to fake a smile. Her face is still wet, but she has changed her outfit. Her pale face is slightly red from the slap and she needs a stitch on the side of her brow too.

"I saw what happened," I say.

"Excuse me?"

"I saw Major Red hitting you." I point at the window.

Ashlyn takes a moment to assess how I climbed out. She knows it's not an easy task. "You shouldn't have done that, June. You could have fallen and died."

"You don't have to worry about me," I tell her. "Why did he hit you?"

"He didn't hit me." Her naive eyes avoid mine. "You misunderstood what you saw."

"Yeah?"

"I don't want to talk about it."

I take a step closer to her, acting like a big sister. "But you're going to tell me."

Ashlyn's eyes widen. She scans my forehead, temples, chin, and then back to my eyes. I feel like she recognizes me from somewhere. Am I famous, like Dr. Suffolk said? Does she know who I am and isn't telling me?

"Ashlyn!" I grip her by the shoulders. I realize how fragile she is. Passive, too. She easily swings in my grip.

"It's nothing, really," she says.

I intensify my gaze, trying to see through her bullshit.

"Okay." She sighs. "Major Red was overreacting to the fact that Dr. Suffolk couldn't confirm whether you're faking your amnesia."

"Yeah? That doesn't give him the right to hit you. And what do you mean when you say he overreacted?"

"Everyone's going to be overreacting today."

"Why?"

"Because of the weather."

"What's new about this shitty weather? We're all trapped here, and I am the most annoyed about it."

"It's getting worse." Ashlyn tries to shake her shoulders free, but she is too soft, or shy, to do it. "They say the ocean's levels are rising."

I let go of her, not sure I understand what she said. "Rising?"

Ashlyn's eyes moisten. "They say there is a possibility of a hurricane. We might die today."

I let go of Ashlyn, feeling sorry for being so hard on her. "I'm sorry," I say, adjusting her collar.

She doesn't reply. I don't think she appreciated my fury. I need to fix that. She is my only way out of here, and I still have to persuade her to help me. The sooner the better. If this rising tide is real, I need to find my daughter *fast*.

She looks like Major Red might have hurt her after all. "You're bleeding, Ashlyn."

She wipes a thin line of blood trickling down to her cheek.

"Let me help," I say, but she steps back. "Listen, I'm really sorry. You said it yourself: I am under the influence of drugs, and I have been under a lot of pressure. But please, don't stop me from making up for it."

The expression on her face changes to that of a sympathetic nurse again. God, she is so nice.

"You know how to stitch a wound?" she asks. "I don't want the other nurses to see this."

"I thought you were nursing me," I tease her. "I'll try my best."

Chapter 28

Ashlyn goes and gets supplies. She's away for only a few minutes while I take another look at the names of medicines prescribed to me. None of them are recognizable to me. I only realize I've been injected too many times. My left arm hurts as I read the chart, so I put it down. I wonder what kind of injury is there underneath the bandages. It would be foolish if I remove them on my own. It could be a serious injury. It could be contaminated. The real issue isn't the pain. It's when I got the bandage. In Ward Four or earlier?

"All done," Ashlyn says. I haven't noticed her entry, nor have I heard the door open. "I brought an anesthetic, but then it's just a small cut. We can do without it. Here are the needle and thread."

"Sounds good," I say. "Do you have any idea about my bandaged arm?"

"It'll be fine. Don't worry," she chews on the words, heading for the bathroom. "Come on. I'd better have you stitch in front of the mirror. I can guide you."

"Yeah, but my arm. What kind of injury is it?"

"Um... I have to check. It doesn't say in the charts. Probably cuts from the accident."

"Accident? You mean the crash?"

"Yes. Come on."

I give up. My arm isn't my biggest concern after all, as long as it doesn't hurt.

In the bathroom, both Ashlyn and I are astonished at my stitching skills—if that's really a skill. She jokes that I may be a nurse in my forgotten life. I surely hope so. It wouldn't explain the gun in my fanny pack, but I'd like to end up being a good person who helps others instead of hurting them.

"Can I ask you a question, Ashlyn?"

"I'll answer if I'm allowed to." Her neck is uncomfortably craned under my hands.

"I am not asking much. I only want to know the location of a place."

"As long as it has nothing to do with the west side of the island."

"Of course not," I say. "It's a place called...the Crib?"

"Is that here on the island?"

Her answer is abrupt. She didn't even give it a thought.

"Yes. Please, Ashlyn, I need to get there."

"How did you hear about it?"

"Um... I heard some soldiers talk about it?"

"I am really sorry, I—"

Ashlyn's voice cuts off mid word. She starts to choke in pain. It takes me a while to realize it's because of me. The inner me, the true essence of who I really am, is pulling on the needle tight enough to make her want to scream. I did it without realizing.

Chapter 29

Ashlyn weeps in my arms like a baby. I loosen my hand on the needle and bounce back against the bathroom wall. It's too late to apologize to her again. I slide down against the door. Ashlyn stands up.

She turns the shower on and says, "I want to help you." Her words surprise me, as I watch her bleeding from the stitch. "I really do. But you have to know how much I will risk doing this."

The shower is noisy, and I can't hear well. But then I realize she has turned it on so no one hears us.

"You don't have to, Ashlyn." I scan the bathroom, looking for surveillance cameras or microphones.

"Listen to me." She almost mouths the words, barely uttering them. "I am not angry with you. I know how much medication and stress you're under." She kneels and faces me. "I'm just a teenager from a small community in Long Island who accepted a mysterious job on this island for a lot of money. I need it to escape my stepfather's hell and go live on my own somewhere."

"I'm sorry. I didn't know that—" I wonder if she wants to elaborate on her stepfather.

"Shut up." Even when she's angry, she is barely angry. "You were not meant to know any of this. My problems are my problems, not yours. I don't want your sympathy."

"I respect that." I lower my eyes.

"Look at me." She grits her teeth, eyes slightly darting upward. I follow her glance but can't see a camera or microphone. "Like I said, I took the job for the money. One year on an island in the middle of the Atlantic. I wasn't allowed to see where they were taking me in that chopper that flew me here. The deal was to take the training as a nurse, do my job, and never ask questions. There are a few other rules I have to abide by. One of them is to never leave the building."

"Is that why Major Red hit you?" I ask.

"Yes. I'm only supposed to leave when I complete my training. This clinic isn't the main business on this island. I hadn't even left. I was just smoking a cigarette in the hall when it occurred to me to look outside, out of curiosity. I am not supposed to do that. Stay in the building until I leave with my check. I'm not supposed to tell you any of that."

"Then why are you telling me?"

"Because I think this place stinks," she says. "I can't figure out why, but I've heard stories."

"Like what?"

"A lot of scary stories. Do you want to know why I was tempted to look outside today?"

"Why?"

“Because I heard a baby’s cries, June,” she says. “Just like you reported when you first came to Ward Four.”

Chapter 30

I need a minute to think about this. Though I haven't yet told Ashlyn about my daughter, I remember that I only heard the baby's cries once. In the forest. So I wasn't imagining that.

"Is that the first time you heard them?" I say.

"No. I hear the cries all the time, ever since I first came here. The other nurses, too, but we're all bound by the contract to mind our own business, or we don't get paid."

"But you're sure the cries don't come from Ward Four itself?"

"That's unlikely. I think it's coming from another place, probably the west side of the island," she says.

"Why unlikely?"

"The part of the shore you arrived from is the closest to the western side, and you heard the cries nearby."

"Is that so?" I try to draw a mental map of the island but can't. "What do you think is happening here, Ashlyn?"

"I have no idea. It's a military base, so it doesn't make sense."

"And you said you're a trainee?"

"Yes."

"And the nurses who finish training are sent to another place on the island."

“True. I doubt Major Red will send me there after today. He is very unforgiving.”

“Did any of the nurses return and tell you what their job was?”

She shakes her head. “They never return. It’s said they go back home once their job is done.”

“What is your training here?”

“Just how to take care of women in need, medically, and psychologically.”

“Only women?”

“All women. Most of them are volunteers. You’re the first real patient on this floor.”

I try not to feel overwhelmed with information. It scares me to try and interpret what’s going on. It scares me to think something bad is going to happen to my daughter. Even if my first impressions about Ashlyn allowed me to trust her, I have to rethink it for a moment. My heart says she is the kindest person I will meet here, but I have to ask her, “Ashlyn, why are you helping me?

She swallows hard. “It’s not the first time I’ve heard about the Crib.”

“Others mentioned it?”

“I’ve heard stories about a nurse leaving in the middle of the night to trace the origin of the baby cries. She never came back. Rumors about a place called the Crib have been around since.”

Babies cries. My daughter. And a place called the Crib. None of this sounds promising. It's unnerving.

"So what do you actually know about the Crib?" I ask.

"Only rumors. I was going to ask you what *you* know about it."

I pull out the oily note and show it to her. As she takes it in her hands, I follow her eyes. Either she is a phenomenal actor or she hasn't seen it before. As she reads, I begin to explain what's been happening to me since I arrived.

"I thought it could've been you for a moment," I say.

"Me? I didn't send it. Why is it written in oil?"

"You're asking me?"

"It's car oil," she says. "My parents have a car in Long Island. It used to leak the same oil, so I recognize it."

"Does all car oil have the same smell?"

"I don't think so, but this one is the same as mine. It's not that unusual. The point is, why not write in ink? It's not like whoever sent this had no means to write it in a normal way."

"You have a point." I take another look at the note. "Does this yellow note mean anything to you?"

"No, why?"

"Is it something you maybe use in the office outside?"

Ashlyn scratches her arm. "I have to check. Do you think it's one of the nurses who's sending you the notes?"

"Or one of the soldiers."

She peeks over my shoulder into the room. “You know how hard it is to get into this room?”

“I can imagine. Who else has the code?”

“Many of us. Nurses. Dr. Suffolk,” she says. “You think it’s him?”

“Not after he sedated me.” I rub my chin. “The only other option is that someone is coming in through the window.”

“It’s very dangerous to do that.”

“I know. I almost fell earlier.”

“The real question is why, June,” Ashlyn says. “Why help you? And why not confront you?” She hesitates. “Are you really a dangerous person?”

“I don’t know.” I lower my eyes. “I mean you saw how I hurt you with the stitches. Maybe I am evil inside.”

“No, you’re not,” she says. “I don’t believe that.”

“I hope you’re right,” I mumble. “But even if you’re not, I don’t care. All I want is to find and protect my daughter.”

Ashlyn holds my hands in hers, like Dr. Suffolk did earlier. “We need to get you to the Crib.”

“How?”

“I think I know someone who knows.”

Chapter 31

The plan is risky, Ashlyn admits. I don't care. I will do whatever it takes to find the Crib, even if it kills me. The storm will kill us all anyway.

It's Ashlyn I am worried about. Though she is determined to help me, I'm just not sure she is up to it.

She leaves the room for a few minutes then returns with a nurse's outfit and a pair of Crocs. The uniform is two sizes too big, but I put it and the Crocs on.

"You have to get out alone, without me, just like a regular nurse," Ashlyn says, standing by the door. "No one should doubt your identity. We're a dime a dozen here, and none of us cares to know about the others. It's all about the paycheck. When we see or hear something we don't like, we look the other way and get the job done."

"But some of the nurses must have seen me coming in," I say. "They'll know I'm not a nurse."

"Only Dr. Suffolk and me saw you. I don't know why, but those were the instructions. You're kinda special, June."

I nod. I'd rather be ordinary and know who I am than a special snowflake with no memories.

"I'm keeping the door unlocked," Ashlyn says. "When you leave, close the door behind you. It's unlikely other nurses will check on you before three hours."

"Why?"

"Injection time."

"What injection is this? Some kind of sedative?"

"Doesn't matter now. All that matters is that no one will notice your absence for a while. Once you get to the corridor, walk casually to your right until you see the elevator. Take it up to the sixth floor." She hands me the chart from my bed. "Take this. It should complete the picture."

"Okay."

"If anyone asks you about your destination, you say, 'It's my turn to check on Meredith.'"

"Meredith?"

"The woman we're going to see."

"The one who knows about the Crib."

"Yes, yes," Ashlyn says. "Every single story about it, trust me."

"Thank you, Ashlyn."

"Ash."

"Sorry. Thank you, Ash."

"That's it." She smiles. "Ah, I almost forgot. Take this." She pins a nametag on my outfit. "I stole it from her locker."

"Brooklyn?"

"A newcomer. She was supposed to arrive yesterday but didn't. Don't worry, I just faked her signature as 'arrived.' It will take some time before someone notices."

"This Brooklyn is almost six feet tall." I point at my oversized outfit.

"Complaining much?" Ashlyn grins childishly. She is excited about the coming adventure. "I'll leave now. Wait five minutes and do as I told you. See you on the sixth floor."

I watch her leave.

Five minutes later, I open the door and step out. This is a much different place than the other parts of the island I've seen. The corridor has a modern look to it, with white ceramic walls and black and white tiles. The light is fluorescent white and reflects annoyingly off the floor. But it's all good, since I can't see anyone walking by.

I walk briskly at first, then remember to make it look like I'm just strolling by doing a boring job. My Crocs squeak against the floor, though. It's an uncomfortable feeling. I'd prefer to make no sound, so I walk even slower.

The rooms on both sides are sealed shut. I can see a code pad on each of the metallic doors. There is nothing hanging on the walls. No charts, ads, or bulletin boards. Plain white walls. The place is too neat and clean, and smells of lavender, I guess.

I reach the elevator and press the button. While waiting, I resist the urge to tap my foot or bite my nails.

The elevator chugs to a stop, but the door doesn't open right away. I feel like I'm missing my gun. Taking a cautious step back, I watch the doors open. No one's inside.

I get in and push the button for the sixth floor. It's the highest. The door takes too long to close. I push the close button again. It's not working. I tap my foot and push the button again. A sudden smell of cigarette smoke attacks me as the door finally starts to slides to a close. Do they smoke in here?

Then I realize what it is. A rugged hand stops the elevator doors from closing.

Chapter 32

A soldier stands before me. With my back to the wall, I am not sure what I should do. He greets me with a dismissive nod and steps inside, taking up space, so much so that I am obliged to move a little to the left.

He stares at the set of buttons but doesn't press any. The door closes. The elevator takes off.

He stands with his back to the opposite wall, checking me out from top to bottom. I look away, wondering if he recognizes I'm not Brooklyn.

"Meredith again?" he says.

I nod, not looking up.

"I wish that old whore would die." He taps his foot on the floor.

I shrug.

"I bet you heard all her delusional stories a million times by now, eh?"

I nod again, briefly meeting his eyes. I feel I should talk. It's not natural if I don't reply, but my tongue is tied.

"All this fiction that comes out of her mouth," he says. "I once heard Dr. Suffolk say she only talks to stay alive."

"She does?" I try to sound loose, imaging I'm a flirty nurse, loudly chewing a piece of bubble gum. I'm under the impression it's what he expects from me, and I don't want to be exposed.

"He said some gibberish about old people feeding on their old memories to stay alive. So much that most of their memories aren't real but weirdly mixed with fiction."

I'm getting my information from a delusional woman? "How would making up stories help her stay alive?"

"You asking me?" He scoffed. "Ask Dr. Suffolk. I think he mentioned it stirs up the mind and prevents it from withering away while we age. Fuck it, I hate Ward Four" He sighs, looking up. "Everyone in this building is insane."

"Tell me about it." I roll my eyes, playing with my hair.

"What would you like me to tell you?" His voice changes, as if purring like a cat. He scans my body from top to bottom like Major Red. I guess my flirtatious vibe is a mistake. Why did I even do it? "We got us a blondie here." He rests both hands on his thick belt, licking his lips.

"I'm not blonde—"

"Rarely do I see such a beautiful nurse in this building of lunatics."

"Thanks." I plaster a fake smile on my lips. I could ask him questions, but that would interfere with Ashlyn's plan.

"I bet you'd like to get out of here too," he continues.

Damn this elevator. Why is it taking so long?

"I could help you leave Ward Four and get to the other facilities, Brooklyn." He grins, staring at my name tag, and probably my chest. "Pays better."

You have got my attention, soldier. Sorry, Ashlyn, but I have to ask him. "Other facilities?"

"Uh-huh." He shoots me another head-to-toe look. "All you need is a soldier boyfriend."

My eyes widen.

"Of course, no one can know about it, if you know what I mean." He winks.

"You're such a player." I laugh, glimpsing a side of myself I didn't know about. "Will you help me leave this building if I say yes?"

He is about to drool. "Anything you want, baby."

I think twice about what I am going to say...but fuck it. "Can you help me transfer to the Crib? I heard they pay more."

He leans back, hands on his belt, with a serious face. It's as if I've offended him, or as if he's figured out I don't mean what I'm saying. "There is no Crib, darling. The Crib is a myth."

The elevator stops. Fourth floor.

He shoots me one last look and leaves, chin up, and walking like a thug. "Whore," I hear him say outside.

I let out a long sigh, not sure what just happened. The way he denied the Crib's existence actually enforced my belief in it. The elevator takes half as much time to reach floor six, but then the door doesn't open for a while.

I push the button again. I wait as the light in the ceiling flickers a couple of times. When the door finally opens, I find myself in a place way different to what I experienced on the lower floors.

Stepping out, I'm in a dim hallway with a fluorescent light flickering in the distance. Not only does it scare me, but it smells faintly of urine.

Chapter 33

"Glad you made it." Ashlyn appears out of nowhere. "Now follow me slowly and do as I say."

"I met a soldier in the elevator."

"Shh, lower your voice," she says. "What soldier?"

"I don't know. Some soldier who flirted with me and offered to transfer me to a better-paying ward if I was his girlfriend, or something."

"Yeah?" Ashlyn grimaces. "That's typical of soldiers with nurses. Did he ask you where you're going?"

"He actually asked me if I'm checking on Meredith, and then got out on the fourth floor."

"Ah, that's the resting floor. Did you tell him you were coming for her?"

I nod. "He called her an old hag and wished she would die."

"Typical." She rolls her eyes. "You did good. Now follow me."

We trudge through a messy corridor. The walls are tinted in green. Old beds and wheelchairs are leaning against them. There are rusty old instruments and equipment.

"Is this place abandoned or what?" I whisper.

"It's the floor where we keep Meredith and a few other old patients."

"Why here? This doesn't look like a clinic."

"I'm not sure. I never come here, and I never ask. This building is said to have been built during World War II. It's all been renovated, except this last floor."

"What?"

"I know, it's crazy." Ashlyn stops, looking lost. "All I know is that most buildings on the island were constructed around 1942. Most of the older patients were kept on this floor. They all died. The few patients they keep here are said to be daughters of those who died."

"Sons and daughters, you mean?"

"Nah, they're only women." She finds her way again, and I follow her. "Meredith used to be a cleaner, but then she went...you know..."

"What?"

"Insane."

"That's why the soldier called this place insane," I say. "Doesn't she deserve better care, then?"

"She does, but I only work here. It's an almost forgotten floor. I hear nurses only bring her food and drinks, plus the occasional medicine. Don't ask me why."

Ashlyn finally stops at a room with an open door. The room stinks. It's horrible. I can't quite fathom this. She points inside at a woman in a wheelchair, staring out the window at the grey weather outside.

We slowly tiptoe into the room.

Meredith has stiff white hair. It's long enough that it's dangling from the back of the chair. Her skin is pale, more cracks and wrinkles than actual skin. Her lips are chapped, and her grey eyes seem to have been blue once—I'm not sure why I think so. Her trembling hands rest on her lap.

"She doesn't like anyone looking at her, so you better ask her from here," Ashlyn says. "Meredith, someone wants to talk to you."

Meredith says nothing but wiggles a finger.

"Hello," I say. She doesn't respond.

"Just go on and tell her," Ashlyn says.

I clear my throat. "I want to ask you about this island, if you don't mind."

"One thousand and one nights," Meredith says. Her voice is husky, a little louder than a whisper. "One thousand and one nights."

I glance at Ashlyn. "Keep talking," she whispers. "I heard most of Meredith's words are riddles.

"Do you know what's happening on the island?" I say.

She keeps up her "one thousand and one nights" chant.

"Do you know what's on the west side of the island?"

"You don't want to know," she finally says.

"I do." I take a step closer. "My plane crashed, and I ended up here. I don't remember anything else. I need to find my—"

"Daughter?"

I think my heart stops. "What did you just say?"

"You should leave as soon as you can."

"She can't," Ashlyn says. "The weather, you know."

"Wait." I step forward, but Meredith's body tenses. Ashlyn grips my hand, so I stop. "How did you know about my daughter?"

A long silence fills the room. Meredith's gaze seems to see beyond the foggy glass. "Nothing here is what it seems."

I pull away from Ashlyn and take another step closer, but now Meredith nervously taps her foot on the floor.

"She will not tell you anything if you upset her," Ashlyn mouths.

"Meredith." I kneel down, wanting to meet her eyes, but I only see her profile. "What do you know about my daughter?"

Meredith only taps one hand on top of her lap, staring outside.

"Is she here?"

Meredith mutters something. I can't make out the words.

"Please, Meredith."

She keeps mumbling. I lean forward, trying to listen, but she tenses again.

"Okay, Meredith. Let me ask you this: did you send me the notes?"

Ashlyn throws me a look. I get it. How would this woman in a wheelchair send me the notes?

I turn back to Meredith and slowly stretch an arm to touch the side of her wheelchair. "Do you have children, Meredith?"

She lets out a moan. A long moan, full of pain.

"I bet you love them," I say. "Right?"

Slowly, she turns her head toward me. Her eyes are drenched in tears that refuse to trickle down her cheeks, as if she is holding on to them for the memories, for solace.

"See?" I reach out and touch her hand. "I miss my daughter, too. Except I don't know anything about her. I don't know her name, not even what she looks like. It's tearing me apart. And you're the only one who can help me find her."

"Horrible things," she says in a feeble voice.

"Come again?"

"The horrible things they will do to you if you don't leave."

Her words send shivers down my spine. "What kind of things?"

"Worse than death," she says.

"What?" Ashlyn asks.

"They will rip you apart." Meredith sobs now. "So much that you will never want to remember who you are anymore."

"Listen." I grip both her hands. "Please tell me how I can find the Crib?"

Meredith's eyes dart over my shoulders. Outside, the corridors are suddenly bursting with the sound of footsteps. Not nurses. Not doctors. Heavy boots treading closer. Soldiers.

Chapter 34

"We have to hide," Ashlyn says between gritted teeth. She darts toward the open door then returns instantly. "We're too late. They're already here."

"I can't go back to that room," I say.

"It's too late, June," she says. "I'm sorry. They rarely visit this floor, and it's impossible they figured out you left the room. Must be the soldier you met in the elevator."

I point at the window. "It's our only chance."

"Are you crazy?"

"We have no choice," I say, then realize we don't have time for debate. I go to the window and pull the latch back. It budges easily. "Come on." I step outside and watch Ashlyn hesitate. Her limbs freeze in place. "I will leave without you if you don't come."

She reluctantly approaches. I pull her hand violently and help her out on the ledge. It's thick enough, as if whoever designed it in the 1940s knew someone would walk on it.

Ashlyn closes her eyes.

"Stop that," I hiss, but wonder if she actually hears me in the pouring rain. "Open your eyes."

"There is nothing to see." She sobs. "It's all grey."

I glance sideways, and she is right. It's like being shrouded in mist. The ledge's edge isn't even clear.

"Open your eyes!" I say.

"I am afraid of heights. I can't believe I am doing this. I'm going to die."

I baby-step her closer to me. Her steps are stiff and rigid. I grip a water pipe to help pull myself away from the window, which blurs in the mist. I guide her hands to the pipe, which she hugs.

"Just don't move," I say.

I have little space and nothing to hang on to. We're both safe from the soldiers for now, but I'm not sure how long we can hold on.

Carefully twisting my neck, I clamp my ear to the wall, hoping I can hear what's going on inside. I hear a loud, muffled argument but can't make out the words. Someone is probably shouting.

"I'll have to take a few steps back to listen," I whisper to Ashlyn.

"Don't leave me."

"I'll just be a couple of steps away."

With Ashlyn in the way, the way back is even harder, but I can hear some of the words now. They're asking Meredith about us. They call her insane, and then insult her about cleaning toilets in the past. Meredith is silent. The soldiers seem to be accustomed to her behavior. One soldier, however, pushes her for answers, calling her "old hag." Then another calls her a bitch.

Beside me, Ashlyn shivers, spitting rain while keeping her eyes closed. I am afraid she'll give in and call for help at any moment.

"Tell me if you saw them," a soldier tells Meredith, then I hear a slap on her face. "Old fucking bitch. You know what we will do to you!"

The horrible things they will do to you if you don't leave.

Meredith's words weigh on me. I think I am going to fall off the ledge. I close my eyes like Ashlyn, hoping the soldiers will soon be gone. I'm not sure I can stand this any longer.

"I'm gonna kill that bitch," a soldier says. I recognize the voice. It's Hecker.

"Stop it. She doesn't know anything." It's Ryan.

"Of course she knows," Hecker says. "Where do you think she went?"

"I don't see how she's on this floor," Ryan says. "Look around. There is nowhere to go."

"Then where do you think she is?" Hecker says.

"I don't know. Maybe she tried to escape to this floor, and then decided it's not going to help her and took the elevator down again."

"So, she is out there on the island?" Hecker shouts. "I told you I don't trust her."

"It's too late for that," Ryan says. "Leave Meredith alone. We're hunting the girl down. She can't have gotten far."

I hear the soldiers leave. They are a bit slower than I'd like them to be. Finally, they evacuate the room. I should give it another five minutes to be safe, but I'm afraid Ashlyn can't hold on that long. Her foot slips.

Chapter 35

The same moment I pull up Ashlyn up to steady herself on the ledge, lightning strikes in the distance. Still holding her, I make sure I am holding the window's edge with all my might, then I stretch one foot back into the room.

"Stay with me, Ashlyn!" I spit out a mouthful of rain. "They're gone, so open your goddamn eyes."

Ashlyn's eyes flip open, her skinny body stiff as a broom.

"Good girl." I gently guide her back without either of us slipping on the wet ledge. "Just keep looking at me."

She does, and I baby-step her back toward the room, one foot at a time. Half of my body is inside now, but if Ashlyn panics or slips, I won't be able to help her. I think I am going to cry myself to death if something happens to her. In my amnesiac state of mind, she is my mother, my daughter, and my best friend. My emotions are that of an infant. She is the first person to lend me a true helping hand since I got on this island. I may have a long past, and a daughter I have to save, but without regaining my memory, I've only got Ashlyn.

"Hang on, Ashlyn. We're almost there."

Most of my body is back inside the room. All Ashlyn has to do is get in. I know how hard it's going to be, so I hold her by the arms and ask her to do it slowly. She pulls up her right foot, and her other slips.

"Ashlyn!" I bend and almost crack my back holding on to her. The way she looks at me as she is half dangling is killing me.

My knees are on fire, rubbing against the wall under the window, but I manage to pull her up. She has her legs on the ledge again. This time, she is alert enough to come in safely.

I squeeze her in a hug once her feet touch the floor.

"Are you all right?"

She nods, spitting water in my face.

I chuckle and adjust her wet hair on her bony cheeks. "We'll have to get you somewhere safe."

"You need to leave the island," Meredith says from behind.

"Stop it." I turn and face her. "I will only leave to go to the Crib, with or without your help."

"One thousand and one nights," she says again, trying to rock her wheelchair.

"Look at me." I kneel and grab her by the jaw. I feel the same chill I felt when I hurt Ashlyn earlier. It's as if I am not myself anymore. "Tell me something useful, Meredith. Do you know anything about the Crib?"

"The Crib is a myth," she says between clenched teeth. "Leave the island now."

"It's not a myth." I pull my hands away and turn. "Come on, Ashlyn. We're leaving."

"The Crib is a myth," Meredith repeats. "So is Manfred Toot."

I freeze. This old woman is messing with my head. "I never asked about Manfred Toot," I say without turning to face her. "How do you know about him?"

She says nothing and continues mumbling her terrible nursery rhyme. I have no idea what it means. Outside, another bolt of lightning strikes. I leave Meredith mumbling absently. "One thousand and one..."

Chapter 36

Ashlyn shows me an old fire escape that we take down, all the way to the ground floor. She is much better now, alert and in the moment. I follow her into the kitchen on the ground floor, and then we hide in a storage room.

"We can stay here for a minute or so," she says, peeking out through the keyhole. "There is a door in the kitchen that leads outside. It's our only way out. I just want to make sure none of the nurses are in the kitchen."

"Good," I say. "Listen, I think you should go back. I'll do the rest of this on my own."

She frowns. "What do you mean, June? We're a team."

"I know, and I really appreciate what you've done so far. But why drag you into this?"

"Because we're like sisters," she says, then shrugs. "I mean friends."

"Yeah, but this could get us killed, and the soldiers were only asking about me, which means they don't yet know you're involved."

"I'm the reporting nurse responsible for you. They will question how you escaped the room. No way you could have broken the door's code without my help. Forget it. We're in this together."

It baffles me how brave she is. I mean, she could be a burden, unable to help herself, like on the ledge, but she either loves me or is fed up with this island.

"You heard Meredith," she says. "She warned us of the things they will do to you when they find you. So we better find that Crib, and your daughter."

Mentioning my daughter is like someone shooting me with a poison arrow. The emotional pain I feel is so intense that I feel a sting in the back of my neck and my shoulders. The pain intensifies when I can't relate to my missing daughter in any way. There is no picture of her in my head. No memory. Nothing that brings a smile to my lips. All I have is the burden of guilt for whatever reason.

"June," Ashlyn says. "Let's go."

I follow her outside. She points at the sliding door in the kitchen. It's still raining outside, and our nurse outfits will be weak protection against this weather. Still, it's better than whatever the soldiers intend to do to us.

"Hey!" someone calls from behind.

Ashlyn and I stop in our tracks. She manages to stay calm, though, turning around to face another nurse.

"Mindy?" Ashlyn does her best to look normal, but if the horror on our faces isn't giving it away, our wet outfits and wet hair does. "I just needed something to eat—"

"Who is that?" Mindy points at me.

"That?" Ashlyn loses her grip on her act.

"I'm Brooklyn." I reach out a hand.

Mindy doesn't accept my gesture. "Ashlyn and Brooklyn. What a happy family."

"Listen, Mindy," Ashlyn says, as I slowly reach for the kitchen table behind me. If I'm lucky, I may come across a knife. "We need to leave. I'll explain later."

Mindy glances behind her, hands in her pockets. I can hear the faint sound of soldiers in the distance. "Relax," she says. "I am not going to tell them about you."

Ashlyn's jaw drops. I realize I've actually found a kitchen knife. I hold it behind my back.

"They're still looking for us?" Ashlyn asks.

"Everywhere," Mindy says. "What did you do?"

"It's a long story. We really need to get out."

"So what's stopping you?"

Ashlyn and I exchange gazes. I'm ready to use my knife if needed. I'm leaving this kitchen no matter what.

Ashlyn tucks her hand in her pocket. She pulls out the oily note and hands it to Mindy.

I'm appalled by her stupid actions, but it's too late.

Mindy takes the note, eyes on me, and then reads it. Her expression is bland. I can't read it. I can only grip my knife harder.

"Who has a daughter here?" Mindy asks.

"Forget the daughter part," Ashlyn says. "What about the rest?"

"Manfred Toot? The Crib?" Mindy squints. "Is this a joke?"

"Joke?" Ashlyn says.

"Of course," Mindy says. "What does this have to do with the soldiers looking for you?"

"None of your business." I step in front of Ashlyn and face Mindy. "What do you mean this is a joke?"

"The Crib is a myth," Mindy says.

I roll my eyes. "Tell me something I haven't heard before."

Mindy senses my tension. "It's a spook story about an evil place that women fear the most," she says, looking over my shoulder. "We all know that, Ashlyn. It's all Meredith's fault, the madwoman on floor six. She is the one who spread it among the nurses."

"Really?" Ashlyn says.

"Of course," Mindy says. "And this Manfred Toot is nothing but a boogeyman. He doesn't exist. Come on, did you ever come across someone named Toot before? Toot. Toot."

I snatch the note back. "Nonsense. Let's get out of here, Ashlyn."

"Yeah, we've wasted so much time," Ashlyn says.

As I turn around, Mindy taps me on the shoulder. I reflexively flip out my knife.

"Whoa." Mindy steps back, hands in the air. "I just thought I saw something in the note."

I notice my hand trembling while holding the knife. It must be the injections they give me.

“Take it easy, will ya?” Mindy says. “I really think I noticed something that will help you.”

Ashlyn snatches the note from my hand and hands it back to Mindy. “Here you go. What did you notice?”

Mindy reads the note again. “If anything is true about this note, then it’s not the Crib or Toot.”

“Then what is it?” I demand.

Mindy meets my eyes. “It’s one thousand and one.”

Chapter 37

"That's it?" I say.

"They sent Hecker to do something there a few times, but he wouldn't tell me what. The place gave him nightmares, he said. Big Red calls the place the one thousand and one."

"Why?" I say.

"No one really knows, I guess," Mindy says. "But wait. Hecker told me the soldiers have a different name for it."

"Which is?"

"The Furnace."

"The Furnace?" Ashlyn says.

"Yeah, but that's all I know." Mindy points at the knife in my hand.

I lay it on the table. I think I have more than I asked for. An explanation of what Toot is, and a location for what might be the Crib. Though my note says to kill Manfred Toot, which dismisses the possibility of it being a number, I have no choice but to follow the thread I've been given to find my daughter.

"Do you know how we find it, the Furnace?" I ask Mindy.

"Hecker said you can reach it walking parallel to the forest outside." Mindy points outside. "Just follow the pine trees."

Chapter 38

Running on the muddy ground outside feels like waiting for a hole to swallow you. The darkness is as deadly. I don't know if I should focus on the ground, the mist, the rain, or the soldiers who could be tailing us.

"Do you think we can trust Mindy?" I ask Ashlyn, spitting out water.

"We have no choice, do we?"

"I agree. Hey, I think we're closer to the forest's edge."

"Really?"

"Can't you hear the faint crashing of waves in the distance?"

"I think so." Ashlyn takes advantage of her skinny figure, maneuvering through the dense trees. "I hope we're on the right track."

"Me too," I say, jumping to avoid a puddle of water. "I still don't get it, by the way. This toot and one thousand and one thing seems a bit crazy."

"What isn't? All this stuff I've heard and seen in the last hour is crazy," She crouches under a canopy, and I follow her. "But then again, soldiers have private numbers on the island."

"So?"

"Manfred Toot being John One Thousand and One means this is a soldier whose name is John and has number one thousand and one."

It's hard to argue with the possibility. I hadn't thought of it. So the man who wants to kill my daughter is a soldier named John, and I came to this island to save her? Did he kidnap her? How could I plan a plane crash to end up here?

Nonsense.

"Wait." Ashlyn ducks suddenly and lies flat on her stomach.

So do I. "What? Did you see something?"

"Soldiers. Can you hear them?"

"No, I can only hear the waves crashing."

"Listen."

"I'm trying, Ash. I can't— Wait, I do."

"Let's wait until they're gone."

We wait. Not only do I hear soldiers, but Jeeps arrive afterward. It sounds like they're still looking for us. The one advantage we have is probably their inability to drive into the forest. It will only buy us sometime, until soldiers decide to walk through. I have a feeling they won't, or they'd have looked for me inside when I first met them. I'd like to imagine their heavy boots and machine guns will slow them down. True, Ashlyn and I will freeze soon in our thin scrubs, but we have no choice.

A few minutes later, their voices grow farther, did they change directions, or do they have a short cut to meet us halfway? It's hard to make out the words, so I don't know where they're heading next. It's hard to imagine they'll head toward the Furnace. How would they know where we are heading, unless Mindy has told them? I bite my lower lip, not trusting Ashlyn's decision to leave Mindy be. We should have locked her in the storage room.

After the soldiers leave, we stand up, covered in mud. Ashlyn lets the rain wash her muddy face, but I stop her.

"What?" she says.

"Use the mud as camouflage," I tell her. "It will keep us invisible."

"Ah." She raises a finger to her mouth. "Like in the movies."

I'm about to crack a tense laugh. "This isn't a movie, Ashlyn."

"Ash," she insists. "I like the name Ash, like Ashes."

"Okay, okay." I wave my hands in the air.

That's when I see the building. It's Ward Four, so far behind us, blurring like a creepy house in a horror movie.

"So we lost our way." She points at it.

"Yeah," I say. "We kinda went in a circle or something. I don't know how."

"I guess that happens in such a disorienting forest," she says. "Come on. At least we know we should go the opposite way."

"You're right. Let's go find the Furnace," I say.

More lightning strikes before I turn and follow Ashlyn. It lights up the form of Ward Four. It's only for a second, but long enough that I glimpse a sign hanging on the top floor. The first two words don't send shivers down my spine: *Ward Four.*

It's the words following that trouble me: *Neurology, Psychiatry and Mental Illness.*

Chapter 39

"Am I a mental patient?" I run after Ashlyn.

She speeds up, suddenly all energetic, maneuvering her small and light figure through the trees.

"Answer me, Ash!" I reach for her shoulder but can't stop her. "What is that I read on Ward Four?"

"You read what?" She stops, rain trickling down her face. She stands on slightly elevated ground, so she looks down on me, though she is shorter.

"I saw the sign on Ward Four. It says it is some mental institution."

She looks like she feels guilty about it but pretends otherwise. "So it's a mental institution."

"You never said it was. Is Dr. Suffolk treating mental patients?"

"So what?"

"Why do you keep answering my questions with questions?"

"Because I don't get the point. The soldiers could come back any moment, but you want to chat about Ward Four."

I hesitate to say the words again. "Am I a mental patient?"

Ashlyn takes a few breaths, looking around. I am not sure if she is scouting or trying to avoid my gaze. "Technically, you are."

"What does that mean?"

"You're an amnesiac and most of your stories are conflicting, so you are, June."

I am at a loss for words. A million questions are in my mind, but I can't utter one coherent sentence. "Come on." She pulls on my hand. "We're wasting time."

I pull away. "Not before one last question," I say. My brain has come up with my biggest fear.

"What is your question?"

"Have I always been in here?"

"Meaning what?"

"Was I never on a plane?"

She shakes her head. "I don't know what you mean."

"I mean, am I imagining things? Are you playing along because I am some patient who's been here all of my life, in this damned hospital on a fucking forsaken island? Is it all in my head? Do I even have a daughter? Tell me!"

"June." Ashlyn chuckles. "You're out of your mind."

"So it's true?"

"No!" She hugs me tightly. "What made you think that? Ward Four has been a mental facility since World War II. Dr. Suffolk mainly handles soldiers with PTSD. There are so many of them on this island."

"Really?" I feel her hand on my back, and it makes me feel love. Not romantic love. Ashlyn's touch calms my pain. Maybe I should have cried earlier, let it all out. Maybe knowing I have a daughter out there whom I can't remember makes me want to scream and cry myself dead. I have kept it all inside, and Ashlyn's tenderness helps so much.

"Soldiers on this island go crazy sometimes," she says. "The loneliness, the bad weather, and, of course, whatever secret mission they are working on here. It's normal."

"But you said you're a trainee."

"I am. They just let us train in the same ward for mental illness," she says. "Who knows? Maybe later they'll teach us to treat disturbed soldiers in the Crib. Just calm down and let's get moving." She touches my face and smiles at me. "Come on. We need to get to the Furnace.

Chapter 40

The more we run, the more Ashlyn gets excited. I let her guide me through the bushes. Not only because of her agility, but because my mind is occupied. Ashlyn's words didn't persuade me a hundred percent. Only one thing stops me from giving in to the idea: the fact that the overwhelming feeling never leaves me. I don't care about the notes, but I can't ignore my gut. In fact, it is what has preserved my sanity until this moment. I suppose a mother's love for her daughter is so instinctual and real that it destroys seemingly insurmountable walls of hardship and memories.

"Look!" Ashlyn stops. "A river."

I stop, bending over and resting my hands on my legs. Following her pointing finger, I see a river streaming out of a small waterfall. "No one mentioned a river before."

"I didn't know it existed, either."

"Do we have to cross it?"

Ashlyn scans our surrounding left and right. "It looks like it."

"Are you sure? I mean you're as lost as I am. Maybe we should find a way around the river."

"That'd be risking bumping into the soldiers," she says. "I'm also lost, but I have a better chance of recognizing something to guide us."

"All right," I'm still catching my breath when I glimpse a canoe by the side of the river. I point at it. "Is this what I think it is?"

Ashlyn sees right away. "Well..."

"A canoe?" I grimace.

"What's wrong with a canoe?"

"It's a bit too convenient, don't you think?"

"What does that mean? Someone must be regularly crossing the river. It actually suggests we're on the right track."

"How so?"

"Maybe this secret Furnace has only access through the river. If so, then a canoe makes perfect sense."

"All right," I say. "Let's do it. We're wasting time already."

I follow her to it. In the distance, I hear the faint shouts of soldiers. There is no point in thinking about it. I hurry to the canoe.

"Have you used one before?" Ashlyn asks nervously.

"Don't be a chicken." I wink, trying to sound calm. "Or is running all you can do?"

She stamps a foot once, like a child. "I trust you, June. Don't drown us."

We push the canoe into the river. It's heavy. Ashlyn jumps in like an adventurous little girl. I wonder if she is an only child, or never left her house before coming to this island. Jumping in behind her, I almost miss the canoe because of the river's strong current.

"Can you row it?" she asks.

"I don't know." I grit my teeth, doing my best with my weary arms. "I'm doing my best."

"Brave big sister."

That weakens my heart. The river is pulling us, fast, and I have no idea how to get to the other side. It would be a shame if we don't make it, because it's not far at all.

It turns out I can row. Maybe I learned that in my past life. The problem is that I still can't reach the other side. The current is too strong. We're flowing away from the pine trees we should follow.

Ashlyn screams. Before I can understand why, something happens. Something I can't comprehend. A sudden, sharp pain in my arms, so sharp I lose my grip on the paddle.

Slowly, I straighten my back. Ashlyn is still screaming. I realize we've crashed against a huge black rock that's stopping us from going down the river.

"Ashlyn, take my hand." I stand up. My legs are wobbly, but I manage. I pull her closer. "Look, this is actually good. I couldn't control the canoe, so we were just floating away from our destination."

"So?"

"We're only a few feet away from the other side of the river. I will climb on the edge of the canoe, so it shifts its weight nearer to the other side. From there, a jump will do the job and we'll be safe. You only need to jump as far as you can. Do you understand?"

She looks at the distance and says nothing. I turn and look. It's not that far. With a little shift from the canoe, we can do it.

"Tell me you understand," I say. "I am not going to let something bad happen to you."

"I will try."

"No, you have to focus, Ashlyn. It's going to only take a split second. Once I am on the edge and about to jump, you will have to jump with me. We can't hold hands. It won't help."

"I'm afraid I'm not going to make it," She lets out a cry, trying to look behind her.

I pull her face back to me and slap her. "Don't do this to me," I growl. "You will not die. I'm here for you."

Ashlyn's neck stiffens. "Are you going to hurt me like in the bathroom again?"

"No." I sigh. "That was a mistake. Just trust in me. Can you do that?"

"Why would you care about me?" She sobs as the canoe begins to shift underneath us. "You don't know me. You don't know anything about me."

"I don't know anything about my daughter either," I say. "It wouldn't stop me from taking a bullet for her."

"I'm not your daughter."

"That's true. But you're my sister, right?"

Her sobbing stops. She nods then hugs me.

"Great," I say. "I will count to three. Three is when I force the canoe to shift its weight. You keep a good eye on it. Once it's nearer to the river's edge..."

God, I don't know what I am doing. It's a mad idea, but I'm a mad girl, aren't I?

I climb out on the rock, one foot on the canoe's edge. It feels like walking on a tightrope. Ashlyn is struggling with her balance. Our weights aren't evenly spread on the canoe now. If one of us gives in, we're dead in the river.

I push with my free leg, and the canoe begins to swerve, slowly. I push harder to loosen it from the rock. It breaks free sooner than I expected. I struggle not to fall backward, but balance by elevating my free leg higher.

"Now!" I shout.

"You said you will count to—"

"I fucked up!" I jump with all my might. "Now!"

I'm in midair for only a second, wondering why I left her behind—unless she manages to jump. Why didn't I wait one more second to explain to her? Or hold her hand? Or even stick with her and not jump?

I don't know.

I grab a rock by the river's edge and hold on to it. The river tugs on my lower body, but I manage to pull myself up. I crawl over the rock for safety.

Panting, I roll on my back, not bothering to look for Ashlyn. Tears trickle down my cheeks before they turn to cries, so painful I think I'll faint. I lost her, and I know the reason why: because if I have to choose between a daughter and a sister, my daughter wins.

Chapter 41

My eyes flip open again...

I am still on my back. It's dark, but I can see shadows over me. The metallic smell of blood is killing me. I keep coughing it out, so I don't choke on it, and I still can't move my left arm.

"Mommy!" my daughter squeals again.

"Hold on, baby. Mommy will protect you."

I realize I can only feel one arm. The right one. But it's jammed under some heavy weight. I'm too weak to push or pull at it. My other arm is either cut off or numb. I don't believe it exists anymore.

Though it's dark, I try to twist my neck to look around. The needling pain stops. I'm such a mess. What the hell is this?

I squint against the darkness, hoping I'll recognize this place I am in, but nothing explains this opening at top or the sound of water. I form a theory: that the plane broke in two, and I'm at the bottom of its tail, sinking into the abyss.

"Help!" I shout. My voice is feeble, and I'm afraid if I talk louder, more blood will seep into my throat and choke me.

But if I'm in the plane's tail, there should be other passengers. Me and my daughter couldn't possibly be the only ones alive.

"H-hang on," I say, but she doesn't reply.

Is she all right?

"Hey!" I realize I don't remember her name. "Where are you, baby?"

The place sinks into pitch-black darkness. The looming silhouette from before blocks the light.

I can smell it. That terrible scent. It smells of oil, the kind used in cars. I'm sure of it now. Where have I smelled this before?

"Who are you?" I try to wriggle my right arm free.

No one responds, but I'm sure someone's there. I also realize that my arm is squeezed under something heavy, but also something fleshy. God, it's under a corpse.

I try to pull away with all my might, but it hurts so much that I'm afraid I could break my only functioning arm.

"Baby?" I call again. "Wh-where a-a-are you?"

The silhouette looms closer. It makes a sniffing sound. "She's gone," it gruffly whispers to me.

"Who are you?" I squint again, trying to make out its face.

"You will never have her. You fucked up."

"Who are you?" I demand, still trying to free my arm.

"You know who I am."

I arch my body upward, trying to reach for it, but my body punishes me with a dose of pain in my bones. "Who the hell are you?"

"I am..." it says, but then the blaring sound escalates to deafening levels again.

Chapter 42

"June?"

Ashlyn's voice brings me back to life.

"Why are you crying?" she says.

I'm panting, unable to talk.

"We did it," she announces. "I jumped."

"But I didn't count." I prop myself up on my elbows. Looking at her, I feel like I'm looking into sunshine. I long to touch her face and be sure this isn't part of my dream.

"It's okay. You fucked up." She chuckles. "We all do. Don't we?"

"I am so glad you're alive." I say.

"I know." She smiles, rubbing her cheek against my palm. "I've never met anyone so happy to see me."

"I'm sure you have," I say. "You just don't remember."

"Maybe I'm an amnesiac too. Though I wouldn't mind starting all over again."

"Why do you say that, Ash? You're young and have your whole life ahead of you."

"You think so?" She looks around. "Even if we find your daughter, I don't think we'll make it off the island. Not alive."

"Don't do this. We're going to be fine. I promise you. Once we find my daughter, and remember things, I'm sure we will get help. Maybe Dr. Suffolk will be on our side. Just don't worry about it."

"If you say so." She stands up. "First, we need to find the Furnace."

I stand up as well and laugh. "You're right. Let's go."

"I don't think we need to search."

"What do you mean?"

She points behind me. "Look."

I turn, almost in slow motion. She's pointing at an abandoned gas station. It could easily be a set from a post-apocalyptic zombie movie: burned, old, and creepily abandoned.

A couple of old Jeeps are parked on one side. One has two flat tires. The other has been stripped and is now a skeleton of what it once was. There is a third one, flipped on its side and burned to the bone. The station is a horror house I don't want to enter at all. One weird thing sticks out and doesn't fit, though. The fuel dispensers. They still look old, but not dead.

"Come on," Ashlyn says. "We've found the Furnace."

"Careful," I whisper. "We're not sure if someone's watching."

"Doesn't look like it," Ashlyn says. "It may have significance for people on this island but doesn't look usable at all."

"The fuel dispensers look intact."

"I noticed. Maybe they still use it? Just to fill up their Jeeps in the middle of the island?"

"That doesn't add up." I walk with her. "Just be careful."

As we take slow steps forward, details come into focus. Everything seems to have been built years and years ago. It's hard to explain how I know, but it doesn't take a genius to know a building isn't from this era.

"It's old," Ashlyn says, reading my mind.

"As old as Ward Four?"

"What do you mean?"

"Ward Four was built in the 1940s, and so was this station, is my guess."

"There is no shop anywhere, like in modern gas stations," she remarks, then points upward. "And look at this, June."

I crane my neck, staring at an old sign hanging over the building's ramshackle door. An old rectangle of wood, burned to black on the edges and skewed to one side. The sign reads: *1001.*

Chapter 43

My hands are loosely hanging at my sides. I don't think I can explain my feelings, if I do feel a precise emotion. It's not just that I've finally realized "Toot" is just a number. It's also not the fact that I've arrived at the place written on my gun, my Kindle, and on the notes. It's the way *1001* is written on the sign.

"It's almost the same handwriting." Ashlyn looks between the sign and the note she took out of her pocket.

"So odd," I mumble, not taking my eyes off it.

"This sign looks old," Ashlyn says. "Not necessarily as old as the building, but it wasn't carved yesterday."

I have nothing to say. How can you say something when your brain has ceased to think? I feel like I'm lost in time and space.

"Are you sure you've never been here before?" Ashlyn says.

"You mean on the island?" My neck is still craned up. "Why are you asking?"

"I don't know. I'm just thinking out loud."

"Wouldn't Meredith have remembered me?"

"She neither confirmed nor denied it. She only urged you to leave as soon as you can."

"The only way I see it is that someone on this island kidnapped my daughter, maybe?" I look at Ashlyn. "And I came to save her?"

"Sounds like a movie," she says. "Still possible, though."

My head is still in a daze. I'm looking at Ashlyn, but I don't quite see her. My eyes are looking at nothingness. A blank vision of emptiness, like white pages of a novel that need a writer's imagination to fill them up.

"Let's not get ahead of ourselves," Ashlyn says. "Let's focus on what we know."

"Like what?" I'm slowly snapping back into reality.

"This place is called the Furnace, which is also an old gas station called the One Thousand and One—for whatever reason."

"Okay?"

"We could assume the Furnace is an appropriate name for a gas station. Gas and fire and stuff, you know. Also, the notes were written in oil."

"Oil, gas station, Furnace. Yeah, I can see a connection, but nothing clear enough to know what's going on." I tell her this without mentioning my dream and the smell of oil in it. I pretend the daydreams are nothing but hallucinations for now.

"You're actually right." She lets out a long sigh. "What is this place? What are we even doing here? This so strange."

"I think we should take a look. It's what we came for."

Ashlyn gives me the eye. "Mindy said Hecker feared this place."

I shrug. This place is so unsettling from outside. A spiraling breeze sends chills down my back. It reminds me of when I first arrived on the island.

"The shore is just a few feet away," Ashlyn says. "I can hear the crashing waves."

"What are you thinking about?"

"Nothing." She looks away.

"Do you want to leave?"

"I said it's nothing, June."

"Do you know a way to leave the island, from the shore, maybe?" I point behind me. "Listen, you don't have to stay with me. If you know a way out, just go."

"I won't leave you."

"No, you're not listening. I'm here for my daughter. I'm not leaving before I find her. You should go and save your ass. What is it? A boat? Somewhere nearby?"

Ashlyn fidgets, looking downward. "We've heard rumors that there is a submarine somewhere by the shore," she says shyly. "Another nurse once managed to escape with it."

"And the soldiers?"

"I don't know. It's a mystery. The older nurses say that whoever operates it could be bribed."

"That's hard to believe, not on this island with all the soldiers."

“I know,” she says. “They’ve always said it’s at the end of the pines parallel to the beach. But you have to cross the forest first.”

“Okay.” I nod. “That’s why you kinda knew where to go, and I had to follow you.”

“I didn’t know. I just imagined the path from the rumors we’ve heard," She looks into my eyes. “It’s not necessarily true.”

“Do you want to go?”

“I don’t know. It’s just the situation we’re in, and—”

“And?”

“I mean, I thought something significant would happen once we found the Furnace, but—”

“I understand. The situation suggests the soldiers will eventually catch us now.”

“I don’t mean to be rude, but we don’t even know where to look next,” she says. “I don’t want to die, June. I mean, I really like you, but now that I feel that breeze from the sea, I’d like to have a chance at staying alive.”

“That’s totally okay, Ashlyn. Go. I understand. It’s just that I don’t see how easy it will be to leave.”

“I don’t see it either, but I need to try,” she says with moist eyes. “I’m afraid to ask you to leave with me, because I know you will not leave your daughter behind.”

“That’s true. I’m not leaving without her.”

"I can get help," she offers. "Once I leave, I can report everything to the authorities."

"I don't think that will work. Listen, I want you to do what you feel like. And I am so sorry I dragged you into this. But my hunch is that this submarine is a myth. Even if it exists and you can actually leave in it—which is just unbelievable—how can you leave in this weather?"

"Okay." She walks away.

"Okay?"

Ashlyn surprises me by walking in the opposite direction of the Suffolk. She is actually walking right into the horror house.

"Ashlyn!" I dart after her.

"Let's be done with this," she says, pushing the door open.

"Ashlyn. Wait!"

She disappears inside, and I follow her. Her sudden change of mind surprises me, and I am a few steps behind her now. I reach for the door, ready to open it, when I hear her shout from inside.

"June! You have to see this!"

Chapter 44

I enter but stop in my tracks right away. There is no office or a counter inside. It's more like a junkyard full of tires and tools. Seems like it's been used as a garage or something. It baffles me how a car got in here. A double sliding door up front explains it. Ashlyn hurries to it and pulls the lever.

"Stop," I reach out. "We don't know what's behind it—"

Too late, confusingly enthusiastic Ashlyn has opened it already.

Nothing dangerous so far. Only strange, like everything else on the island.

We're staring at some garden.

It's dirty and looks like it's been a perpetual autumn in here. The plants are brown and yellowish, not to mention everything seems dry and dead in spite of the continuous rain. But that's just part of the picture.

Ashlyn walks farther into the garden. In front of her, there is an old wall. Brick and mortar. It's abandoned but doesn't look as old as everything else. Most of it is covered in crawling vines and bushes.

"What do you think this is?" I say.

"Looks recent."

"Built clumsily and uneven."

"Probably in a hurry."

"To stop someone from leaving or to separate something behind it?"

"I can peek through a few brick holes here and there," she peeks through the bushes and vines.

"What do you see?"

"Haven't looked, but we don't need to."

"What do you mean?"

She points at the far left of the wall.

"A door?" I squint.

"A rusty iron door." She approaches it. "The plot thickens."

I'm not sure why Ashly would use a phrase like the *plot thickens*, but I assume she's manipulating herself into thinking this is an adventure not a nightmare so she can handle the pressure.

I say, "Do you want me to go through first?"

It amazes me how she thinks part of this is a game sometimes. "Nah, I can do it." She says.

I doubt it but admire her challenging herself. I watch her pull on the door with all her might. It squeaks. I immediately look around, afraid this will grab someone's attention. She pulls on the door again to fully open it. I don't know why, but I stand cemented in place. Something about seeing her open it freezes me. I don't even approach. Something tells me I don't want to see what's behind the wall.

Ashlyn steps inside. I am expecting her to take her time and tell me what's there. My expectations are wrong. She screams as soon as she enters.

I watch her jump back. She bends over, resting a hand on the wall as she begins to vomit.

Still paralyzed, I ask her, "What is it, Ash?"

She continues puking her guts out, then raises her eyes to meet mine. "I think we found the Crib."

Chapter 45

I try to unchain myself from my fears and slowly trudge toward the door. A rotten smell attacks me. It intensifies the closer I get.

"What's inside, Ashlyn?" I ask, ashamed at my cowardice.

She vomits again. Her small frame is in pain. She wipes her mouth with the back of her hand then signals for me to look for myself.

My breathing gets heavier as I walk through the door. My stomach churns. The mist thickens inside this walled place. All kinds of scenarios run through my head. I wonder if we're on the west side of the island now. It occurs to me that the soldiers weren't trying to catch us, but instead stop us from seeing the Crib for ourselves.

The mist clears a bit. My eyes widen, and now I see.

Everywhere I tread, corpses are piled up in front of me. This place, though vast, isn't big enough for them all. Skeletons are almost knotted into each other. Pyramids of macabre bones show up every few steps. The smell is overwhelming. Most skeletons are incomplete. They look like they have been burned.

"I think that's why they call it the Furnace." Ashlyn coughs, standing by the door behind me. I don't think she can force herself inside again.

As for me, it's as if my legs can't walk me back anymore. Once you're in hell, there is no way back. I keep looking, trying to understand. Is this a cemetery? Who are these dead people? Who burned them?

All of a sudden, I stop and balance myself on the edge of a hole dug in the ground. Then I realize the carnage that happened in this place. Those bones forming pyramids aren't set on the ground but piled up from large holes in the earth. Whoever killed these people hadn't planned to kill as many. I feel like I'm back in time, witnessing the aftermath of the Black Death in Europe.

I walk around the hole. Endless cans of gas are scattered on the sides. Some empty, some not. That's what the gas station is for. This place really is a furnace.

"I think you should get out of there, June," Ashlyn says.

I keep going. Further ahead, I begin to see clumps of burned flesh. They smell the worst. Those victims are recent. Whatever this is, it's not a shameful genocide from the past. It's an ongoing crime.

I change direction, still advancing. I don't know what I am looking for, but I need a clue. I need a reason for this darkness. Not a reason. Nothing will ever justify this. I need an explanation. A motive. How is it possible someone could do this?

Something greenish shows in the dark. It sticks out like a flower in a pile of ashes. It gives me a little hope. I realize it's the first real color I've seen inside this place. The rest is every different shade of ash. I rush toward the green, accidentally stepping on something fleshy. I don't look down, and cup my hand over my mouth and force myself to inhale ashy air as I walk toward the green.

It's clothing. I can see clearer now. But it's not just one set. There is another. And another. So many. The same green gown, over and over again. They're hospital gowns, but not the same as the one I wore on my first day on the island. Similar, but darker green.

What does it mean? They burn patients on this island, here in the Furnace. Why?

Accidentally, I kick something. It's also something green, but small, and it's not clothes. I kneel down and pick it up. It's a wristband. It's metal and has a number carved on the side. Ten. And a name. A woman's name: Janice.

A terrible premonition occurs to me as I come across more wristbands all over the ground.

I bend down and scoop up as many wristbands I can. The hair prickles on the back of my neck as I read the names:

Joan Murray, number 28, Ready.

I pick up another.

Juliane Koepcke, number 345, Ready.

And another.

Vesna Vulovic, number 1004, Ready

I don't know any of them, but I keep hearing a sound in my head. The sound of crying babies.

"June? Found anything?"

"I think I did." My heart is pounding against my chest. I feel like a fish out of water, unable to breathe. "I can't believe this."

"What is it?"

I can't tell her. She will freak out. I think I've read over fifty names now. All women. Not a single man. I fall on my knees. Dear God, what is happening on this island? The baby's cries aren't all I hear in the back of my head. Now I hear Meredith taunting me: *The horrible things they will do to you…*

I bend over but don't vomit yet. The weight of truth is pushing me down, closer to the dead. I crawl on all fours, hysterically picking up more wristbands and reading the names. It's impossible.

"Answer me, June. You're scaring me."

I am as scared as her, if not more. More wristbands. Some unreadable from the fire. Thirst attacks me. I feel like I am dehydrating, out of fear, not lack of liquids. I fall flat on my face. Imaginary photos of every woman fly before my eyes. Why the hell is someone burning women on this island?

Then a dark, dark thought comes to me. I am staring at the wristbands, realizing why I've been collecting them. What if one of them is my daughter's?

Chapter 46

I can hardly breathe. My brain reels with possible explanations, but none of them are plausible enough. I don't even have the slightest idea what to do next.

"June!" Ashlyn is panicking outside. "Are you okay?"

"Don't come in here, Ashlyn," I snap. "You don't want to see any of this."

"Believe me, I know."

I force myself to stand. My back resists my wishes. I drop the wristbands on the ground. "I'll be back in a second."

"Good," she says. "Because there's something else I need to show you."

"Okay. Okay." I convince myself that I'm trying to calm her down, when in reality I am trying to calm myself down.

"No, really," she says. "I mean, I don't know what I smell inside, but I hope it doesn't have anything to do with this."

"This?"

"Please come and see."

"I said okay." My voice is as stiff as old piano strings.

Her words are barely audible over a sudden gust from the ocean. I think she says, "It's the walls..."

I can't make out the rest. I don't think I even want to. The breeze intensifies the awful smell. It's sickening. I try my best to confirm whether this is the same awful smell as in my dreams. I can't.

"June!"

I turn around. Maybe it's best to leave.

"The walls!"

I walk over the mucky ground, with no intentions of looking down. Ashlyn stands by the wall looking sideways. I guess she means the cemetery's wall, but from outside. She keeps pointing against the heavy rain.

A sudden beam of light slices through the darkness. An artificial beam of light, circling the Furnace from above. I should be scared, but instead I freeze again. I can see the piled-up corpses clearer now. I didn't want to see this. It was much easier in the dark. I raise my hands in the air and surrender. For a moment I don't care about the soldiers coming to capture me — or even kill me — as long as I get out of this dark, dark place.

I look away and force myself to walk a few more steps to the iron door.

Ashlyn pulls me down by my sleeves. We duck together behind the wall. She points at the source of light. A lighthouse in the distance. "It's a watchtower," she says.

The loud blare in my ears attacks me again. I am not sure if it's real. I clamp my ears with my hands and shrink my posture against the pain.

"It's so loud," Ashlyn shouts. I am surprised she can hear it. "A warning siren. I hear it sometimes when I'm in Ward Four."

"You can hear this?" I shout back, hoping she will say yes, that it's not all in my head.

She nods. "It sounds like a car's honk."

"Yes!" I say. She is right. I couldn't put my finger on it earlier. It does sound like an incredibly loud honk from some car. But how can it be?

"So this means they found out we left the ward?"

"Must have been Mindy!" Ashlyn says. "Or how would they have found out?"

I glare at her. We've both been so naive, thinking Hecker's secret nurse lover wouldn't give us away.

"But listen," Ashlyn says. "Whatever happens to us, you have to see the writing on the wall—"

An amplified voice from a loudspeaker interrupts, "Please come out, Miss June."

"You have to—" Ashlyn's voice is fading to black in the back of my head.

I don't care about the wall. I changed my mind. I don't want to be caught. I want to find my daughter. "We have to find a way out," I say.

"But the wall—"

"Forget the damn fucking wall," I shake her violently again. "You have no idea what I've seen in the Furnace. Meredith was right. You have no idea what they will do to us."

The horrible things they do to women.

"I think I can imagine it," Ashlyn says. "If you just look at the sign on the wall."

Though all I want is to escape now and to protect Ashlyn, I turn my head and follow her gaze. Her face twitches in the rain and her lower jaw shivers as she points at the wall. I squint, not sure what I am looking at. Yes, there are a few signs on the walls. Hand painted in red. Inverted crosses, I think?

Red inverted crosses like the small one on my gun?

Ashlyn demands my attention, as we wait for the light from the tower to shine onto the wall. It does, ever so briefly, but long enough for me to realize it's not an inverted cross. It's an even much more worse sign. My mind has only tricked me to see it as an inverted cross, so I wouldn't panic. But now that I see it, this island scares the shit out of me.

I return my frozen gaze back to Ashlyn. Images of the women burned in the cemetery flood my vision. The sign on the wall explains, in a vague way, what happened here. At least it's proportionate with the atrocity of the crime.

Ashlyn nods, horror dripping from her face. "Swastikas."

"I saw," I say with a dropped jaw. "But how is that possible?"

"It explains the grey uniform," she says.

God in heaven, what is this place? The soldiers' grey outfits remind me now of the Nazis SS uniforms, except they have stripped them of additional stripes and insignias. This makes no sense at all.

I don't have time to ponder that. I'm too late to even find a way out of this situation. Silhouettes of soldiers loom out of the forest. Heavy squelches of their boots sound in the mud, as they come for us.

My whole being is chained to the insurmountable horror in Ashlyn's eyes. *The horrible things they will do to you.* I scream at her, summing up all my confusion into one word. It's an order. Precise and short, "Run!"

Chapter 47

Ashlyn doesn't think twice about it. She takes off, running aimlessly in the dark. This is when I realize it was a mistake. I shouldn't have told her to run. The moment she does, soldiers start shooting at her.

"No!" I scream.

The shooting continues. My God. What have I done?

I stand up and dart after her, but she's already gone. The forest ahead is dark. The cemetery behind me is as dark. I can't find her. Which direction did she go? I'm worried that if I summon her, they'll know where she is exactly when she replies. But I have to find her. I am so fucking confused. How can I save her?

I wave my hands in the air. "No. You want me, not her!"

The shooting doesn't stop.

I tell myself I'd hear her moan or make a sound if she gets shot, but I'm not sure this will be the case.

I keep waving my hands at the sky. Then I hop in every direction, not sure where the soldiers are. "Take me! I'm here. You're looking for me."

The strobe of light shifts left and right in consecutive movements.

"Here!" I wave at the lighthouse.

The light stops, focusing on me. I'm at the center of the stage now. Never have I thought that light would scare me more than darkness. I swallow hard. My arms are still in the air. I resist the urge to close my eyes and say a prayer I don't remember. Nothing should stop them from shooting me now.

At least, I saved Ashlyn's life.

"I'll turn myself in," I shield one hand against the light. "Just don't shoot her."

The shooting stops. Heavy footsteps trudge in the mud all around me. *The horrible things they will do to you.* I wish they would just kill me, and not burn me like the women in the cemetery.

The footsteps get louder the closer they get. A shadow forms out of the light from the strobe. A soldier with a machine gun. It's Hecker.

I shiver when I see him. He is gritting his teeth. Veins are visibly pulsing in his neck. "I knew you were not who you told us you were from the beginning," his tall frame shadows me, up close and personal. "I hate it when I'm right."

"I know, I know," I lower my gaze. "Just don't shoot her. Take me."

"Is this another game of yours?" Hecker breathes his anger into my face.

"I'm not playing games," I insist. "Take me. Let her live, and I beg you, tell me where my daughter is."

Hecker roars with laughter, addressing the soldiers surrounding me. "Did you hear that, boys?"

The soldiers laugh back with harassing comments about how they wasted time finding me when they had important work to do.

"Come again?" he asks me.

"I'm begging you to let Ashlyn live."

"Who is Ashlyn?" He takes a step closer, his gun touching my thighs. I'm not sure if it's intentional.

"The nurse." I pull my leg away from his machine gun.

"What nurse?"

"The goddamn nurse who you were shooting at," I stomp a foot while my shoulders tense.

"Ah," Hecker says and takes a step back. "I guess we were shooting at her."

I grimace, still not looking up to him.

"We're not here for her, anyways," he says. "We're here for you, Miss June," he snickers. "You shouldn't have escaped Ward Four."

"Yeah? And let you kill me?"

"We weren't going to kill you," he says. "Not if you'd obeyed the rules. Don't leave the ward. Don't look west. Wait for the storm to subside. Why was that so hard? Now you've seen too much. Things got complicated. I personally think you're not who you say you are."

"I'm sorry. Just promise me Ash will be okay."

"Ash?"

"The goddamn nurse."

"Ah, her name is Ash," he says. "Don't worry about her. Now are you coming with us willingly or are you going to resist me?"

"Do I look like I have a choice?" I raise my gaze to meet his eyes.

"Good. You will stay in Ward Four until the weather gets better, and then we'll send you back home, wherever the fuck that is."

"Do I have your word?" I raise my eyes to meet his.

"You're infiltrating a top secret military base, Miss June. We've been generously patient with you, and we don't accommodate women ever. So don't offend and ask me to give you my fucking word."

I want to comment that they don't accommodate women because they burn them in the Furnace, but I don't. What if they're not sure what I've seen? He said I've seen too much but didn't mention the dead women in the cemetery. The soldiers caught me and Ashlyn on the outside wall, so I have to count on the possibility that they think we've not seen inside. Also, the rain has washed the muck from her face, as I can't feel any from lying flat on the floor inside the furnace. Otherwise, I doubt he'd ever let me leave like he promised.

I surrender to the soldiers approaching. They look like alien beings in the light. Two of them hold me by the arms, ready to show me to the Jeep.

"Good girl," Hecker grins and spits his gum out. "We'll take you to Major Red first. He wants a word with you. Let's go."

"Wait," I say. "Where is Ashlyn? I'm not going anywhere without her."

"About that," Hecker cracks his neck left and right. He says nothing, looking at the forest.

Words refuse to form in my mouth.

"I have to tell you something, Miss June." He follows.

Now thoughts refuse to form in my head.

"My soldiers aren't the brightest dudes, sometimes."

I make an effort to stand still. I make an effort to open my mouth. My jaw hurts so much, "What do you mean? Where the hell is Ash?"

"It was an accident," Hecker says. "Ash is nothing but ash. I guess her name preceded her fate. She's gone."

Middle

Chapter 48

Mercy Medical Center, New York

FBI agent James Madison Floyd stared at the window but couldn't see beyond the rain outside. He lifted one hand and wiped the foggy glass from his side. The rain was lighter now, but not for long. New York's weather had always surprised him. It defied forecasts and expectations year after year. But this nonstop pouring in the middle of June was a tad unusual.

He bent his bulky frame forward to watch the rain trickling on the glass but saw his reflection instead. Damn, he'd gotten older. A little paler for a black man, too. He ignored his reflection and looked past it at the rain again. He enjoyed it. At least it made him feel like he had a friend in this hospital. The raindrops reminded him of the tears he was suppressing behind his eyes.

At fifty-five, he was in great shape. His coworkers had always feared him. He was too brash, they'd said. A man who feared nothing. Not that it was entirely true, but his impressive résumé played a role in their perception of him.

In the past, he had played essential roles in saving lives all over the world. He'd never shed a tear in a battle—the same way he refused to cry now. Great men died in Floyd's presence, serving their country and trying to save others' lives. He'd never flinched. His only focus was on getting the job done.

In the bureau, they called him the Rock. But right now, Floyd didn't feel like a rock. He doubted he would have the grit to keep his tears inside any longer.

He turned and glanced at the woman lying speechless on the bed. Comatose, eyes closed, and breathing shallowly. The minimum breaths to stay alive, he supposed.

She was about his age. She wore a lime-green hospital gown. She ate and drank from a tube. And never said a word.

In fact, she hadn't moved for three years, stretched out on this coffin the doctors called a hospital bed. She was the dearest person to his heart. Her name was August.

Since her accident, Floyd had spent most of his time next to her. He'd have spent every minute of the rest of his life next to her, but he couldn't. Not with the loneliness he suffered watching her being neither dead nor alive.

Doctors had advised him to stay positive. When he'd asked about her chances to wake up from her coma, they always looked away without a definitive answer. Later, he'd learned the answer was almost never.

"I'm here, August," Floyd whispered. "In case you can hear me."

August just lay there, breathing monotonously. He could never fathom the difference between a coma and death. Patients had no means to interact with their loved ones either way. Death wasn't just about leaving the world but leaving loved ones in this world.

Floyd usually pretended she answered him, so the conversation didn't die. "I want you to know that I'm always here."

Some doctors claimed that she could hear him. At least feel his presence. If he'd learned anything in this hospital, then it was that doctors didn't know jack-shit.

If August could hear him, why hadn't she made a sign? A cough. An infrequent breath. Blinking eyes or a wiggling finger. None of that ever happened. She only lay there, trapped inside her head, inside a world he didn't know anything about. Sometimes when he talked to her long enough, telling her about his day, he had to watch the rise and fall of her chest to make sure she hadn't died...yet.

"I love you, baby," he said, then sat at the edge of the bed and gently rubbed her left arm. She used to like that when she was conscious, but told him he had rough hands and that his touch was too strong. They laughed. Good old times.

Floyd let out a short sigh then stretched his arms behind his back. He still wasn't used to prolonged sessions doing nothing. Being on call was bliss, or he would have gone crazy.

Sometimes he wasn't sure why he was here beside her. What was the point? What was the use? She wasn't healing, and he truly doubted she felt his presence.

One of the younger doctors had asked him to pull the plug on her. Floyd had given it some thought. Keeping August alive had nothing to do with beliefs or morals. He just couldn't imagine living without her. At least her body was still intact, and he could still look at her on a daily basis, as selfish as it sounded.

Floyd's cell phone rang. He recognized the caller. It was Karl Dixon from NTSB, the National Transportation Safety Board of America. He picked up immediately. Back to work.

"Dixon?" Floyd said. "Tell me you have good news."

"I have, sir," Dixon said. "We've found the plane."

Chapter 49

I am taking a shower in my bathroom in Ward Four. Not that I need to, but mingling my tears with the water helps me calm down. As for the blood on my hands, I doubt it will ever wash away.

The women's blood in the cemetery, Ashlyn's blood, and hopefully not my daughter's—I try my best not to think about the last part.

Right now, I wear my guilt over Ashlyn on my skin like tight latex, suffocating me.

With closed eyes, I can see what happened after Hecker told me of Ashlyn's death. It plays like a movie in my mind.

It started with me kicking one of the soldiers in the groin and pulling myself free from the other. I crouched as Hecker tried to catch me and hurried toward the forest.

All the screaming in the world could not fix the aching inside. Guilt sometimes feels like a dull, useless knife. It won't cut, no matter how hard you want to use it to slit your wrists.

The strobing lights searching for me went crazy in every direction. I ran in curvy paths to evade them, and also because I couldn't tell where I was heading exactly. A vague sense of the path Ashlyn had taken guided me into the darkness. But like in the movies, I ended up stumbling over her dead body.

I dropped to all fours, reaching for her, attacked by the smell of her blood. Her body was still warm, but unresponsive. I couldn't bring myself to touch her. Most of her pale face was covered in blood. It looked black in the dark, not red. She lay on her back, her legs askew, reminding me of every other woman I'd seen in the Furnace.

God, she was so young. She could have done so many things in her life. She'd been here to make money and better her life. Most of all, she'd offered to help me when she knew it would kill her. I'd been foolish bringing her into this. Selfish! What had I done?

I closed my eyes and wished to die, but then reminded myself of a daughter I was supposed to save. There was a moment when I doubted everything, even the existence of my daughter. From the beginning, none of this has made sense. My insanity would be the only plausible explanation or conclusion.

"It should have been me," I whispered, reaching for her, and instead of giving her a proper burial, I gave her a hug goodbye.

I squeezed her to me with all my might, wondering why I loved her so much. Of course she'd helped, and she was a lovable person. But my feelings surpassed that. I really loved her. If she had been any younger, I'd have suspected that she, in some convoluted turn of events, could have been the daughter I was looking for. But I couldn't have given birth to a girl. I would have been too young.

Or could I?

I let out a cry. Pain ran through my veins instead of blood. Part was because of Ashlyn's death. Part was for my confusion. I'd come to a point where I prayed this all would be a dream, so I could just wake up from it in the morning.

I could hear the soldiers arriving again. This time I was too tired to fight. Ashlyn gave one last cough, spitting blood on me. I shrieked. I'd thought she was gone.

I held her closer, thinking she had a chance to make it. "Help!" I shouted, wishfully asking for a savior on this godforsaken island.

But Ashlyn didn't look like she'd make it. She knew she was dying. I could see it in the empty look in her eyes. She'd given up, and in some wicked way, she seemed to like it. She wanted to leave this island, even if the afterlife was her only solace. Ashlyn had only returned briefly to tell me something.

I lowered my head and pressed my ear to her lips. She talked in sputters and staccato. I think she said: *"You were right about the babies."*

Then she fell back, staring into the side of life we'll all stare at eventually, once and for all. Then Hecker silenced me with the butt of his machine gun on my skull.

Now, as I turn the water off and get out of the shower, I can't help thinking about my purpose in all of this. Drying off,

I remind myself we all need a purpose in life. Mine is finding my daughter. And it's not because of the yellow note I received about a man called Manfred Toot that I am supposed to kill. It's because I *know* that I have a daughter.

If I were in conversation with a stranger, they'd ask me how I know. All the logic in the world will not give me the right answers. The only thing I know is what I feel. A mother always knows. And when I held Ashlyn in my arms, the feeling came down on me like lightning. Amnesiac or not, I do have a daughter, and she is in great danger.

My only hope to find her will be to find the Crib. The Furnace isn't the Crib. It just can't be.

And then comes the swastika part. Could this island be some sort of a Nazi camp, one no one has ever heard about? One that has been kept secret for more than seventy years? It shouldn't make sense, but it is my only plausible explanation. I have little historical knowledge about the world seventy years ago. Meredith would have more answers, I guess. She has been here since World War II. Ward Four was built in World War II. So the island is that old.

So are the soldiers here Nazis? Can't be. There are no Nazis anymore, right? Neo-Nazis, maybe. But what would they be doing on this island? Does this have anything to do with the sect Major Red talked about? If so, how do I fit into all of this? And what the hell is this island for?

A knock on my bathroom door interrupts my thoughts.

"Miss June," some soldier says. "Major Red will see you now."

Still naked, I tell him I will be ready in a few. I hear him leave, then stare at my reflection in the mirror again. The girl staring back at me knows what I am about to say. She agrees, nodding. She knows that whatever darkness I suspect is inside me has to come out now. If I can use a gun, then I'll have to use it. If I can be threatening like I was with Ashlyn in the bathroom, then I will. If I want to find my daughter and save her, I have a feeling I will have to kill someone in the process. No wonder I came here with a gun.

Chapter 50

Mercy Medical Center, New York

James Floyd listened to Dixon's update about the plane that crashed in the Atlantic yesterday. The man apologized for not finding the plane sooner but blamed it on the horrible weather.

"Actually, there is a possibility of a coming hurricane," Dixon explained. "So I was thinking maybe the rescue team should wait a few hours."

"And lose the chance of saving the lives on the plane?" Floyd said. He didn't like Dixon much, but that had nothing to do with the job. "Of course not."

"I don't think anyone can survive this, if you ask me," Dixon argued.

"No one thought Poon Lim would survive the South Atlantic for 133 days on a log made of wood," Floyd said.

Poon Lim was a legend to everyone in the NTSB, a true miracle. He was a Chinese sailor who survived alone in the South Atlantic while working as a second steward on the British merchant ship *SS Ben Lomond* when it was sunk by a German U-boat on November 23, 1945.

"Poon Lim was an exception," Dixon said. "Miracles don't happen every day."

"Miracles always happen," Floyd said, losing some of the authority in his voice. He held his wife's hand tighter.

"How about my men?" Dixon asked. "They could die saving the passengers."

"It's their job. They didn't sign up and get the appropriate training for shits and giggles."

Dixon kept silent. Floyd didn't mind. He had been sharing silence with his wife for three years now. A precious silence.

"Floyd," Dixon said, "the probability of finding survivors is less than one percent. It's not worth it. I'm not saying we're packing up. I'm only asking for a few more hours on hold."

"Dixon," Floyd said, then stood silent for a few heartbeats. "You're fired."

"What?" Dixon's rage was instant. "You can't do that. You're FBI, not the NTSB. The only reason why you're involved is to see if the plane crash was a terrorist attack."

"I think you'd be surprised to learn that I care about survivors more than discovering if it's a terrorist attack," Floyd said. "Lives first, conclusions second. If you don't cooperate now, I will make sure my report mentions it."

Dixon's rough breathing crackled in the speaker. "Yes, sir. We're on our way to the plane crash right now."

"Full squad. Divers, ROVs, and choppers," Floyd said. "I want a full list of everybody you find. Survivor or not."

"Of course."

"An accurate list, Dixon. No fuckups like with TWA and 9/11." Floyd remembered those days. The FBI and NTSB had messed up the names on the list and caused a lot of pain for the passengers' families. He didn't want that to happen again. He knew from experience that saving one soul would make all the families happy, even those who'd lost their loved ones. The magic of hope, of saving lives, was like no other.

Putting the phone aside, Floyd pulled his wife's hand up to his mouth and kissed it. "Normally, I would only care to know if the plane crash was a terrorist attack," he told her, hoping she really did hear him. "But I know you'd want to save survivors first, even if it's just one."

Chapter 51

Major Red greets me at the door. He looks surprisingly concerned. He takes my hand between his two clammy burned palms and says, "I am so sorry, Miss June. So sorry about Ashlyn. It was a mistake."

I find myself speechless. Not in awe, but in horror. In a state of suspicion and disgust. I've come here, prepared to shout and spit in his face, even look for my gun and threaten him with it. But he shows such fake sympathy? I am wondering what kind of sick game is on the table now.

In an instant, I pull my hand away. Something about his touch suddenly makes me want to throw up. A peculiar fear goosebumps all over my skin. It reminds of my dreams.

"Please sit down," He pulls a chair out for me, not commenting on my behavior. "Would you like something to drink?" He taps me on the shoulder. I push his filthy hand away.

He doesn't react. He isn't angry. What the fuck is going on?

I watch him sit down behind his desk, noticing the slightly foul smell on him fade out with distance. What is that smell? Like the soldiers, it's so familiar but I can't seem to identify it.

"We're burying Ashlyn tomorrow," he says. "Though it's forbidden, and the coming storm is our priority, we'll have a big funeral for her outside — if the weather gets better of course."

He makes it sound like it's her birthday tomorrow. Silence still overwhelms me. I can easily jump over and pull the gun and put a bullet in between his eyes.

For Ashlyn.

I have enough pain and guts to do it. It only scares me to leave this world without fighting for my daughter.

Then a snowflake of a thought floats before my eyes: *is it possible that Major Red is Manfred Toot?*

He looks like someone I want to kill. It's not farfetched in my book. Looking at him, I don't see why not. He's operating this island. He knows what it's really about. Everyone fears him. Wearing his grey soldier's outfit with no insignia makes me think he really is a Nazi. A neo-Nazi. Or a follower. Or admirer. Who gives a shit?

"I have the soldier who shot Ashlyn on trial," Major Red says. "My orders were to find you both and bring you back."

I know it's not true because there were too many soldiers shooting at the poor girl and me.

"You see, Ashlyn was sick." He says.

I purse my lips, and cross one leg over the other. Let's hear more of those lies. Silence is sometimes the best trap to catch a liar.

"A lot of nurses on the island suffer from isolation," he explains. "They go toot in the head, if you know what I mean." He circles a forefinger in the air, around his left ear.

Did he just used the word *toot* to describe insanity? I blink, thinking I've imagined it.

"One of our doctors says it only happens to women," he says. For the second time, I smell that stench of his hatred or disrespect for women. "Statistically, women are prone to madness more than men."

Next thing, he'll try to persuade me I am insane as well.

"I have always preferred male nurses, but it was Dr. Suffolk's advice to hire women. He claims no one can understand and contain pain like women. That's why he sent you to Ward Four and assigned Ashlyn to help you." He lets out a condescending laugh then lights up a pipe and starts to puff. "Dr. Suffolk always points out the fact that men, with all their strength and power, could never bear giving birth to a baby. As a doctor, he thinks giving birth is the hardest thing in the world."

I continue my silent mourning over Ashlyn.

"I suppose Ashlyn told you the consequences of being the sole survivor of a plane crash?" he says. "Cloudy thinking, delusions, and sometimes insanity. It's true."

"Are you saying I am insane?" The devious man pulled the words out of my mouth.

Major Red chuckles. “Of course not. You’re confused and need to rest. That’s all.”

No one confuses me as much as you do, Major Red.

“Tell you what, Major Red.” I lock eyes with him. “Let’s cut the crap. What is this island? Where is The Crib?”

Chapter 52

“I don’t know what you’re talking about.” Major Red puts the pipe aside. “I told you the Crib is a myth, perpetuated by the crazy woman on the sixth floor. What was her name? Ah, Meredith.”

“So you’re not telling. Okay, forget about the Crib.” I stand up and ram the desk with my hand. “How about the Furnace? Are you going to deny it, too?”

“Not at all. The Furnace is real.” His face dims. “It’s some kind of a cemetery where hundreds, if not thousands, of women were buried in War World II.”

“So you admit it.”

“Admit what, Miss June? That this island was a secret Nazi concentration camp in the war? It’s true. How? I am not sure. We discovered that place a few years after we arrived. We thought this island met our needs—which I’m not obliged to tell you about. The Furnace is where they burned their prisoners. Is that what you want to know?”

“That’s it? Are you denying you have anything to do with it?”

“I don’t have to deny anything,” he sneers back at me. “Like I said, I am under no obligation to tell you anything. We’re not the horrible people you think we are.” He stands up. “The soldiers like to call the Furnace the 1001, named after the sergeant who discovered it."

"What was that soldier's name?"

"Sergeant Manfred Toot, a.k.a. 1001, his number in the camp, a bit similar to *toot* in lowercase letters."

"What kind of nonsense is that?"

"I think it's only nonsense because you refuse to believe it."

"Where is this Manfred Toot now?"

Major Red laughs, looking downward and shaking his head. "Why do you think you have the right to interrogate me, when you're most likely the suspicious egg on this island?"

I ram the desk again, in desperation for an answer this time. "Is Manfred Toot still on this island?"

"You're such an annoying woman, Miss June. Manfred Toot's information is classified at the moment. I will tell you nothing about him." He raises his eyes to meet mine again. "All you need to know is that he found the bodies buried deep in dry earth. It's like the Nazis wanted the bones to decompose as slowly as possible—maybe a sinister way to show us what they had done to our grandfathers and grandmothers."

"You're lying. Making a story up on the go. Most of the skeletons didn't look old. I'm not even sure if it's possible those bones survived that long. Seventy years? Are you kidding me?"

"Miracles happen."

"Bullshit."

"Why, Miss June? Haven't you survived an unsurvivable plane crash yourself?" His gaze defies me and strips me from top to bottom again.

"That's not the point. I know what I saw. There were clumps of flesh everywhere."

"That was probably mud. I am told that you need to rest."

"And the horrible burning smell?"

"That's because I send my soldiers to burn the place from time to time, so the stench won't reach the wards. We just discovered it last year and never had the time to do anything about it. All we did was build the wall."

"The wall? Now I'm sure you're making this up. The swastikas?"

"What about the swastikas? My soldiers drew them to remind us this is what Nazis did, not us."

"You're just messing with my mind. You're twisting every fact into unbelievable circumstances."

"Coming from someone who claims she doesn't remember who she is and has a gun in her bag."

"Don't start." I wave my hands in the air. "What about the hospital gowns? They looked fresh."

"What hospital gowns?"

"They were scattered all over the place. Lime-green hospital gowns, right next to the wristbands."

Major Red rolls his eyes. "What wristbands?"

"I saw them in the Furnace, next to the dead women." I point at the window, not knowing left from right. I realize I have no grasp of where I am exactly. Ashlyn must have reached the Furnace through sheer luck. "Take me there, and I will show you. Hundreds of wristbands with women's names on them."

"I don't know what you're talking about," he says. "Let's hypothetically say there are wristbands—why is it a problem that they have women's names on them?"

"The skeletons are only women. Not one man has been burned in the Furnace."

"How could you possible know that?" He isn't asking. It's a statement. "I can't take this anymore. I have much more important things to take care of. My whole island is threatened by a possible hurricane, for God's sake."

I take a step back and slump into the chair, mad at myself. What is happening to me? Am I really mad? Is that it? The blaring sound attacks my ears again, and I am forced to cover my ears and close my eyes.

"I've been as nice as possible to you because Dr. Suffolk asked me to," Major Red says. "But I am growing increasingly impatient with you. I can't believe you're accusing me of being a Nazi who is burning women in a gas station. In fact, you're the one I am suspicious of. You claim you're amnesiac, and we haven't proven this yet. How do I know you're not lying? If all you want is to remember who you are and go home, why are you snooping around the island, sending a poor nurse to her death? You carry no identification and I have no proof you were even on the plane. To top it off, you carry a gun. Not just any gun, but a gun with a swastika stamped on it. Who is the Nazi now?"

His words are distant and muffled under the loud blaring in my ears. I think I need medication, but for what exactly? Hearing voices?

Major Red's accusation seems plausible, but so are my suspicions. I can tell him about my daughter, but he would definitely think I'm crazy then. I could tell him about Toot, but what if Toot is so important to him, would he end up killing me or something?

I am overwhelmed with the terrible feeling of wanting to disappear. Kill me, bury me, send me to hell, and reincarnate me as a new person into another world with a less complicated life, away from the island.

"Stop that blare!" I shout at Major Red.

"What blare?" he shouts back, tense and irritated.

"This sound. Can't you hear it?"

"I hear nothing unusual, Miss June."

"It's that blare I keep hearing. I heard it when Ashlyn and I were at the Furnace. She heard too. It's like a loud horn."

"I hear no horns," Major Red says. "What kind of horn is so loud you need to cover your ears? Be reasonable and admit you're sick. You need to go back to Ward Four."

Like a withering migraine, the loud blare fades into oblivion. It's a bit sudden, I have to admit. Is it time to admit something is wrong with me? No, this can't be. My gut feeling tells me I have to hang on.

When I open my eyes, Major Red is gripping the phone and dialing. "I'm sending you back to Dr. Suffolk. He has to tell me if you're faking your amnesia, and those sounds you hear, or not."

My guard is down. I'm so tired. It's not a bad idea to see Dr. Suffolk again. I wait in my seat until soldiers arrive and I surrender. They seem gentle with me this time. I guess I've become so pathetic to them.

Walking along, I replay Major Red's reasoning in my head. One word stands out all of a sudden, and I pull away from the soldiers again. "Did you say there was a swastika on my gun?"

"Please go, Miss June," he says. "Talking hasn't solved anything."

"Answer me," I demand. "My gun had an inverted cross on it, one that belonged to some weird sect from the eighties or something."

Major Red smokes his pipe again, leaning back in his chair. "An inverted cross?"

"Yes." I approach the desk again. "Pull the gun from the drawer. I will show you. You were the one who pointed it out."

"I did point it out." He nonchalantly pulls out the gun and throws it on the table in front of me. "Look for yourself."

His confidence scares me. I'm sure it was an inverted cross. My hands tremble a little as I reach for the gun. This is going to be a deal breaker. My sanity is on the line here. I pull the gun up and look at the inverted cross, except it isn't. It's a swastika.

Chapter 53

Somewhere in the Atlantic Ocean

Karl Dixon watched the plane wreckage from the passenger seat of the chopper. He is unable to fathom what could have happened. Plane parts floated everywhere. The raging ocean and wind had scattered them all over the water, so much so that he was almost sure this rescue mission was already a failure.

He was using fog-proof binoculars—purged of air and filled with dry nitrogen that did not condense on internal surfaces during rapid temperature changes—to get a better look. The results weren't spectacular, though. Thick fog like this rendered even "fog-proof" binoculars useless sometimes.

Several other choppers hovered nearby. An immense crew of rescuers had just arrived, but Dixon couldn't see all of them due to the fog.

"The nose and cockpit exploded," an officer told Dixon from below. "Passengers are floating everywhere. Most seats are dislocated, if not burned or sunk. Looks like the plane's tail sunk perpendicularly, like the *Titanic*."

"How far below?" Dixon asked.

"Hard to tell now. It's almost impossible to send anyone down there. You should come here and see the ocean spitting piss onto us."

"Did our remote-operated vehicles arrive?"

"Yes."

"Try a side-scan sonar and laser line-scanning to find passengers."

"Copy that. I'll report pictures of survivors we find for identification."

"I doubt you will find any," Dixon said. "I've seen tons of crashes. Nothing like that. Certainly, not in this kind of weather."

"You think it's a terrorist attack?"

"No doubt about it," Dixon says. "And the only way we know for sure is to get to the tail before it sinks into the bottom of the ocean."

"I'm not sure what you're asking," the officer said. "I'd prefer to concentrate on one mission. Either I find passengers or coordinate with the boys from the FBI and investigate a terrorist attack."

Dixon disconnected. He needed a moment to think it over. He knew Floyd wanted a list of passengers to report to the press and families. The press had been pushing for answers on CNN, FOX, and the BBC since yesterday. Al Jazeera had asked for the passenger list, claiming there had been two important investors from Qatar on board, flying from London to New

York. Floyd had always cared about the deceased's families. So typical and naive of him. Dixon figured the old man thought that confirming a relative's death as fast as possible was the least they deserved.

But Dixon had seen this enough times to know it was a fuckup either way. The only outcome that families wanted was to hear their loved ones were alive, which was almost never the case.

Even if their loved ones survived, they were usually disabled and wished they had died. Dixon always thought he was the right man for Floyd's job, but he ended up in this horrible position, taking orders from a dreamy man who believed in miracles that never happened. People thought he was saving lives, but all he did was report dead people, empathetically. He hated Floyd for pushing him out in this risky weather.

He clicked his radio on. "Tell you what, put the terrorist investigation on hold."

"So it's a rescue mission. Copy that. Anything else?"

"Actually, yes. I want you to send the rescue divers down."

"But they wouldn't make it in this weather."

"Floyd says we have to send them," Dixon said. "It's his call if they die. I am following orders."

Dixon rested the radio on his lap and then rubbed his chin. Normally, he would have consulted Floyd. All the old man had said was to find survivors. He had no idea divers would die if sent into the water now. Dixon didn't care. He didn't like Floyd, and it was time the old man retired in disgrace.

Chapter 54

I'm stretched out on the couch in the clinic, waiting for Dr. Suffolk. My thoughts have been haunting me since I left Major Red's office, but they're useless now. I've come to a fork in the road where I don't know what to think or which path of clues to follow.

Dr. Suffolk stands tall over me while I am on the couch. It's judgment day. Now or never. We're going to know who I really am right here and now. I want to know, so badly. Not like last time, when I seemed reluctant and worried.

"How are you, June?" Dr. Suffolk says, tilting his head as if staring at a skewed picture on the wall. "You're certainly no ordinary patient."

"Of course I'm not," I mumble. "None of your patients are sole survivors with amnesia, carrying a gun with a swastika."

"Witty and beautiful." He smiles and sits opposite me. Though his ease is appreciated, I find it fake and out of context. Nothing is beautiful about me. "Everything is going to be all right. Don't worry."

"That's what you told me the last time."

"I can't win with you, can I?" He chuckles and glances at a dossier with my name on it. "Look, I'm not going to look at your test results—not yet. I'm not going to question any of your actions, either. You know why?"

"I don't."

"Because I'm your doctor. I don't care about your attitude outside, nor do I care about what you've done. I want to help you remember who you are."

It sounds good, but I am not sure if I can trust him anymore. Even though my heart tells me he is a good man, I'm the most paranoid girl on the planet right now. I am afraid, even of myself—my real self.

However, I realize the handsome doctor is my only chance. I prop up on my elbows and whisper. "Dr. Suffolk, if you really want to help me, tell me what this place is."

I lock eyes with him.

He says, "You want to know what this island is?"

"Yes, please." I get closer, smelling his scent, stretching my neck, and tolerating the ache in my exhausted body like a champ.

Dr. Suffolk gets closer too. Our faces are a few breaths apart. He has beautiful eyes. "This place, June"—he swallows—"is none of what you think."

"What is that supposed to mean?"

"It means all you have to do is breathe." He glances sideways and back to me. "Just breathe."

I sigh and lie back in frustration. I'm sure he is lying to me. I rest my hands on my chest as if I am a mummy, dead and gone. "I'm ready for your hypnosis. Shall we begin?"

"That's a good start," Dr. Suffolk says. "But not yet."

"I thought this was all you and Major Red want, to know who I am, if I am a terrorist or a spy sent to discover the secrets on this island." I roll my eyes.

He laughs. "Reason is: I can see you're afraid."

"Afraid?"

"Yes, June. You're afraid to know who you are. You think it's not obvious, but it is."

I make sure I'm still staring at the ceiling, so my eyes won't give away that he is spot on.

"It's common among amnesia patients," he says in that soft and caring voice. Does he use it on all his patients? "As more time passes without remembering who you are, you're building a new persona, which you're starting to fall in love with, so much that you begin to fear you're not the good person you've convinced yourself you are."

The man reads my mind. I don't know how. "What makes you think my new persona is good?"

"Are you kidding me? You left your room in your horrible medical condition, convinced a nurse of a conspiracy going on here, then escaped soldiers and managed to cross the river to the Furnace, all in the name of doing the right thing. You've definitely built not only a good persona, but a heroic one."

"I'm not a hero." I shrug. "I'm just a mother looking for her daughter."

Dr. Suffolk says nothing, long enough to force me to look at him. I'm surprised he is expressionless.

"Did you hear what I just said?"

"That you're not a hero? Yes."

"That wasn't just it. I said I have a daughter and need to find her."

"Okay, what else did you say?"

I said I have a goddamn daughter. What the fuck is wrong with you?

Dr. Suffolk tilts his head, waiting for me to answer him. The words I speak about my daughter seem to be all in my head. He does not hear them.

I feel like I want to sink deep into this couch and be buried forever. Two more times I try to tell him about my daughter, and he can't hear me, as if I'm saying nothing.

"So let's begin, anyway," Dr. Suffolk finally says. "I'm going to ask you a few questions with no hypnosis. Questions that will hopefully refresh your memory."

I nod, staring at the ceiling, realizing I might have not looked at him at all. What's happening to me?

Chapter 55

Dr. Alan Suffolk has been asking me questions—that's if I'm not insane and imagining things.

Some questions are simple, some complicated. I'm actually starting to feel better. It's a relief to look back at the events that have happened since I arrived on this island. It's like popping outside my stuffed head for a breath of fresh air.

I reveal all that's happened like a movie in slow motion. I even tell him about the oily messages I received, risking that he may still be an enemy. I tell him about Toot, but he doesn't seem interested. I tell him about my daughter again, and still it's like he is unable to hear this part. I could scream and kick all I want, but it's like it never happens. I'm starting to realize that it's me who never tells him about her. I'm afraid it's all in my mind. I'm afraid my brain thinks my daughter would be in danger if I told Dr. Suffolk.

Dr. Suffolk believes most of the incidents to be hallucinations, induced by an after-plane-crash effect. Again, he recites this theory about how it's not easy being a sole survivor. How there is a whole new science about it. Except then he adds a disheartening fact about how I may spend the rest of my life with these hallucinations. He won't be able to know for sure until I remember the events of the crash.

Lastly, he compliments my energy levels after the crash. Most sole survivors tend to be introverted and silent for long periods. All bullshit and nonsense that I don't want to hear.

But then he says, "Now, about those baby cries you heard." He rubs his chin. "I have a few questions for you. Please try to be open-minded as I ask them."

"I'll do my best."

"Do you think you may have kids?"

A hysterical laugh of madness forms on my lips. I tell him I have a daughter, and of course he doesn't hear me. I give in until he speaks again, as helpless and insane as it sounds.

"The reason I ask is because of the cries you keep hearing," Dr. Suffolk says. "So try to pressure your mind for answers. It's unlikely that you will remember, but the feeling of having a child may hit you."

I answer him again, but he doesn't react.

"An infant, maybe?" he offers. "One who kept you awake nights?"

I close my eyes. He isn't going to hear me. Let him talk. Maybe this is going somewhere.

"An infant in a crib?" he says. "Could that be it? Your brain has confused memories with hallucinations?"

My heart pounds faster. Could it be that the doctor is right? Am I imagining cries. And a crib? I feel my closed eyelids twitching, Dr. Suffolk's voice in my head.

“Maybe you want to be a mother, June, and have daydreamed about the baby crying in the next room.”

I feel like I’m sinking deeper into my couch now, into a place that could be my memories. Every girl wants to be a mother at some point, I suppose. I try to focus on scattered images of my past. The more I squeeze the thought, the more I realize how it resonates with me. I find myself walking in a dark hall. A place not on this island. And there it is. The baby crying. I follow the sound, knocking on too many locked doors. Then I find one open. It’s a child’s room. But the room is dark. I can’t see as good as I need to. But it’s not hard to locate the source of the cries.

A baby.

In a crib.

Slowly, I step toward it, reaching out. I’m about to look into it and see the crying infant. Here I come. I think the doctor is right.

Suddenly, the floor beneath me cracks and I scream, free-falling. All the way down, I can still hear the baby’s cries. If I focus, I might save it. But then I realize I am illogically strapped to a chair at the bottom of that circular place again. The sound of water is all around, but it’s not the ocean. It’s the plane. I think I’m in the bottom of a well, or a fissure in the earth. I’m not on a plane. The loud blare is definitely the horn of a car. A Jeep, actually. I think so. The looming figure is all over me again. His foul scent is the smell of the oil itself. The oil from the car that's blaring. The oil on the messages.

I jolt up straight on the couch, in tears, with nothing to save me from my troubled mind but Dr. Suffolk's arms.

"I think I've never been on a plane," I whisper in his ear.

"You'll be all right." He holds me tight and says, "Breathe, June. All you have to do is breathe."

Chapter 56

Mercy Medical Center, New York

Floyd's phone rang while he was eating lunch in his wife's room. It was Dixon.

"Two hundred and thirty passengers were on the plane. It's a massacre down here."

"In this weather, I'm not surprised," Floyd said. "Any survivors?"

"None so far."

"How many passengers did you find."

"All but twenty-seven. We'll try and match their identities, but trust me, some are only fragments of what they used to be. We'll do it when we're back in New York."

"No. You'll identify the corpses now." Floyd put down his fork and stared at the passengers' families on TV. "We have to ease the families' pain. Waiting and not knowing is a horrible thing." His eyes shifted to his wife.

"Floyd. You're not being rational. We've already lost one of our divers. The longer we stay here, the more of my crew I will lose."

Floyd's jaw twitched. All his life, this had always been the hardest decision. Sacrificing one of his men to save civilians, or cherishing his men, whom he'd trained for years, and sacrifice the civilian. If interviewed on national TV, he'd be obliged to say civilians were above all others. Which was a great lie. These men, soldiers, divers, or pilots had families as well. Floyd would've normally ordered his men back for one simple reason: the possibility of a survivor was infinitesimally slim.

"Sir?" Dixon said impatiently.

Floyd was silent, unable to decide, his eyes fixated on his comatose wife.

"There is no need for our men to die," Dixon said. "This rescue mission is dead. There will be no survivors. It's impossible."

Floyd said nothing, still staring at his wife. He realized Dixon was right. But he also realized that giving up hope on the survivors meant he'd have to give up hope on his wife as well.

Floyd simply didn't answer.

Chapter 57

"You'll be fine." Dr. Suffolk is still squeezing me in his strong arms, now gently brushing his hand through my hair. "Just keep breathing."

"I think I'm going crazy." I hiccup into his shoulder.

"It's okay. You don't have to pressure yourself."

"It sucks not knowing who I am."

"None of us really do." He breathes out one of his light chuckles. "I've been trying to know me for almost forty years now."

I find myself chuckling too. He sure has a way of looking at the world.

"Memories are nothing but names and incidents that could have been twisted and turned into circumstances beyond our grasp," he says. "You don't choose your parents or name, for instance. Yet you have to live with them. Who we really are and how our lives came to be are two different things."

"You make it sound so easy."

"Why not?" He holds my head between his hands, staring into my eyes. "You have no memory of who you are, but you know you were brave enough to survive a plane crash."

"I'm starting to think Major Red is right. I was never on that plane."

"So what? You survived something. Every day alive is a gift, proving you've survived the one before."

Words like these make me want to totally trust him. But if I do, I will need to believe all the lies Major Red told me as well. I'm going to overlook the fact that I'm unable to tell him anything about my daughter for now. But what about all those women burned in the Furnace? I find it hard to believe that people on the island are the good guys, like Dr. Suffolk wants me to believe.

"Can I trust you, Dr. Suffolk?"

"I'd like to believe that," he says. "Sometimes I don't trust myself."

I'm astonished at his vulnerability. Is it real? An act? Or is he just a good doctor doing his best?

"I have so many questions, so much fear—so much that I've lost track of what I really want to accomplish here." I say.

"Don't we all?"

"Yes, yes." I plant a gentle finger on his mouth. His smoothness is starting to annoy me. "But I need a theory or an idea about what's going on."

"Why? It'll be over when the storm subsides. We'll know all we know about the plane in the news, and you will know who you are and go home."

I've not thought about it this way. In my mind, the storm will never come to an end. Besides, if a hurricane is really on the way, we'll be gone forever.

"Listen." I collect my thoughts again. "I'm not asking much. I want to tell you about my daughter."

Dr. Suffolk leans back. His face dims a little. It's like he is staring into a lost memory while looking at me. As if I'm not there.

"Did you hear what I just said?"

"Yes, I did."

"And?"

Dr. Suffolk stands up, walks toward the window, and looks out at the trickling rain. "I'm waiting," he says.

"Waiting for what, Dr. Suffolk?"

"For the question you want to ask me."

The anger and frustration build inside me. I can feel heat rising in my throat. "Fuck this!" I stand up and stamp my foot. "How can you not be hearing this?"

Dr. Suffolk doesn't look back. Now I'm not sure if my outburst of emotion was real. Does he not hear my cussing, or is he ignoring me?

"The rain outside is my only friend sometimes," he says. "It reminds me that I'm not alone in this room."

"What did you say?" Tears trickle from my eyes. My life is utter madness. I'm not even sure he said that. I'm not even sure I exist.

This has to stop.

This has to stop.

This has to...

"June?" Dr. Suffolk says, still staring at the window. "What's your question? What did you want to ask me?"

Chapter 58

Mercy Medical Center, New York

Floyd had finally made up his mind. It was a long shot, but now he felt good about it. "Identify all corpses now, in the field," he told Dixon. "Don't call me back without the names of the missing twenty-seven passengers."

"But—"

"I will take responsibility."

"What good will it serve me when you take the blame after my rescue team dies?" Dixon asked.

"They signed up for this," Floyd said. "They know the drill. We all signed up for this."

"You son of a bitch," Dixon said. "Why don't you get your fucking FBI ass down here and die with us, instead of nursing your fucked-up wife!"

Silence saturated the air after Dixon's rant. Floyd wasn't the type to burst out in rage. His steadiness and stability had made him the man he was today. This wasn't the time to get back at Dixon and curse at him, nor was it the time to tell him about the three bullets Floyd took in the field, one close to his heart, to remind Dixon of the dangers he'd confronted throughout his career.

The one thing Floyd could fire back for was Dixon doubting the recovery of August—not that Floyd actually believed his wife would regain consciousness, but he didn't want to hear it. In times when facts cut like a knife through him, hope was the steel shield under his skin. Hope, even false, made the world go on.

Floyd also considered Dixon's dilemma. Many people signed up for jobs without imagining the consequences. Then, when the shit hit the fan, they folded under the pressure. Be it a doctor, a rescue team, or even a mother giving birth to a child, the responsibilities they eventually faced were the true test of life. Dixon didn't have that. He'd been a victim of his ego, unable to live under the radar, saving lives every day without someone praising him in the news. Saving lives was the noblest job, yet the most underrated.

Floyd's reply to Dixon was short and simple: "It's an order, Dixon. God be with you."

Dixon had hung up already, knowing how devoted Floyd was. The old man put his cell phone on the table, doubting himself for a moment. It'd always been like that when making a decision. People wanted to think that men like him were rock-solid-sure about their decisions. It was far from it. Each decision was usually a choice between two evils in Floyd's world, including the option to pull the plug on his wife or not.

He stood up, walked over to his wife, and held her hand. He bowed down, planted a kiss on her cold forehead, and whispered, "Tell me I'm doing the right thing, August."

When she was alive, August had said that his job wasn't about saving many lives. Just one life was a victory. She'd concluded that saving lives wasn't always feasible. In major accidents, people died. One saved brought hope back into the heart of the masses. That was all they needed.

Like always, August didn't reply, assure him with calm words. She didn't even sigh or blink, like doctors claimed would happen someday. Nothing about her changed, and Floyd hoped to God that Dixon was wrong about her situation.

Floyd turned and faced the silent TV. He'd put it on mute earlier, but now raised the volume. He listened to the latest news about the plane crash. Most of it was fabricated and untrue. He hated news channels with their over-the-top stories and speculation. Everything had to have a meaning behind it. Everything had to be a conspiracy. One channel claimed this was a terrorist attack—something Dixon would suggest. The channel said there had been terrorists on the plane. Women, they said. The suicidal type.

Bullshit.

Floyd knew for a fact that none of this was true. No investigation had taken place yet. They hadn't even released a list of passengers. Besides, why was it hard to believe that a plane had crashed in such terrible, unexpected weather?

Another channel caught his attention, though. He watched the families at the airport, demanding to know if their loved ones were alive. He couldn't imagine the pain they were suffering. It made him realize he couldn't pull the plug on August. He had been in so much pain, and yet she hadn't really died yet.

With the remote in his hand, he sat down and listened to families pleading with the authorities to save their loved ones on Atlantic flight number 1001.

Chapter 59

I'm in the bottom of that fissure in the earth again. Now I'm sure it's not the plane's broken tail. It's like a huge well or something; the sound of rushing water is everywhere. The water is underneath me, but I can't crane my stiffened neck enough to see.

The stinking smell of oil is everywhere. Oil from some old Jeep, I suppose. And, of course, the blare of the horn is a continuous, cacophonous torture in my ears. If it stops, I think I can call for help. But it never stops.

My body is still weak. I can't move it. My hand is squeezed under someone's body, and I can't pull free. My left arm hurts like hell. I'm not sure if I can't feel my legs or if the pain is too strong to comprehend. An accident has definitely occurred somewhere, but how, I have no idea.

I close my eyes and try to listen beyond the loud blare, but it's futile. Above me, in the far distance, beyond that opening in the fissure, I can faintly see the sun. Shy and obedient behind the darkening mist. I wonder if it's not the sun but fire. And again, I can't tell.

All the way down, the walls are dark silhouettes upon darker silhouettes. I can't tell what they're made from. Whether they're natural or man-made.

Down here, I'm strapped to some seat. I suppose this is a car seat? It's a plausible idea. The belt runs diagonally from my shoulder down to my hip, not around my waist, like in a plane.

How did this happen? How did a plane become a car?

None of that really matters. It's the fear in my heart that's killing me. That fucking feeling of needing to save my daughter. It's so strong that I can't deny it. How can I be insane and feel such strong emotion?

"Baby?" I call for my girl, ashamed I don't know her name. Ashamed of leaving her behind. Ashamed of things I can't understand.

A drop of oil splashes down on my face. There is no mistake about it. Then another. I try to glimpse its color as it falls but can't do it in this darkness.

My throat tightens when I understand what the oil means. It's always related to that looming, dark figure. It has arrived. I can smell its preposterous stink. God, it scares me so much that I think I'm peeing myself now.

"Who are you?" I shiver.

"You know who I am," it replies. Low and dull and mocking. The embodiment of evil.

"I don't. What do you want?"

"I want what I've always had."

"What's that supposed to mean? Do I know you?"

"You've always known me."

"You're Manfred Toot?"

"Whatever you'd like to call me, I'm fine with it," it says. The looming veil of darkness blocks my view of the sky above.

"Get away from me!"

It keeps getting closer. "Can you hear the baby crying?"

"I can't." I try to unstrap myself by twisting my body.

"Beautiful cries," it says. "Let's make babies, you little whore."

The words make me want to vomit. What did he just say?

Then he drops a bomb on me: "Let's make Nazi babies."

Chapter 60

Kicking and punching, I wake up screaming in a bed that I have never seen before. This certainly isn't Dr. Suffolk's clinic. It looks like yet another hospital room, but a much more advanced one than in Ward Four.

The tiles on the floor look like a chessboard. I haven't set foot on them yet, but they look cold. Actually, it's the whole room that's too cold. The four bare walls surrounding me are pale blue. Machines are set against two of them. Nothing special, except the one thing that jolts me off the bed immediately.

It's the fact that the bed I'm on is set in the middle of the room, like an operating table.

With a hand on my chest, I keep staring at it. A set of fluorescent lights are fixed above it. Lines of metallic instruments are set on a tray next to it. This is definitely an operating room.

I suppose I fainted in Dr. Suffolk's clinic and they brought me here. Why an operating room? Where is Dr. Suffolk?

I run to the door, which is pale blue like the walls, only visible because of its white frame and a white box with a keypad.

Trying to pull or push open the door doesn't do the trick. I am locked up again, like in Ward Four, only this room feels like a place for illegal experiments—or maybe I've watched too many movies.

An unusual calmness comes over me, though. Maybe because I've been through so much shit on this island. It's not the first time I've woken up to a shocking surprise. All that comes to mind is that the charming Dr. Suffolk deceived me like everyone else—for the second time, actually. I'm wondering if appearing to not hear me speak about my daughter was a trick.

From the corner of my eye, I see a window. Weird to find one in an operating room, but what hasn't been weird lately?

The window, though two-sided, is long and thin but I think I can still make it outside. My slow footsteps slap my bare feet on the chessboard tiles. It's not the nicest of sounds, but it feels like a dread-filled soundtrack to what I'm about to see through the window.

I find it easy to open. Weird again. All I have to do is twist the handle, but then I realize that only side opens. The other is rather locked. I miscalculated the size, now wondering if I can unlock the other part to widen my way out. I peek through the open part. It's an unexpected view outside, inducing optimism and pessimism at the same time.

Almost all the wards are visible, but from the back. That would be the optimistic part—realizing that I am probably on the west side of the island now. The pessimistic part is the question that presents itself: why was I brought here, and what is this building?

Is this the Crib? It doesn't look like it, but I can't tell without leaving the room.

Below me, the entrance to the building is vacant and calm, as if no one lives here. I can't see anyone nearby, either. Just a few soldiers guarding the wards in the distance. None of them guards this place.

I search for a bathroom. I spot it and hurl myself inside.

I'm standing in front of a mirror again. Here I am, wearing another hospital gown.

This one is green... just like... Wait... Fuck... No!

Beads of sweat form on my forehead.

My reflection shows me wearing something that confirms my fears. It shatters my reality so much that I don't trust the mirror and turn to see it on my flesh.

Shit.

I'm wearing a metallic wristband, like the women in the Furnace.

This can't be happening.

I try to pull it off, but I can't. It needs a key to unlock it, I guess. It's heavy, too. I lift my arm to take a closer look.

What are you looking for?

Shit. Shit. Shit.

There is a name on the wristband, just like every other woman I saw burned. It's carved in capital letters.

I read it:

JUNE WEST.

Then, a little lower, in red marker:

Ready.

Chapter 61

Mercy Medical Center, New York

The news pleased Floyd. Dixon had done a good job. Some of the found corpses were matched to identities on the list of passengers. Not just that. The brave divers had managed to find most of the twenty-seven passengers in the plane's tail at the bottom of the ocean. Most passengers had been strapped to their seats, unable to free themselves. Whatever had happened to the plane was quick enough that no one could do anything. A few passengers had managed to free themselves, though. They'd been found, either floating upon wreckage or underwater.

Dixon's men were exceptionally fast. Even Floyd hadn't expected results that quick.

"How many haven't you found?" Floyd asked Dixon on the phone.

"Three," Dixon shouted, the sound of the chopper deafening behind him. "If my list is accurate, they're all girls. Ages between twenty-five and forty."

"Young women," Floyd said, wishing they were alive. "Great job, Dixon. I'll be waiting for the last three girls."

"I was thinking you can populate the list now," Dixon suggested. "Didn't you want the families not to be left in the dark?"

"Yes, but I need some time. I can't risk three families going crazy not knowing. What if the three girls are dead? I can't play with their feelings and let them think they're alive and then prove otherwise. The list needs to be completed. At least try. If not, I'll have to populate it. Also, a little more time will allow us—"

Dixon murmured something that Floyd couldn't hear with all the noises behind him.

"Don't give up yet, Dixon," Floyd said. "You and your men did a heroic job. It's always the last mile that counts. Three girls, and your job is done. God bless."

"I still think we should abort," Dixon said. "Three girls don't mean anything. The list isn't accurate, as well. We're counting corpses, not human beings. Some of the families will know their loved ones are dead, but we'll never be able to identify them. I have half torsos here, Floyd."

"What are you suggesting?"

"I can check off the three girls as found. As dead. No one will know. It'll be between me and you."

"And repeat the mistakes of TWA in 1996, when we messed up the names of passengers and caused those families all that pain?"

"*You* messed up on 9/11," Dixon argued. "That was your fault. Still, everyone thinks you're a hero."

"I panicked. It was an unusual plane crash. We hadn't been trained for such a catastrophe then. But flight 1001 is what you and your men trained for at the NTSB. Sure, it's almost a suicide mission in this weather, but it's our job."

"My men will die."

"They're my men, too."

"Last three girls don't matter, Floyd."

"They're last but not least."

"Dead people don't matter."

"We don't know they're dead."

"They will be."

"The dead matter."

"Why, Floyd?"

"Because they remind us we're alive. Because their loved ones need closure."

"Shit, Floyd."

"If I were younger, and even though it's not my job, I'd have flown over there and hit the water with all the divers," Floyd said.

"Fuck you, Floyd. You're an arrogant prick. We should be investigating this crash, not saving bodies. Fuck you."

Dixon hung up.

Floyd didn't flinch. He'd been in the field and knew the stress and fear and their consequences.

He put the cell phone away and stared out the window, hands laced behind his back. "Dixon could be right, August," he said. "It scares the shit out of me. I don't think I can forgive myself if the last passengers turn up dead and divers die for nothing."

Of course, August didn't respond. He pretended to be talking to her, knowing he was talking to himself. Maybe it was time he resigned. He was an unstable man who shouldn't carry such responsibilities. A man craving the resurrection of his loved one should not have been granted the honor of deciding the fate of other people's loved ones.

"Please," he said, not knowing whom he was talking to. Was it August? Himself? God? The universe? "Please grant my men the honor to save at least one last girl."

Chapter 62

I sit on the edge of the bed with one of the weird metallic instruments from the operating table. This one looks like it can kill. It strongly resembles a shard of glass. I can see my reflection in it, and I have to grip it carefully, so I don't get cut. I tap my foot impatiently, sure of the feelings I am experiencing. Whoever enters through the blue door first to check on me is an unlucky son of a bitch.

No more Mrs. Nice Girl. I need to take things into my own hands. Where is that girl who attacked Ashlyn and was ready to twist her arm to get information?

Staring at my wristband, I make an effort to connect the dots. So my name is June West? The low-life scumbags knew my name all along. It's impossible to build a story behind that fact, but why else would they write my last name as West? Not that I recognize my last name, but I can't think of any different conclusions.

I wonder how much of this was planned in advance.

Also, what does it mean: ready?

I can only think of Meredith's words: *The horrible things they will do to you...*

I could keep thinking forever and still not find the right answers. It's time to get moving.

I hear someone punching the numbers in the pad outside. I hear a click. In she comes. Another nurse. She is a little older than Ashlyn. She plasters that fake Dr. Suffolk smile on her face and asks me if I ate.

I can't hear her, only watch her mouth moving. My senses are blurred with thoughts of revenge and self-protection. I don't want her poisonous words to seep through my brain and make me end up doubting myself. I don't know what's going on here, but there are a bunch of Nazis on this island who will eventually burn me in the Furnace for reasons beyond me.

The nurse stoops to pick up something from the floor. In a flash, I stand up and wrap my arms around her neck and almost stick the instrument into her neck.

She wriggles under my grip and utters a muffled scream. I slap her on the mouth then scratch her with the instrument. It's a sharp motherfucker. Like a twisted razor. Blood drips out, but not much.

I. Don't. Give. A. Fuck.

"Don't scream," I whisper in her ear. "Just tell me where I am. What does this wristband mean?"

Stiffening, she grits her teeth, as if locking the words inside.

"I will kill you."

She grunts incomprehensible vowels.

"I knew you wouldn't tell me." I kick her in the back. She falls to her knees. I pull her hair hard, yanking her neck back before she utters another scream. It amazes me how fast I unbind her long hair and stuff it in her mouth to silence her. I'm watching myself become the girl I think I have always been. Someone I was so scared to meet, not knowing she was my savior all along.

The nurse chokes. I feel nothing. No empathy. No worries she could die in my hands. I slap her violently on the face.

"Where the fuck is my daughter?"

Her eyes widen, but she puts so much effort into locking her secrets inside.

"Don't test my patience."

She still doesn't talk. I hit her hard on the head with a tray from the table. She falls to her side, unresponsive. It seems too easy, but she isn't moving.

The thought of having killed her doesn't stop me from emptying her pockets. No ID. No personal belongings. Nothing but a magnetic card and a syringe ready for use. Maybe it's some sort of a sedative.

Tucking the syringe and the card away, I go back to the door and slowly open it. I crane my neck out the gap and check the corridor outside.

Empty.

Is this place deserted or what?

I take a deep breath and step outside, pulling the door behind me. This is when I realize I am still in my gown. I forgot to wear the nurse's clothes like I did with Ashlyn. What's done is done. I need to find out what this place is.

Barefoot, I take cautious steps, brushing my shoulder against the wall next to me. I can always find a storage room or something to hide in.

To my surprise, I glimpse lights coming from other rooms all along the corridor. Faint yellow lights. Which means the doors aren't locked like mine. I wonder if there are patients in these rooms, but everything is dead silent in here.

I deliberately try to slow my breathing, so I don't panic. My aim is to reach the closest room and peek inside. I tiptoe forward, glancing back occasionally, and finally hear something. I was right. I was always right. I hear a baby's cries. Real cries. Not figments of my imagination. This time they are so real that they cut through my soul.

Chapter 63

Mercy Medical Center, New York

Trying to kill the boredom of silence, Floyd rifled through his wife's handbag. It's a heavy bag that no one had bothered to empty or look into. He'd brought it from their house some time ago when doctors suggested the proximity of her belongings might bring back memories. The same old bullshit.

The bag contained August's favorite books. She'd always been an avid reader. In her last days before succumbing to her coma, she had insisted he bring her some of them. All paperbacks, with dog-eared pages and fading covers. August didn't like e-books.

He tried to remember that one book she really liked but couldn't. The one she'd been crazy about, so much that she'd travelled to meet the author. Remembering names had been a struggle for him lately.

Floyd wasn't much of a reader himself. Never fictional books. He only read manuals and reports, usually concerning his work. Most books were crap, written by men who knew little, if any, about real-life complications.

August devoured fiction. Romance, fantasy, thrillers, you name it.

Now, standing before piles of books he had shelved on the window pane, he still didn't understand the purpose of fiction. He thought he never would. What was the point of deluding oneself and escaping into a world that wasn't real? To him, such books were filled with incorrect information, impossible circumstances, and mythological heroes that wouldn't last half a second in the real world.

He ran his hand over the books and closed his eyes, then pulled one up to his nose and inhaled its scent. August loved her books getting older. She read some of them twice, and thrice, and loved them even more.

Floyd didn't care. He wasn't inhaling the books, not really. He was inhaling his wife's scent. Traces of her scent, of her mind, of her passion, of what made the woman she'd become. She had touched these books a thousand times. She hugged them while falling asleep. Sometimes cried all over the pages. He loved this.

"You should read to her."

"Excuse me?" Floyd turned, looking at the nurse standing by the door.

"Dr. Hope says reading books to a coma patient is one of the best things to help their mind stay alert," the nurse said.

Nurses loved Dr. Jessica Hope. Floyd had always been skeptical about her last name being Hope. He wondered if it'd been made up to manipulate patients into recovery.

"She said reading books to your wife might be better than holding hands," the nurse said.

"Read to her?" Floyd glanced at the book in his hand. "Will that help August?"

"Of course. It'll keep her mind working and alive." The nurse picked up August's medical chart from the edge of the bed. "I'm surprised Dr. Hope never told you about it."

"Maybe because she knows my opinion on such things."

"Meaning?" The nurse read the chart.

"I don't believe in pseudoscience."

"Ah, I understand. Of course, we don't really know what's going on with most coma patients. I'm just telling you what studies suggest."

Floyd wondered if a nurse was qualified to discuss a sensitive subject like that, but he couldn't help but ask. He'd do anything for August. A deal with the devil would do. He didn't mind. "What did these studies find?"

"That keeping a coma patient's mind busy is the most important thing to keep them alive, and hope for recovery," she said. "The trick is to shock the brain into alertness, like an adrenalin shot we stab drug overdose patients with, or the patient's probability of going into the rabbit hole of their own mind increases."

"Rabbit hole of the mind?"

"She'll be dreaming and making up stories in her mind. Nonsensical stories that will give her purpose in the beginning but drive her mad in the end."

"What happens to a coma patient if they get mad?"

"I didn't quite mean mad. What I meant is that the mind is a mystery. Sometimes it works in our favor. Sometimes it's our greatest enemy."

"I'm not sure I understand."

She put the chart back and smiled at him. "I'm only suggesting you read to her, Mr. Floyd. It will increase the chances she wakes up."

"You talk as if waking up from a coma is the usual."

"Not at all. To be honest, the odds are always slim. But it happens—happened—before. Why would we give up hope?"

Floyd's eyes shifted toward the TV set on mute. The nurse's words rang in the back of his head: *Why would we give up on hope?*

How was he so determined to save the last three passengers from the plane crash, but not believe in his wife's recovery?

"I have seen it with my own eyes," the nurse continued. "I have seen patients blink an eye or wiggle a toe after hours of someone reading to them."

"You did?"

"I know you don't believe me, but..."

"No." Floyd waved a hand. "I don't necessarily think it's pseudoscience. I will begin reading to her."

"Excellent." The nurse's smile broadened.

"One more thing, please?" Floyd said.

"Yes?"

"I'd like to meet with Dr. Hope and learn more about the reading thing."

"Of course. She is in an operation right now. Once she's done, I'll let her know." The nurse nodded. "Have a nice day, Mr. Floyd."

Floyd waved then glanced at his mobile phone. No word from Dixon, which meant he hadn't found the three passengers yet. A good opportunity to start reading to August. First, Floyd had to remember which book was her favorite. He wanted to read the closest words to her heart.

If he could only remember the title.

Chapter 64

The cries are near. Lovely baby. A newborn? I spot two nurses carrying an infant in the distance. I crouch and hide in the shadow of a bed on wheels left empty in the corridor. The nurse with the baby in her hands looks happy talking to the other nurse. I can't see any more, though, so I wait until they disappear into another corridor.

I tiptoe toward the nearest open room. There is the constant low drone of a machine thrumming through the walls. Also, the muffled voices of patients and nurses everywhere. Suddenly I realize this place isn't as empty as I thought, but I can't make out any words.

Stopping before the first door, I slowly stretch my neck forward and peek inside. It's a copy of mine. Same walls, windows, and big bed in the middle. Except there is another woman inside. She has cocoa-colored skin. She's lying on the bed and breathing cautiously, as if a doctor instructed her to do so. Some sort of training, I assume. Not sure why I know this.

The woman is wearing a gown like mine. There is one more important thing about her: she is pregnant. Probably in her last months.

Gripping my razor harder, I'm not sure what to do. The woman looks alone in the room, but will she shout or push an emergency button if I approach her? Is she a friend or foe?

This place still baffles me. A woman giving birth on an island where they burn women to death?

Shit, I wasted time thinking and didn't catch the woman noticing me. I freeze in place and show her my razor in case she is about to scream or call for help.

She doesn't. Her bulging eyes remind me of a rabbit's. A scared rabbit.

She raises a forefinger to her mouth and says, "Shhh."

So she doesn't mind my venturing through the corridors? All she asks is that I don't say a word.

When I am about to take a step closer, she points at the corridor and shakes her head. She doesn't want me to enter.

Call me paranoid, but I stare into her eyes for a moment to assess if she is fooling me like the rest. I don't think she is. How do I know? She projects fear in her eyes. I bet she has been whisked away into this awful place, not knowing what is really going on.

"I need to ask you something," I mouth.

She grits her teeth but says nothing. All she does is point to the right side of the corridor.

"Okay." I nod, not sure what is waiting there for me. "Okay."

Further into the hall, I wonder if I should have insisted on talking, but what if she'd called for help then? She was kind enough to not expose me, but maybe she wouldn't have been as kind if I'd risked her child's safety.

I stop by the next room. There is another woman. She is also pregnant. This one is pale white and reminds me of Ashlyn. She shushes me, just the same.

I can't stand this. I can't stand being so confused.

The pale woman points at the corridor. This one is really scared, tears in her eyes.

I feel apprehensive as I see more pregnant women in each room I stop at, almost not giving a shit about the sound of my flapping feet anymore, or if I get caught. What the hell is going on here?

The women keep directing me further and further away until I see my destination: an entrance to another section, labeled *Operations.*

I hear the two nurses coming back. I duck as I see them cross the hall in the distance. They're laughing casually and don't head in my direction.

Once they disappear, I stare at the operating room. This is where the women wanted me to go. Cautiously, I push the door, enough to glimpse inside. There is so much to see, but the closest is my obstacle to entering. Another nurse. I realize I have to disable her and claim her identity.

The ease with which I wrap my hands around the nurse and choke her until she faints disturbs me. It disturbs me even more when I realize I'm also capable of doing it without making much noise. Have I done this before?

It doesn't take me much time. It's almost effortless. I lock the door from inside and start undressing the poor girl. I don the nurse's outfit, tucking the magnetic card and syringe in a pocket. I have a feeling I will be using them.

I pull her to a metal cabinet full of bandages and stuff her inside, bending her body in strange ways. I ball up my hospital gown and throw it in as well. I can't pull off the wristband, so I hide it under my sleeve.

I peek through the keyhole. Outside, a nurse walks by with a crying baby in her arms. Time to go out and face whatever awaits me. I put on my poker face and open the door, following the nurse with the baby.

Not many nurses are in this corridor, which is broad enough to handle two hospital beds side by side. The air conditioning here is almost freezing.

The nurse turns right into a smaller corridor. I follow her. A nurse walking in the opposite direction greets me. I nod, realizing I'd better pick up one of those surgical masks, like the one she is wearing, from a nearby basket.

I do. It makes my mission even easier. I only have to fake the look in my eyes, which most people aren't good at reading anyway.

The nurse enters a room. I slow down and pretend to keep walking ahead. From the corner of my eye, I glimpse her swiping a magnetic card through a slot in the wall, waiting for a door to slide open, and then passing through. I make sure none of the other nurses are around, then turn and enter the room, now empty.

I lock the door to the room behind me, then pull out the magnetic card. A green light shimmers on the wall, and a hologram of a digital pad appears on the wall above it.

I guess the card isn't enough. Now I am stuck again.

It occurs to me to use 1001 for the passcode, but it seems unlikely. What happens if it's wrong and a warning sounds all over the place?

I take a step back and scan the room. Maybe it holds the answer to the passcode. I don't need to look long, because something on the wall to my right catches my eyes.

A chart.

It takes me some time to understand what it really is. At first, I see the baby names. Hundreds of baby names are assigned to different years. *Popular names*, it says in one column. Someone here is interested in popular baby names by year, starting from 1945. I don't know why, but the back of my neck heats up.

I near the chart on the wall, almost forgetting all about the door I want to enter. The names are endless. The chart becomes much more complicated when I focus on the details. One part interests me the most, though.

A few small papers are pinned to the wall next to the chart. According to the heading, these are babies born in 2018, and the names suggested for them. I have a feeling a lot of answers are on this piece of paper, but I can't even figure out what this is all about. Aren't the babies' parents supposed to choose the names?

The paper says there are around ten babies born each week. Some of the babies' chosen names are circled in red.

Something else is circled in red. A calendar. I have a feeling I should understand something right away, but can't. The calendar has certain months circled: January, April, May, June, or August.

What the hell does this mean? What happens in these months? Why are they important?

The sound of nearing footsteps tick-tocks in the back of my head, but I am too consumed, and confused, by the chart I'm staring at.

The footsteps are getting louder. Someone is at the door.

I rip the chart down. I will fold it up and tuck it in my back pocket. But just as I am about to do that, I notice a scribble at the bottom of the report:

Babies survival rate: 50%

Abortion rate: 50%

Mother's survival rate: N/A

Note: Awaiting permission to send to the Furnace.

Chapter 65

The door flings open. Quickly, I fold the chart and tuck it in my pocket then straighten up. The woman at the door, probably a senior nurse, glares at me.

"What are you doing here?"

I don't know what to say. My mind is still distracted by the baby names on the chart. I still hold the magnetic card in my hand.

The nurse comes forward and scans me from top to bottom. Her eyes linger on the card. "Are you new here? Never seen you before."

"Just arrived a few days ago." I nod, faking the naive newbie-girl look. "Don't know how to use the card."

"Yeah?" she says. "Who's your handler?"

Handler? "Dr. Alan Suffolk," I say, risking everything.

"Of course." She rolls her eyes. "His nurses are the most naive, always." She snatches the card from my hand and inserts it into the slot. She waits for the green hologram and then types in the passcode.

I don't get a chance to read it. She's bigger and taller than me and blocks the view. I wonder if she'll ask me if I know the passcode, but she doesn't bother. She pushes me into the white room ahead. "We have too many babies to deliver today, so we need all the nurses available."

"I am glad to help," I mumble, and step inside.

Deliberately, I slow down until I hear the door close behind me. I don't want to seem lost.

I am in another deserted hall. Everything is white in here. The walls. The equipment and the desks. Only the chairs and a bed on my right are metallic. The drone I heard earlier dominates the room. It sounds like a generator.

Farther in, human sounds begin to rise. Rooms on the left and right. I hear another baby's cry.

Furious, I push through one of the double doors and stand still. What stops me is a complicated image of the things I have feared since I arrived. My mind tries to reject what I see, but there is no escaping. It's all in front of my eyes.

Ahead of me, behind a window, I see doctors operating on a woman. Some of them are holding strange metallic instruments in their hands. A doctor hands a baby to the nurse on the left. The nurse holds the crying baby and gently hushes it. The doctor says something to the other nurses, and they pull a blanket over the mother on the table from head to toe. I can see she is wearing a wristband.

Frozen in my place, swallowing and sweating, I don't know what to do. One of the doctors seems to be the one everyone looks up to. Then I realize the nurses and doctors are congratulating him.

On the mother's death, or the baby's birth?

He shakes hands with a few then takes off his head covering and pulls down his surgical mask. That's when I suppress a shriek. The doctor is Major Red.

"Bastards!" I totally lose my patience. I have no more time for puzzles and games. Whatever is happening here, it's not right. I run to the nearest door leading to the operating room and storm inside. One of the nurses tries to hold me back. I punch her in the face.

By the bed, I pull the blanket back and stare at the poor woman. Dead. She has a brutal cut in her midsection and clots of blood are seeping out.

"What the fuck did you do to her?" I turn and slash at another doctor. I pick up another sharp instrument and slash at Major Red.

Chapter 66

Soldiers storm into the room, flashing their firearms. No one worries about contamination in here.

A soldier pushes his gun against my back and I fall to my knees. My magic weapon of justice falls on the floor. Its metallic sound fades into oblivion, and so does my hope. I realize how alone I am on this island. So many people around me, and not one of them deserves to live. I miss Ashlyn.

"That was so reckless of you, Miss June," Major Red says, my knife having slashed diagonally across his face. It's strange how my instrument went over the same old scar I'd seen earlier. He waits until the soldiers truly get hold of me, then kneels down. "Why do you keep doing these things?"

I spit on his face. I don't want to listen to his manipulative excuses, to him trying to convince me of my insanity. I am so beyond that. I know I am not insane.

Major Red wipes my spit away, his face reddening slightly. He doesn't look as angry as I'd expect him to be. I stare at his ugly face and then...

Then...

The back of his hand. This can't be true. How didn't I notice this before? There, on each knuckle, I see a tattoo. The same small red tattoo. A swastika.

My mouth hangs open for a few moments. All kinds of questions spin in my head.

He smirks, as if enjoying that I noticed. Then he stands up. "Take her back to her room."

"She hurt one of nurses badly and locked her inside a cabinet," a soldier says. "She should be sent to—"

"I said to her room." Major Red glares at him. "Make sure she doesn't leave this time. I'll deal with her later."

My numb feet drag behind me on the floor as the soldiers pull me. I wriggle and swear and spit on them, but they're like robots, nonreactive to my insults. On the way back, I glance at the pregnant women in the open rooms again. They are terrified. Most of them look away as if they have never seen me before.

"What's stopping you from opposing them?" I ask them. No one says a word.

Then, when I am close to the corridor that leads to my room, I see it. The horror of it all. Another large room behind thick glass. This one isn't an operating room. Nor a patient's. It's a room full of newborn babies. The soldiers' hands I once resisted are now my solace. I grip them hard, so I won't fall to my knees. My eyes are still on the babies. The infants whose mothers probably all died on operating tables like where Major Red stood. Mothers who eventually ended up in the Furnace.

"Is my daughter in here?" I drool the words, nearly incoherent. "Who is Manfred Toot?"

The soldiers don't answer me. No one will answer me on this island. One of them sticks me with a syringe in my neck. I'm wondering if it's the one I stole from the nurse. The world begins to shutter all around me.

The babies are still crying. A large sign on the wall spells it all out for me. It reads in bold, neon-lit letters: *Welcome to the Crib*.

Chapter 67

Mercy Medical Center, New York

Floyd read to his wife but had noticed no changes so far. Every few pages, he raised his head from the book and looked at her. Nothing. He reasoned that he was an impatient man. Improvement wouldn't happen so fast. He just wished August would wake up and take him in her arms and save him from this brutal world.

The things he'd seen in his life were enough proof.

A few recent missions with the FBI came to mind. One of them stuck out more than most. The discovery of a neo-Nazi organization planning to plant their members in American government.

How was that possible? Nazis surviving this long? What kind of hate against humanity drove such an organization?

Floyd shook the memories away. Right now, even while he was reading to August, he hoped the last passengers of flight 1001 had survived. At least one. Just one. So they weren't just loading corpses into a chopper and taking them home to wailing families. *Please, God, if you're really there, make their efforts count.*

It wasn't long before he realized that he couldn't really stomach the book he was reading to August. He'd have preferred informative non-fiction, but August hated those.

He stood up and shoved the book back in the bag. Not that he had given up on hope for his wife's recovery. He just figured that if he was going to tolerate a fiction book, he better read her favorite. That book he'd seen on her nightstand so many times. That book she'd gushed about and begged him to read.

If only he could remember its title now.

He felt guilty, not paying attention to the books she loved. It was a common human fault, not listening to loved ones. A song he used to listen to in his youth came to mind: "Don't Know What You Got (Till It's Gone)" *by* an eighties rock band called Cinderella.

Book after book, cover after cover, he tried to remember that favorite book of hers. He recalled her telling him that this book had changed her life. Something he never understood. How could a book change a life? Only experiences, blood and sweat, and repeated heartache changed a person's life. Or so he believed.

He wondered if there was a book that could change his mind, not his life, about books. One paperback fell on the floor, and he knelt to pick it up. He wiped away a faint trace of dust and realized he remembered this one. Floyd picked it up, wondering if this was some kind of a divine intervention.

It wasn't entirely fictional, he remembered. The real story was of a skydiver whose parachute didn't open. She'd crashed straight on the ground. Only the endless spikes of adrenalin caused by hundreds of red ants stinging her kept her alive.

Floyd stared at the book for a while. It was barely a believable story, but the FBI had confirmed some details back when August asked him about it. The real woman had ended up in a coma for a long time, but she woke up eventually.

Was this really a divine sign, to find the book August loved the most? What did she love about a woman in a coma before she went into one herself?

"The woman in this book woke up." He stole a glance back at August.

Fighting the tears, he sat on the sofa opposite her, chains of hopelessness wrapped around his heart. "Wake up, August," he said. A whisper, really. "If you can hear me, I beg you to wake up. I'm lost without you, babe."

Of course, she didn't. Nor did she blink or wiggle a toe.

He checked his cell phone and wondered why Dixon hadn't called yet. He put the cell away and sat down to read August's favorite book.

He began by reading the title out loud:

The Last Girl.

Chapter 68

Everyone around me is trying to sell me all kinds of lies. Nurses try to explain things to me. That none of what I saw is what I think I saw.

They wipe away my sweat and change me back into the hospital gown. I can't resist. They already sedated me again.

"Dr. Suffolk didn't just say you need to be locked up," one of them tells me. "He said you needed better medical care, the kind you can get in Ward Four."

"You shouldn't have spat on Major Red," another says. "He is a good man."

"Get out!" I say with a numb tongue, but my anger must be showing in my eyes, because I see the nurses step away, as if I am a disease. "Major Red is a liar. So are all of you. Isn't this island supposed to be a military base? I believed there were no women on the island, let alone pregnant women. What do you want with the babies? What the hell is going on in here?"

"She's lost it," a third nurse says.

"You think?" a fourth comments with a nasty chuckle. "This woman has been a nut case since she arrived."

I spit out more words from my brain, not sure they're reaching my tongue. "Goddammit. What did you bitches inject me with?"

One of them whispers in my ear, “We aren’t bad people. On the contrary. I think it’s you who is bad. Anyway, Dr. Suffolk will see you again soon.”

Chapter 69

I spend the next hour or so awake. Whatever they've given me, it semi-paralyzes me. I can't even move my eyes, as if I am in a coma. I'm staring at the bland color of the ceiling, trapped in my head. It's an awful feeling to be imprisoned in your own mind.

The worst thing about it is how much calmer and collected I begin to feel. I don't want that. What is it that I've been injected with? My left arm hurts like hell from under the bandages.

Time feels like killing myself with a slow and dull knife. How long has it been? It doesn't matter. The sedative is wearing off. Soon I'll be free again.

While I wait, I begin to count sheep.

Then I decide that counting sheep is for people with memories.

I resolve to do it my way. Instead of counting anything, I keep repeating:

Kill Manfred Toot.

Kill Manfred Toot.

Kill Manfred Toot.

Until the unbearable blare in my head returns and cracks my skull in toot—I mean in two.

Chapter 70

I stand by the bed, drinking all the water I can. Needing energy, I follow up by gorging on all the food the nurses brought in on the tray. I need my strength. I have a plan.

It's a dangerous plan, but it's not like I didn't already do it with Ashlyn in Ward Four earlier. I will climb out the window and walk on the ledge outside. Victorian buildings have big ledges. I guess I am lucky. I will have to slide myself outside the half open window somehow, since the other part doesn't open.

Before I get to the window, I scan the floor, foolishly hoping for another oil message. There isn't one. I wonder if this means whoever sent them before has no access to the Crib.

In just a few minutes, I am out on the ledge. How? Suddenly I could easily open the locked part. I wonder if whoever sends me the notes did that, trying to help. I plaster my hands to the wall, not looking down. I move only as far as the ledge goes, briefly sneaking glances to feel my way. My gown is soaking wet. I begin to shiver. It's nothing. Practice makes perfect.

The cold in my back chills me, tempting me to slip and fall. Step after step, I am waiting for my hand to grip a window frame. From where I stand, it's hard to tell how far away the nearest window is.

What if there are no windows to other women's rooms? I have two choices: either believe in the existence of a window and keep going or slip and break my neck on the ground below. That would be a shame: an amnesiac dying thinking she is someone else. In that case, I wonder what happens to me in the afterlife, if there is any. Will they count the sins of the person I am now, or the one I was then?

The edge of the window almost cuts at my hand. I almost slip again, unable to grip the window's wet frame.

I hold on. The window is slightly open, which makes no sense in this weather. I don't question such illogical things anymore.

Recklessly, without scanning the room from outside, I take a leap of faith and jump inside.

Chapter 71

The room's door is locked, so I don't have to worry about someone spotting me from the corridor. It's another copy of my room. The woman on the bed in the middle is pregnant. I saw her when I stepped out in the corridor earlier. I remember her. The cocoa-colored woman. The first one who hushed me and told me to advance.

She freaks out when she sees me again.

"Silence," I say. "I will not hurt you."

"You have to leave," she whispers. "I want my baby to live."

"Listen." I pull her hand up and read the name on the wristband. "Adriana—"

"I will not listen. You have to leave." Her accent is South American, or so I believe. No time to chat about her nationality.

"You will listen to me," I whisper with ferocious intensity. "I will not leave before you tell me what is going on in here."

"No. My baby doesn't deserve to die. I know I will, but I want it to see the world."

"Of course your baby has to live." I nod. "But why do *you* have to die?"

"It's the law of the Crib. All the women here know it. Stop asking questions and leave."

"Only if you tell me everything. Who brought you here? How long have you been here? Why are you giving in to death?"

Adriana stares at me, breathing heavily. "You're crazy."

"Try another one. Been told that too many times."

"I will say nothing. You had your chance. Me and the other pregnant women showed you to the operating room."

"So?"

"You should understand everything by now."

"Understand what? I saw Major Red delivering a baby, and the mother was dead on the operating table." I try to remember what else I saw. "And I found this chart, sorted by years, with names of babies on it." I flatten it out and show it to her.

"I know what this is." She looks away again.

"You do?"

She refuses to speak, loathing my existence in a strange way I can't comprehend.

"What is this? A calendar? Why are these months circled? January, April, May, J—"

"June and August." She looks into my eyes.

"June and August?" I tilt my head. "How do you know that?"

"You know."

"I know what? Why should I know? Major Red said today is the fifteenth of June. He said he didn't believe my name is

June." I can't catch my breath, recalling the events. "Then I wake up with this wristband on my hand. It says my name is June West."

The nurses are outside. Adriana peeks behind me at the door then back to me. "You have to leave."

Though I'm exhausted, afraid, and trembling, I raise my hand and slap her back to the pillow.

I slap her again, in case she decides to resist. I pull the emergency button from atop the bed then tell her, "If you don't tell me, I'll push the button. I don't give a shit if the nurses come and punish both of us. I'm just an angry woman, looking for her child. But you. Look at you, Adriana. You'll lose your baby."

"What kind of bitch are you?"

"The bitch that won't give up."

Adriana takes a deep breath. Her eyes are moist. "I am like you," she says.

"Like me?"

"I have no memory of who I am or how I arrived."

"And the other women?"

"The same," Adriana says. "We don't know how we got here."

"Tell me more."

"We were told we were the sole survivors of a plane crash."

I suppress a morbid shriek. "All of you?"

She nods. “I had a few sessions with Dr. Suffolk. Tests. All in the name of helping regain my memories. He kept saying he’d hypnotize me, but it never happened.”

“And?”

“Like the other girls, I heard about the secret submarine by the shore, and how it was my only hope to escape this island,” she says. I remember Ashlyn telling me about it. “I failed. They caught me and brought me to the Crib.”

“Did you see the Furnace?”

“No, but I heard. Other girls saw it.”

“Please continue.”

“More tests. More drugs. Illusions.” She trembles. “Nightmares. Unspeakable nightmares.”

“What kind of nightmares?”

“I don’t want to talk about it.”

“Please, Adriana.” I glance behind me. “We have no time.”

“Nightmares about a man called Toot.”

“And?” I fist my hands to keep calm.

“Manfred Toot.” She begins to cry. “I don’t want to—”

“Please, Adriana.” I sink to my knees and gently grab her hand.

She pulls away. “A few days later, I wake up and the nurses tell me I’m pregnant.”

“A few days?”

"I'm not sure. Could be months. The hallucinations. The nightmares. Time slipped. I couldn't tell what was real from what wasn't."

"I totally understand."

"The nurses showed me the charts, if I remember correctly. It said I've been almost nine months on the island, but it felt like a few days."

"You're sure you weren't pregnant when you first arrived?"

"I think so. It's all so blurry." She raises her crying eyes to meet mine. She even reaches for my hands now. She holds tightly to me. "I didn't care about all of that. I wanted to know who the father of my child was."

I hold tighter to her, feeling stupid I didn't ask.

"The nurses told me it's the same man who impregnated all the other women."

I'm speechless. I need a second to think it over. I can't fathom what she has told me. How can I connect the dots? An uncharted Nazi island that somehow survived World War II without anyone knowing about it. The island is ruled by an American man, Major Red. The soldiers, doctors, and nurses are mostly American, too, but the pregnant patients are from all over the world. They impregnate women and take their babies. The mothers have to die, and it's one man who impregnates them all. This is stranger than fiction.

"Have you ever met this man, Adriana?" I say.

"No, but I know his name." Her pupils dilate with fear. Black fear, the color of the oil I keep smelling. "They call him Manfred Schmidt. Also known as Manfred Toot."

Chapter 72

Mercy Medical Center, New York

"We found two passengers out of three," Dixon informed Floyd on the phone.

The old man held his wife's favorite book in the other hand and said, "Alive?"

"Of course not," Dixon retorted. "Dead, Floyd. One of them without legs."

Two out of three narrowed it down to the possibility of one survivor. It wasn't far-fetched. Statistically, most plane crashes killed everyone on board. Rarely did a few people survive. A sole survivor in a plane crash happened more than twenty percent of the time, though. The kind of strange fact that had always puzzled Floyd.

"I have to tell you, Floyd," Dixon continued, "in this weather, I'm going to give up on that last girl."

"Last girl?" Floyd squinted, staring at the book in his hand. It seemed like too many coincidences had happened around him recently. The fact that August's book fell from the bag, and that its title was *The Last Girl*, which seemed similar to the current situation of the last passenger on the plane. He didn't want to read much into this, as he'd never believed in such things.

“The last three passengers were girls, remember?” Dixon said. “So we call her ‘the last girl’ around here.”

“Appropriate name, Dixon. Find her!” Floyd hung up.

He tapped the book in his hand and said to his wife, “Let’s pray the last girl is alive, August. I’m going to keep reading to you. Let’s see if a book can save a life.”

He continued reading the book aloud. A few minutes in, he was shocked by how much he liked it.

Chapter 73

I'm still holding Adriana's cold hands. Mine are as cold now. Footsteps sound nearer outside the room. I have to get back on that ledge before the nurses arrive. I can't stand against them alone. Besides, I still have no aim. No purpose. No solid conclusion to what's going on. Too many questions, so little time.

"Do you know anything else about Manfred Toot?"

Adriana's eyes widen. She looks away from me again, lowering her neck onto her chest. It's as if she wants to crawl into a fetal position but can't do it. Instead, she covers her stomach with both hands.

"You said you haven't met him. I know." I lean forward. "But do you know anything about him? Did any of the other women tell you something? Do you have any idea why he impregnates women?"

She tenses, refusing to look at me. I'm not sure she is breathing anymore.

"Adriana, I've been looking for this man for some time. I don't know why, but I have reason to believe I should kill him. I need to know who he is. At least tell me where I can find him."

"You can't kill him."

"Let me be the judge of that. Where can I find him?"

"Nor can you find him." She drools on the pillow now, as if she is having a seizure. "Toot finds you. Once to impregnate you. Later to kill you."

"Why?" I try to shake the stiffened skeleton of a woman. "Tell me why, Adriana." Behind me, I hear the nurses getting closer. "Please." I kiss her forehead. "I need to save my daughter."

Adriana cries painful hiccups, still drooling onto the pillow.

"Adriana, you'll be a mother soon. You know how it feels," I say softly. "I'm a mother myself—at least, I think I am. I need to save my daughter. This Toot man will hurt her. You're my last chance to save her. Do you hear me? Think of my child as if it were yours. *You're a mother, Adriana.* You know how it feels."

"What does your daughter look like?" she says.

"I have no idea. I don't remember anything. Just like you."

"What kind of mother doesn't remember her daughter?"

"I—" I wish I could answer that question.

"Do you know what they do with the babies here?"

I swallow hard, not sure I want to know, but then I realize this could lead me to my daughter's whereabouts. "Tell me."

"You'll never find her," Adriana says. She stops crying. It's as if her body froze all of a sudden, but she can still speak.

"Don't say that," I say. "I know I've been cruel to you, but please don't tell me I'm not going to find her."

Outside, the nurses are loud enough to be only steps away from the door. I have no choice but to abandon Adriana. I stand up and reluctantly hurry for the window. It'll be a temporary escape. I'll have to come back and find out more.

"Remember to breathe," Adriana says into her pillow. I can't tell if she is talking to me. "Just breathe."

Though the door is going to burst open any second, I'm hesitant to leave, hoping for a payoff. "Is there is anything else you can tell me, Adriana?"

I'm surprised that she answers right away. "Try to find the submarine. It's your only way out."

"I'm not leaving without my daughter." I grip the edge of the window to start my escape.

Adriana spits one last thing before the door opens: "Your daughter is so close," she says. "Closer than you could even imagine."

Chapter 74

Somewhere in the Atlantic Ocean

"We've found no one so far," the diver shouted on the radio.

Dixon couldn't see clearly from his position in the helicopter. No way in hell he'd get down near the wreckage himself. Up here, he had the advantage of escaping in case the weather went full-on berserk.

"We can always dive deeper," the diver continued. "It'll be a tad suicidal, but my men are brave."

"Brave enough to die?" Dixon said.

"It's their job. They know what they have to do."

"All that for a fucking last girl," Dixon mumbled. "Damn you, Floyd."

"If I may ask," the diver said, "since when do we let the FBI tell us what to do?"

"Since we fucked up on the TWA flight." Dixon squinted, trying to get a better look with his binoculars.

"Ah, of course," the diver said. "That was a fuckup. No wonder it remains unexplained what really happened."

"More than twenty years ago. Can you wait a sec, please?" Dixon said, staring at his phone. He'd received a report from his men and read it. "Listen," he said to the diver. "Did you find a seat 37A?"

"Let me check," the diver said. "Yeah. A single seat. It somehow broke off the row and sank deep below."

"Was it empty?"

"Yes. Why?"

"Any signs of its passenger having survived?"

"Could be. The strap was cut violently. I suppose someone was panicked and couldn't unbuckle."

"My team speculates it's the last girl's seat."

"Shit," the diver said. "So we actually have to dive deeper."

"You don't have to," Dixon said. "Just tell me it's impossible in this shitstorm and I will report it."

The diver was silent for a long while. Dixon wondered why people wanted to be heroes. It was just a last dead girl. Who cared?

"Gimme a minute," the diver said.

Dixon could faintly hear him talk with his men.

Thirty seconds later, the diver returned to the speaker. "We should scan the ocean in a ten-mile radius, in case she is hanging on to something the waves swept away."

"You mean use the trawlers."

"Yes."

"All right. Just get this done with so we can go home," Dixon said. "Does this mean your men can't take the dive?"

The diver hesitated. "Frankly, none of them wants to risk it."

Dixon grinned. "Wise call."

"I'm sorry, it's just not worth it. One girl. Who's she gonna be in the end?"

"No one special, really." Dixon glanced at the girl's name. "Trust me, she's not even average in the human hierarchy."

"This stays between us, right?" the diver said.

"Of course," Dixon said, taking a deep breath, happy he'd be back home with his wife and kids soon. "Just send me some technical issues that'd prevent your men from taking the dip, and I'll report right away—"

"Wait a second, please."

Dixon waited impatiently. What could have happened?

"Shit!" the diver said.

"What's going on?"

"Two of my men are going to take the dip."

"What?"

"They volunteered. I can't stop them, or they'll report it. Honestly, the dip is dangerous, but doable if you're good."

"They'll fucking die."

"Don't blame me. It's their call. Besides, dying is our middle name in this business."

"What the fuck?" Dixon couldn't believe it. Some people were morons. Who'd want to risk their lives for one girl that didn't mean anything?

"Put them on," Dixon roared.

"Excuse me?"

"At least tell me their names. I'll talk to them."

"Jack and Irene."

"Jack Irene?" Dixon was about to type the name into his phone. "And the other?"

"No, you misunderstood. Their names are Jack and Irene."

"Irene? The other diver is a girl?"

"Yes. She's badass."

"I can't understand why this Jack and Irene want to risk their lives."

"It's their job," the diver said. "I'm proud of them, I have to say. They're also engaged."

"Fuck me."

"Their wedding is next week, sir."

Dixon was going to vomit. "Next week? Do they understand there might be no wedding after this call?"

"They do, sir. Some people just love to save lives."

Chapter 75

Out on the ledge, I try to move in the opposite direction to my room. Unfortunately, a thick brick wall blocks the way. I have no choice but go back to my room for now. It's a tough call, but climbing around the brick wall is a huge risk. I'm not suicidal. Far from it, now that Adriana confirmed I have a daughter.

Your daughter is closer than you could even imagine. What did she mean? Why so cryptic?

Though I've climbed outside before, it's much harder this time. My mind is on a rampage. Adriana. The women in the other rooms. The Crib. Manfred Toot impregnating these women. The plane crash. Either I'm naive and stupid or a big portion of this story doesn't make sense.

Step after step, my only concern is my daughter's location. Adriana said I should take the submarine Ashlyn mentioned. Once I find my daughter, I'll take her to the submarine. I know the way. It's a naively optimistic plan, but it's all I've got. I have to hang on to something.

My right foot slips.

I grab a pipe and my left foot plays acrobat to help me hang on to the edge of the ledge.

Wake up, June. You can't fuck up, now that you're sure your daughter exists.

Hanging, I close my eyes to calm down. My weight is tearing my muscles apart. The rain makes it harder for my left foot to hang on any longer. I need to gather my strength and pull my right leg up again.

The pain is too strong. I grit my teeth and try not to scream or call for help. An image forms behind my eyelids. A movie plays before me.

A memory.

A red flicker forms at the end of my tunnel vision. A man. He isn't dressed in red, though. He is covered in blood. He is coming for me. I'm going to pee in my pants. I've never been scared of anyone the way I fear him. I loathe him. I can't see his face, as it's covered in blood. He is laughing. Getting closer. Nearby, someone is crying. A girl. *"Mommy! Mommy!"*

I'm trying to locate the girl but realize I'm alone in here. Where is here? Shit. I know where here is. Not quite, but it's a room. I've seen it before.

I can't breathe. I can't breathe.

The man is getting closer. He wears...

I can't breathe. I need to learn how to breathe.

The man smirks at me and says, "Are you ready to deliver?"

Breathe, just breathe. It's going to be over soon. Where is that little girl calling for her mother? And why the heck is he wearing a Nazi uniform?

My eyes flip open. What the hell was that? I think it's my first real memory. My first true clue about who I am. I can't recall who this man is, but I think I have a clue about the girl's identity.

As I'm about to take a deep breath to pull myself back on the ledge, I realize I've already done that. Both my feet are fixed on the ledge. I'm only a few inches away from my room.

Almost automatically, I find my way inside. My room isn't empty, though. Dr. Suffolk and several nurses are waiting for me.

Chapter 76

Mercy Medical Center, New York

For an hour straight, Floyd couldn't stop reading. Time flew by, and he felt immersed in the story, so much that he sometimes forgot to read out loud for August. He felt like he knew every character by now, sympathized with them, cried and laughed with them. It was as if he'd been sucked in through a looking glass made of paper and ink. He enjoyed it so much that he contemplated taking the day off—which was impossible, of course.

Floyd found the author's voice enticing. He appreciated her not being a wordsmith, or he'd not have eased into the story. Every twist or surprise or cliffhanger challenged a new emotion. In short, he could not believe a work of fiction could make him feel alive.

Though he was curious to read her biography, he decided to do it later, in case it would spoil anything about the book. He'd glimpsed her photo though. A blonde woman with thick glasses. A perfect nerd, he thought.

One thing that surprised him the most was that the protagonist wasn't even a man. Not that Floyd was a sexist—he'd seen women kick ass in the field; a young diver named Irene came to mind—but he just didn't expect it.

The Last Girl's protagonist was a girl in her teens. *Lord in heaven*, Floyd thought, *the horrible things that have been done to her.* The book was mind-bending, and presented as real-world survival story, even though Floyd knew it was mostly fiction. How would anyone survive an accident like this woman did?

Chapter 77

Dr. Suffolk's smile is gone. So is his beauty. Hands in his pockets, he stares back at me like an interrogator.

I'm sitting on my bed, all wet, since he denied me a shower or a change of clothes. I'm shivering, teeth chattering. He looks fed up. I watch him pace back and forth.

Then he stops.

"June, we have to talk."

I hug myself to warm up. "You want to feed me more lies. I know all about this place already."

"Know what about this place?"

"Whatever criminal conspiracy is going on in here. Nazis, pregnant women you burn after they give birth to one man's seed—"

"Stop it."

"Stop what? I saw everything. I saw Major Red. The evil doctor. The babies. What the fuck are you doing with the babies?"

"Stop. It." He grits his teeth.

I'm not scared. Showing me his other face is a shock, but it will not stop me. Whoever he is, he seems to be following orders from Major Red.

He kneels and tries to charm me with his smile. It's not working. "Would you listen to me for a minute?" he says.

"I'm not stopping you."

"Okay." He sighs. "I will tell you everything."

"I don't need to know everything. Just tell me where my daughter is."

"We'll get to that, in time. Let me ask you a question first."

"Enough with this crap—"

"How come you trusted Ashlyn with your life so quickly?" he says, cutting through my stubbornness. He knows how guilty I feel about Ashlyn.

"What do you mean?"

"Look at you. You're scared of everyone on this island," he says, sounding reasonable and calm. "You're basically a classic case of amnesia: a person without a memory wondering on which side of the fence they're on, the good or the bad." His words grow slower with every sentence, as if he's hypnotizing me. "It's normal. It's human instinct. We all want to know whether we did good or evil by the end of the day. It's a universal question."

"What does this have to do with trusting Ashlyn?"

"It doesn't fit your personality," he says. "Think about it. You trusted no one, but when you met Ashlyn, not only did you trust her, you loved her."

"I—"

"Don't jump to conclusions. Give it a thought. Dig deeper inside and think about it."

"It's—"

"Ashlyn was no different from nurses like Mindy. There was a reason you trusted her so fast."

"She was naive. Lovable. She was—"

"Why do you think she wanted you to call her Ash?"

"What?" I grimace. I haven't answered his first question. What is he trying to prove? "She liked being called Ash. What kind of question is that—"

"Did she?"

"I'm not a liar—"

"Do you see the correlation between the word Ash and the Furnace?"

"I don't like this conversation."

"How did Ashlyn die?"

"Your soldiers shot her." I'm trying to look away, but he shifts to look me in the eyes.

"That's not what you told me in the clinic."

"Fuck you." I look away again.

"I'm on your side, June." Dr. Suffolk shifts again to face me. "I'm trying to give you the answers you seek."

Looking into his eyes, I can't see the doctor I met before. His eyes are bland. Emotionless. Unforgiving. "You told me you found Ash burned," he says. "You said the soldiers burned her in the Furnace."

"I didn't say that."

"Try to remember."

"I have only a few recent memories. Do you think I don't remember how my only true friend on this island died?"

"Why did you call her Ash?"

"What's wrong with you? What kind of question is that?"

"Ash is a word that's related to furnaces. You burn something and ashes are everywhere," he says. "Ashlyn, a.k.a. Ash, died burning in the end."

"In the end?"

"The end of your story."

"You're pushing it, Dr. Suffolk." I stand up and turn away. "I'm not insane."

"You know what they call this in fiction?" he says to my back. "Foreshadowing."

"Please leave." My teeth chatter. "I need to take a bath and change clothes."

I feel his breath on my neck behind me. "Why did you not ask me what foreshadowing is?"

"I don't want to know."

He swiftly stands before me again, staring at me, his eyes moist and tender now. "Foreshadowing is a writing device that hints of events that will happen later in a book."

"What the fuck are you talking about?"

"You wanted to know what's going on. I'm telling you, June."

"Telling me what, exactly?"

"I'd prefer it if you come to the conclusion yourself."

"You're fucking with my mind, that's all."

"Please," he says. "Help me help you."

"I don't need your help."

"You need all the help in the world."

"Where is my daughter?"

He ignores the question like always and reaches for my left arm, the bandaged one. I push him away and head for the bathroom. He grabs me by the bandaged arm. Violently. He pulls me closer.

"My arm hurts." I let out a painful moan.

"Yeah?" he says. "If it hurts so much, how come you used it to climb on the ledge outside."

I scoff. "I'm a big girl. I tolerated the pain."

"I don't see how." He squeezes my arm harder.

The pain inflames my body, so much that I almost buckle. "Ruthless asshole." I spit on him.

"I didn't want to be," he says. "You wanted answers, and I'm trying my best."

"Your best what?" I pull away again.

This time, the nurses get me. Six of those bitches. They're all over me. I'm stranded. I'm cold. I'm so pissed off.

"In your condition, you could have never climbed the ledge outside." Dr. Suffolk approaches me. "Not with a damaged arm like this." He begins to undo the bandage while the nurses keep me in place.

"Are you saying I've never climbed the ledge or escaped to the forest?" I ask.

"Like I said." He finishes undoing the bandage. "I want you to come to the conclusion yourself." He points at my arm. "Look, June," he says. "Look at your arm. Look so you understand why you had it bandaged in the first place."

"I didn't bandage it," I retort without looking. "I woke up in Ward Nine and found it this way."

"You've never looked at it before?"

"Once, when I was on shore."

"What did it look like?"

"I couldn't see. Blood covered every inch of it."

"Then it's time for you to look. Now!" He points at my arm.

Slowly, I look.

I'd be lying if I said what I see makes sense at all, because it does explain a lot of shit. I raise my eyes to meet his. "What is this supposed to mean?"

"It means there was never a plane crash," he says. "Never a nurse called Ashlyn, or the Furnace, and certainly there's never been Nazis."

Chapter 78

Mercy Medical Center, New York

Floyd drank some water to soothe his throat. He wasn't used to reading out loud for so long. It still amazed him how much he enjoyed the book, and he hoped to God that August enjoyed it as much.

"No wonder you loved this book so much," he told his wife. "It's so well written. I can see now why you admired that girl so much."

He sat back to continue reading.

"I mean, the protagonist of the story, she is one hell of a girl," he said to August. "A German girl who was the sole passenger to survive a plane crash. Her flight was on a commercial airliner that was struck by lightning during a severe thunderstorm and broke in midair." He tried not to scoff at the author's over-the-top imagination. With his expertise in the field, he never saw such accidents, but he liked the book. There was no need to spoil the beautiful writing and the well-told fantasy.

Floyd stared at the rain outside for a moment and smiled. "The girl in the book was seventeen when it happened. She reminds me of you, baby. I imagine you as brave as her when you were young." He didn't want to bring up the fact that

August couldn't conceive children. He loved his wife dearly, so much that it had never bothered him.

He continued, "After the plane crashed, that seventeen-year-old girl was still strapped into her seat. She'd survived the fall with a broken collarbone. God, what a hell of a story. She also had a gash to her right arm, and her right eye was swollen shut. Then she tried to find her mother, who'd been seated next to her. She couldn't find her."

He turned back to face August. "The girl survived for eleven days. Eleven days. My God. She located a small stream and waded through knee-high water downstream from her landing site. Luckily, her father had taught her how to survive such places when she was younger. My kind of father. Good on him." Floyd let out a long sigh, imagining he'd have taught his girl the same, if he'd ever had one. "She knew that following the stream was her one chance to come across civilization. It also provided water, not only for her survival but for cleaning her wounds. She couldn't sleep at first because of the insect bites, worried she'd end up infected. Then she found a boat moored near a shelter—it's fiction, after all." He rolled his eyes. "Then finally she came across a couple of travelers who finally helped her to a place called"—he opened the book to read—"ah, Tournavista District. Then a local pilot took her to Pucallpa."

Floyd closed the book and sighed. "What a story. It's told with such detail and emotion. I felt like I was there with the girl, rooting for her, wanting her to make the right choices," he said, staring into nowhere, picturing the story in his mind's eye. "I know I just read you the story out loud, August. I also know you know this story by heart. I'm only reciting it because the most fascinating part is how she managed to survive. I mean, all the technical details are much appreciated—and she was very lucky. It's the part about her hallucinations that I find fascinating."

Floyd stood and walked to his wife's bed. He sat next to her, talking as if she were alive and kicking. "The hallucinations, August. Do you hear me?"

August didn't show any signs. Nothing about her changed. But he still hoped.

"Isolated and shocked, the young girl used her mind to save herself. She began seeing hallucinations. Scary things in the woods. Shattered memories attacked her. Instead of going crazy, she turned them into a story. Can you believe that?"

August didn't move.

"What the nurse told me about you needing your mind stimulated might be right," he said. "It's like the girl in the story. She used her mind as company. As her best friend. She hallucinated so she could survive. She basically let her mind entertain her. Of course, there were consequences. She ended up mentally unstable for years." He lowered his voice and leaned forward, whispering, "But it kept her alive, August."

Being so close to his wife confused him. Her scent brought up too many memories. Bittersweet memories that could make him cry. He slowly stood and retreated to his chair again. "There is still more in the book. Another survival story, I believe. I'm going to read it to you." He opened the book and was about to begin reading when a question came to mind. Why was his wife's favorite book about a girl who used hallucinations for survival?

"Mr. Floyd?"

Floyd turned and saw it was Dr. Jessica Hope.

"I believe you wanted to see me."

Chapter 79

"I'm insane?" I say to Dr. Suffolk. It's not a question, as much as an objection.

"Insanity is different," he says. "This isn't insanity."

"Then what?"

"Look at your arm again."

"I know what I saw on my arm," I growl. "I just don't understand. It all felt so real. Ashlyn was real. The Furnace. Adriana. All of it. Are you real?"

"I am, June," he says. "Major Red, too. Some of the events are actually real. It's just that when your condition worsens, you go deep down into the rabbit hole, and we have to live with it over and over again."

"Over and over?"

"You've been in my clinic for three years. This is the third time we've had to live up to your made-up story, trying to help you."

"We?" I'm embarrassed by the look on the nurses' faces.

"It's okay. We're here for you."

"So I'm just a crazy loon, running around with conspiracy theories in my head?"

"Don't call yourself a loon, please. Each time, you have a different story. We try to cope with you."

"Why cope? Why not send me back to my ward?"

"Because we believe you can recover if you face your fears."

"That's a ton of nonsense, what you've just said."

"It's not the first time you've told us that."

"I don't believe you. Are you trying to tell me each person on the island is playing along so I get better?"

"In reality, you've not met many people," he says. "In fact, you haven't left this room in three years."

I can't believe I'm hearing this. My brain refuses to comprehend it.

"Like I said, when your condition worsens, you go down the rabbit hole."

"I just came in from the window outside." I gesture at my wet clothes. "You were waiting here for me."

"Not true," he says. "You came from the bathroom." He points at it. "You took a shower with your clothes on. People in your condition do it all the time to wake up. If you open the door, you'll find the shower is still on."

I can't hear water from where I stand, but I'm not going to check. I know I'm not insane. I know this is a game.

"Why am I like that, then?"

Dr. Suffolk shrugs and exchanges brief looks with the nurses. "Something...happened to you when you were a child."

"What kind of something?"

"Let's not get into it now," he says. "It will worsen your condition. Besides, you will remember it once you're better."

"And my daughter?"

"Let's not bring this up now—"

"My daughter, Dr. Suffolk," I demand.

He takes a long breath then says, "She's dead."

"Fuck you!" I don't know why I spit this out whenever I'm not ready to accept reality.

"You lost her when you were younger."

"What?"

"You just don't want to give up. I feel for you."

I'm breathing fast and unevenly, unable to unchain myself from the nurses' grips. "When did this happen? How old was I? How old was she?"

"Your daughter was never really born, actually," he says. "You had an abortion. That's why your story has a lot of impregnated women in it."

"No," I say. "I know I have a daughter. I know."

"Calm down," Dr. Suffolk says.

"I have a daughter, and I have to protect her from Manfred Toot."

"There is no Toot."

"Of course you'd say that."

"I can prove it."

"Then prove it."

"Look at your arm again."

"I looked once," I say. "I saw the wounds. I know what I am. It doesn't prove Toot doesn't exist."

"They're not wounds," Dr. Suffolk says. "They're needle marks."

"I know what the fuck they are."

"You're an addict, June. Always have been, since you were fourteen. You're disturbed. Please accept that."

"So I did cocaine and flushed my life down the rabbit toilet. I get it." My voice pitches up. It hurts in my lungs. "I'm the dirt of the earth. I'm scum. But I know I have a daughter. I know there is a Toot who wants to hurt her."

"How do you know?"

"My heart tells me," I say. "My mother's heart tells me."

"There is no Toot." He grabs me by the arms, but tenderly. "Listen to me. You're a cocaine addict. You had an abortion because you were fourteen years old and didn't want the baby. You feel guilty about it. But it's all over. Please wake up."

I'm stiff like a broom in his hands. "You said you can prove there is no Toot. Then prove it."

"Toot is not a name," he says. "And you know that."

"What is it, then?"

"Charlie."

"What?"

"Snow."

"Snow?"

"Rocks or stones."

"What the—"

"Crack, coke, or...toot."

I loosen up. It rings true. A blast from the past.

"A toot of cocaine," Dr. Suffolk says. "It's an expression. You've blamed yourself for the cocaine addiction for years. Blamed yourself with sleeping around with every bad boy with tattoos. That's why you created Manfred Toot, a beast that takes lives and impregnated you and killed your child. Your daughter was dead before she was born."

End

Chapter 80

Mercy Medical Center, New York

Floyd watched Dr. Jessica Hope check on his wife. She was mid-thirties with an athletic body. A blonde with a sharp nose and chiseled jawline. She wore thick glasses and looked exhausted, but she apparently loved her job. He'd known her for a while and noticed she'd almost never left the hospital.

"Your wife's vital signs have improved," she told him.

Floyd took his time smiling. Not that he didn't want to. He just didn't want to hang onto false hopes. "What do you mean?"

"A steadier heartbeat. No fluctuations," she said. "Probably because her beloved husband never leaves her bedside."

Floyd smiled feebly. "I'm a bit skeptical about my presence helping her."

"I noticed," she said. "Also, the nurse told me." She tucked her hands in her white coat and approached him. She stood next to him, staring out the window then pointed at the book in his hand. "Then why are you reading to her?"

Floyd stared at the book. He'd somehow forgotten about it. It had been a good read, he had to admit to himself. Only disadvantage was that waking up from the fantasy world of ink and paper was a disappointment. “The nurse told me reading to August helps keep her mind alert.”

“But you said you don’t believe in your presence helping her, let alone reading books to her.”

“I’m human.” He smirked like he had a toothache. “I don’t always act on my beliefs.”

“It’s because you’d do anything for her.” She gently touched his arm. “Even if it contradicts your own beliefs.”

Floyd shrugged, looking out the window. “Of course. I’d do anything to bring her back.”

“She hasn’t gone anywhere.”

“True.” He nodded. “But I miss talking to her.”

“You know what I think?”

He turned to face her.

“Though you claim you don’t believe, you actually do,” she said. “Deep inside you, there is this nagging voice that calls for hope and miracles.”

He couldn’t debate her, so he remained silent.

“You’re a practical man. Your men use science to search for surviving passengers from the crashed plane now. Your life is calculated and factual with no room for glitches or errors.”

“I hate glitches and errors.”

“I love them.”

“Excuse me?”

“In my book, glitches and errors are miracles,” she said. “Wouldn’t you love for a glitch to wake up August?”

He nodded again.

"It doesn't matter how much you resist the idea. We all believe in something bigger, an unreasonable hope that defies all the science in the world."

"Are you telling me that, scientifically, August will never wake up, but that I should still hope by reading her the books she loves?"

"I didn't say that. In fact, *scientifically*, she *feels* you and maybe hears you when you're beside her. Studies have shown us this, but not conclusively."

"If it's not conclusive then it's not scientifically proven..."

"Yet," She raised a finger. "Science is like a baby. It still crawls. It's still new. And it needs nurturing."

"I'm not here to debate you, Dr. Hope," he said. "It's good to know that August's vital signs improved, but it's not because of me. I've been nearby for the last three years"

"It must be the book then. You have never read to her before."

Floyd was about to counter the argument but felt he couldn't. The book did mean a lot to August.

"My grandmother used to tell me that books save lives," Dr. Hope said.

"My men in the field save lives."

"It doesn't mean that books don't," she said. "Do you know why we tell stories?"

"To kill time?" he said.

"No." She chuckled. "We tell stories to share."

"Share what?"

"Experiences, life, and dreams, and sometimes a few facts."

"This book is fiction." He pointed at the one in his hand.

"Fiction is only facts retold," she said. "Fact is what inspires fiction. They feed each other."

"Sounds like too much of a twist on words to me." He glanced at his phone back by the chair, wondering why Dixon hadn't called yet.

"Words are fuel for our thoughts, and thoughts are the basis of creation," she said.

He tried not to belittle her by laughing. He was a polite man but had no interest in poetic metaphors and over-the-top quotes about life.

"Let me ask you this," she said. "How long have you been reading to August?"

"A few hours."

"The book is that good?" She winked.

He chuckled. He had to give it to her. She didn't give up, just like August.

"Actually, it *is* that good," he said. "I was about to read the second part. The first was about a courageous girl who survived a plane crash."

"Sounds promising."

"She not only managed to survive for eleven days but used her hallucinations as fuel to keep her mind from collapsing—" Floyd realized he'd just agreed with Dr. Hope's assumptions.

"See?" She winked again. "The girl used the power of fantasy to survive the real world."

"Hmm. It's still fiction."

Dr. Hope grimaced all of a sudden. He didn't want to offend her. Her belief in fantasy fueling reality seemed to be a dear idea to her, though she was a neurosurgeon.

"I'm sorry," he said. "I didn't mean to—"

"It's not that." She put a finger on her chin. "Did you say the girl in the book survived using her hallucinations?"

"Yes."

"What was her name again?"

"Uhm.. Koepcke. Juliane Koepcke," he said. "It took me a time to pronounce it. German."

"Show me, please." She snatched the book from his hand and read the title, then she raised her eyes to meet his. "Is this your wife's favorite book?"

He nodded, wondering what the fuss was all about.

"Mr. Floyd, this book you're reading..."

"What about it?"

"It isn't fiction," Dr. Hope said. "This really happened."

Chapter 81

My daughter is dead. I've been chasing shadows of regret. I was once a mother, the worst mother of all.

Dr. Suffolk tells me I need to be alone and think things over, maybe remember and confirm he is telling me the truth. My next dose of medicine is in one hour. Turns out the syringes are sedatives that help me with my withdrawals.

Until three days ago I'd been advancing my recovery, until I slipped again and fancied a toot of cocaine. No one knows how I obtained it, but they suggested that I certainly like to call my secret dealer Manfred Toot.

Why Manfred? They have no idea. I'm the one who knows but can't remember.

I ask him about the correlation of forgetting and cocaine. He drops some medical terms on me, and I end up with no definite answer.

I end up asking for permission to take a bath and change my clothes again. My mind is too much on fire. I'd like to think that soaking myself in water will cool it down.

He leaves, and so do the nurses.

A few minutes later, I'm in the bathtub, not quite present, not quite alive.

The water pouring into the bathtub is hot, but I'm still cold. My body and soul are numb to exterior circumstances. The world is spinning around me, yet it's still. I'm alive, yet I'm dead. I'm June, yet I'm not summer.

Fuck, I hate my mind so much. I wish I could live without it for a while. It doesn't leave me alone though. It offers me another suggestion: what if I fall asleep and slide deep underwater and just die? Will dying ever solve the mystery of living?

Thankfully my body opposes the idea, and I keep my head rested on the edge of the bathtub, staring at the ceiling again.

It's a white ceiling. A blank slate, like a movie screen, just before they put the projector on. How I wish this could be my life. How I wish I could just write it from scratch. A new beginning. A new novel. I'd write a happy beginning, a perfect childhood. A rough middle, crisis and learning and growing up. An even happier ending, modest but with children and grandchildren and the feeling of having contributed to the world. Then I'd scribble the words *the end* at the bottom of the last page and send it for publication. And for years after I'm dead, people will remember me. Yes, how I wish I'd be remembered, not for being a crack whore, or even insane, but for having left a unique footprint on the map of mankind.

"Fuck me to the grave," I mumble, washing my face with water.

I look away from the ceiling. None of my memories have come back yet. Nothing but assumptions, and facts told by people I don't trust. I glance at the needle marks on my hand. If one thing is definite it's my addiction. There's evidence I can't deny. I'm an addict, a slave to the needle, and the worst kind of mother.

Tears trickles down my face, like water from a stone. Did my daughter really die when I was a teenager? Did I fuck up her life by being a crackhead whore at fourteen?

Your daughter is closer to you than you could even imagine.

Adriana's words ring in my head. A momentary hope flutters in my chest, but I remember... Adriana doesn't exist. I've been in this room for three years. I've never left. The walls of concrete are simply the inner walls of my brain. I can write on these walls all I want. None of it will ever be real.

I've been trapped inside my brain, trying to escape my shameful past. A prisoner of my own regrets and addiction.

An agonizing chuckle chatters out of my chest when I remember the phrase *a toot of cocaine*. Oh, the mysterious ways the mind works.

I find myself looking for a sharp instrument in the bathroom. The nurses told me they made sure I never had one, since I've attempted suicide a couple of times in the past. Dr. Suffolk explained that this is why I imagined the sharp shard of glass as an instrument on an imaginary operating table. I was feeding my suicidal needs, that's all. Now, that I've seen the room outside my bathroom has no operating table, I can't argue about it.

Yet I stand up and look for a sharp instrument.

My naked figure in the mirror supports Dr. Suffolk's story. Tattoos everywhere. Tattoos I've never seen before—or so I deluded myself into thinking.

The needle marks cover the length of my lower arm. Some are big enough to be cigarette burns. Maybe they are. Something tells me they're called *track marks*. Maybe I'm remembering. A few of them show on my left hand, left leg, and left thigh. I'm right handed, so I must have been injecting myself. Maybe for years. There are also cuts on my right thigh. Not needle marks. Razor cuts. I've been cutting myself.

How haven't I seen any of this before, or is it that we only see what we want to see?

Like a stranger, my skinny figure approaches the mirror. She hates me, but I don't hate her. I want the best for her. She won't let me. She is my past. I'm her future. But she is going to win. My daughter is dead. There is no point in arguing with her—or living.

I glance at the only thing I'm wearing. The wristband. I check it out one last time:

June West. Ready.

At least I didn't imagine that, whatever *Ready* means. As for my name, it makes sense now that I remember the soldiers asking me not to look *west*. My name is June West. In my crack-head, toot-infested reality, I made sure I never saw my real self. Just like in the mirror.

I wanted to live my fantasy of a good mother trying to save her daughter. I didn't want to look at west.

The real June West.

Me.

I bang my head into the mirror and enjoy my cracked reflection. I locate the sharpest splinter and pull it out. My grip is too tight. I'm bleeding already. Slowly, I'm bringing the edge toward my wrist. It's time to end this mess, but then the loud blare in my ears returns...

Chapter 82

I'm back in the fissure. In that place in the bottom of that place I can't accurately describe. The blaring horn is as loud. I'm so sure it's the horn of a car now. Its noise is so amplified that I imagine it's very near.

The water is covering half my horizontally stretched body. Soon it will cover me. Soon I will drown.

My body is weak. I can hardly move. My eyelids are drooping, giving in to the pain. I have nothing to rely on but my will to live. Where does it come from? I have an idea.

My right arm is still stuck underneath that dead person next to me. I have no energy to look again but try to see his face.

My left arm seems numb. Knowing it's the arm I shot with cocaine, I force myself to look at it. My neck burns with pain. I think part of it cracks. Now that it's twisted sideways, I don't think I can move it back again. I see my arm. It's there. It's not cut. I just can't feel it because of the needle stuck in it. I must have just had my fix. Or is it that I'm overdosing and dying?

I don't think so.

I might be dying, but not because of the drug. I've been in some kind of accident. The man next to me has something to do with it. Did I fall out of the plane into a fissure in the earth? What a silly thought.

A breeze reminds me there is a world outside. I look up and see the faint opening. It's nighttime. A shy moon looms behind some faraway clouds. The sound of waves is audible in the distance. I hope I'm not imagining it.

"Mommy!"

Her voice brings a tear to my eye. I know she isn't there. She is dead.

I close my eyes, praying for her. May my daughter have a good afterlife, if there is one. May she forgive. May I burn in hell, so she can live.

Her voice disappears. I still feel the pain, whether she is near or far. It's never going to be all right, either way.

When I open my eyes, the light above is partially gone. The silhouette of a man is blocking it. He is back. I can't see his face or what he is wearing. I feel that I know him. His smell is the same. That of oil from a car. Images of the Furnace attack me. The tires and car tools I saw there. Is he a mechanic?

"Let's make babies." He snickers, sounding drunk or high. Why not—maybe he's an addict. Maybe he is my dealer.

"What do you want from me?" I manage to say. "Who are you?

"Don't you know me, Tootsie?"

"Tootsie?"

"Tootsie is what they call young American brats, don't they?"

His silhouette gets bigger. I think that at a certain angle, I'll be able to see his face.

"Mommy!" My daughter's voice returns.

I'm afraid this man will hurt her, and suddenly I realize he is the same man from the memory I had on the ledge. I realize the girl's voice is the same too.

BUT YOU HAVE NEVER BEEN ON THE LEDGE!

Though I know I'm not awake—whether daydreaming or hallucinating or remembering—it feels so real. Undeniable. How do I know? The fucking pain is so real.

"She won't hear you." The silhouette snickers again. "Mommy is dead."

What the fuck did he just say? I don't understand. I wriggle, trying to pull my right arm from under the man next to me. It still won't budge. I want to kick the silhouette, but I can hardly move my legs. All I can do is spit on him.

"Bitch!" He roars with anger and rams a hand into my face.

Blood spatters out and I feel my guts churn.

"Let's make Nazi babies." He grunts, coming closer. "Just like I did with her—and the others."

I shiver at the smell of his sweat. I shiver at almost knowing who he is. What this is. I shiver as I realize what he meant by "Mommy is dead."

He spells it out to me, as I sense warm fluid running down my thighs. "If you call for your mommy one more time, there will be no toots for you again."

Chapter 83

Somewhere in the Atlantic Ocean

The two divers, Jack and Irene, sat by the boat's edge, ready to put on their masks. They held to each other as the boat rocked to the pissed-off ocean and the angry wind.

"Sure you want to do this?" Jack said.

Irene nodded, checking on her oxygen tank.

"I need to hear you say it," Jack insisted. He was twenty-six and had his life ahead of him. So was Irene. It wasn't his idea to save the last girl. He'd have preferred to go home, prepare for their wedding next week, instead of a coffin sent back to his family in Portland Oregon if he didn't make it tonight.

"I want to do this." Irene, the love of his life, shouted against the wind. "It's our job."

"It's also a hundred other people's job."

"They're cowards," she rocked to the boat. "We're not."

"I don't mind us being cowards and living long enough to have children and raise them."

"You don't have to come, Jack," she said. "I can do it."

"You think I'll leave you?" he said. "Till death do us apart, remember?"

"We haven't taken vows yet. You can still walk," she said. She wasn't angry. He knew she loved him. But Irene was Irene.

She would not let anyone die on her shift without making sure she did all she could. If there was still a last girl, she had to try to save her.

"What if that last girl doesn't deserve to live?" Jack tried to persuade her otherwise.

"We save lives, Jack, not nuns or saints."

"I fucking love you," he said, ready to put on his mask.

"Me toot," she said.

"What did you just say?"

"Me too," she repeated. "Stop talking. Let's go get her."

Jack reached for Irene and grabbed her closer, risking a fall from the boat, and kissed her as hard as he could. It wasn't a gentle kiss. A rough one with all the intensity he had. As if saying goodbye. As if implying it could be their last kiss. He was sucking her soul into his and she took his in as well.

"I wish you kissed me like that all the time," she teased him.

"I promise I will if you promise not to die," he said. "You're fucking twenty-two years old. We could have children and—"

"We could grow old together, I know," she said. "But what do I tell our children if they asked me what I do for a living?"

"You saved lives, that's what you tell them." Jack said, realizing Irene had trapped him into a corner again with her smart words.

She tilted her head with victory. "Then let's save lives, Jack, or we'd be lying to our future children."

She took the jump. Jack had to follow, looking for the last girl.

Higher in the sky, Karl Dixon watched them with his binoculars and muttered, “Stupid millennials. They think they can change the world.”

Chapter 84

"Miss June!"

I'm back in the real world. Someone is calling for me. The voice is coming from outside my bathroom door.

I'm still standing, looking at my hand. This daydream, whatever it is, hasn't change my mind in the least. Whatever story it suggests, I'm not sure I want to know.

"Miss June." The voice outside is a man's.

I stare at the glass' sharp edge. It's close enough to my wrist. I could just cut and forget about everything.

"I have something to show you."

My hands are trembling.

"It's important."

I remind myself that I should trust no one on this island.

"It's Ryan. Sergeant Ryan, remember me?"

My hands stop. *Hang on, June. I'll take care of you,* he told me when I first arrived here. A false promise.

"Please open the door."

I can ask him what he wants. What this is all about. Only if I can trust him. Where has he been all this time?

"I've got your Kindle."

Yeah? There is no Kindle. I must have made it up. Another item I borrowed from my life and used in my fabricated story.

It has to be. Maybe they offered me a Kindle here in my isolated room so I could pass the time reading. It's not far-fetched to assume I love reading. I'm probably a hell of a fiction reader who read hundreds of fantasies and decided to create my own. A lonely addict girl in a hospital room for life. What can she do but imagine, make up stories, believe them?

"We've figured out the password," Ryan says. "Don't you want to know what's inside?"

Here we go again. It's all in my head. I'm not wasting time now. I've been like a pendulum rocking between reality and fiction. I have no strength to rock anymore.

"June?" Ryan says. "I shouldn't be here."

I wish he would go away. Killing myself is a private matter. I'm not comfortable doing it while he is behind the door.

"Listen to me," he says. "I have no time. I'm not supposed to contact you."

A question pops in my head: is Ryan even real, or is this the part of my brain that cares about my survival, trying to stop me from dying?

"They were worried you kept secrets in the Kindle, but found none. I made up an excuse to pass it on to you. I wanted to see you."

Dammit. My cocaine head is a genius storyteller. Why is it doing this? Do I need another fix? I decide to oppose it. There is no Ryan.

“Please let me in,” the fictional Ryan insists. “I can help you.”

Breathe, June, just breathe, I tell myself. If I breathe, the voices in my head will leave me alone and I can just end this.

“Open the door, June.” My fictional Ryan won’t leave me alone. “Whatever they told you, it’s not true.”

Have I broken the mirror? I feel so dizzy, staring at a black future.

“Your daughter is so close,” The fictional Ryan says. “Closer than you could even imagine.”

My hand freezes. The noises in my head subside. A hollow silence fills my world. I can hear the droplets of blood from my forehead falling into the sink.

I admit that I want to believe his words, the same Adriana said earlier. My fictional characters are giving me too much hope. It puzzles me how real it feels.

“Open the door, June,” Ryan insists. “I’m real. You’re not crazy. You’re troubled, but I can help you. You’ve been through so much. I should’ve helped you from the beginning.”

I glance sideways at the door. My eyes slide down to the bottom. I see someone’s shadow underneath.

I turn sideways and reach for the doorknob. I twist slowly with both anticipation and fear.

A fluorescent light pools in through the slightly ajar door, spanning wider as I pull it open.

Sergeant Ryan—I don't know his last name—stands in front of me. He is alone. No one else is in the room. A look of shock dawns on him when he sees me naked. I don't feel naked. I feel fucked up. His stare stops at the shard of glass in my hand.

Holding my Kindle in his hand, he sighs long and hard. "God help us," he says. "I caught you in the last minute before you..."

"What makes you think I won't kill myself?" I say. "I only wanted to make sure you're real, that you actually told me that my daughter is closer than I could imagine."

"She is."

"My daughter is dead. Abortion when I was a fourteen-year-old crackhead."

"I know."

"You do?"

"Yes. I'm not fully aware of your history, but I heard it happened."

"Then why are you fucking with my mind?"

"I'm not. You have another daughter."

I try not to give in to another plot twist in my shattered reality.

"Adriana was right. Your other daughter is closer to you than you think."

"Adriana isn't real."

"She may not be true, but it doesn't change the fact you have another daughter, here on the island."

"What did you just say?"

"Look." He points at my wristband. "What does it say?"

"*Ready*."

"Do you get it?"

"I don't."

Ryan reaches for my naked body with his hand. I should have known he was another pervert. I'm not sure why I let him, though. He reaches for my stomach and gently rests his palm upon it. His hands are warm. He slowly smiles, not with his mouth, but with his eyes. It's a genuine smile. "Your daughter is closer to you than you could even imagine."

Chapter 85

Mercy Medical Center, New York

Dr. Hope had to answer a few questions from a nurse before she returned to Floyd. At first, he watched August breathe in her sleep. He wondered if she actually felt better. Or was this whole reading thing Dr. Hope's way to calm *him* down. He knew some doctors used all kinds of psychological tricks to keep people from panicking. He did the same, lying to families of the deceased passengers to help them cope.

He tapped the book in his hand and wondered if this was what fiction was all about. A legal way to blow off steam. To immerse oneself in the emotions we sought day after day. To escape reality and heal our wounded souls. To recharge our human batteries by hypnotizing ourselves into believing the unbelievable.

He thought about stories of revenge, superheroes, and the impossible.

In his line of work, he'd learned that the basis of human evolution was based on imagination, from paintings on the inner walls of caves to the quest of living on Mars. He'd also learned imagination had its dark side. Terrorists and extremists were as immersed in their imagination, only darker ones that permitted them to kill others based on differences, race, and hierarchies.

"I'm back," Dr. Hope said. "I have little time. They'll need me somewhere else soon."

"I appreciate you taking the time to talk to me," he said. "So how come this book isn't fiction?"

"Ah, that," she said. "I suppose you didn't read the back cover."

"I did—only now."

"Most people think it's fiction at first. Somehow the publishers shied away from mentioning it's a true story—stories."

"That's odd. I can only imagine true stories sell more."

"Not if they're borderline unbelievable. People didn't think the survival stories in this book were. People tend to resist believing in miracles."

"So truth is stranger than fiction, after all." He tapped the book.

"Surprised? That's what I've been trying to tell you. Never give up hope."

Floyd smiled. Not so much in agreement, but hope. "So what happened to Juliane Koepcke?"

"Like you read. She became a mammologist, and she is still alive and kicking at sixty-something."

"Such a joy of a story. She must appreciate life like no one else."

"Just a German girl who survived LANSA Flight 508," Dr. Hope announced proudly, as if Juliane were her best friend. "And it happened so many years ago, in 1945."

"Nineteen forty-five?"

"Oh, wait." She adjusted her glasses. "No, I meant 1971. I tend to mix up dates sometimes—too much work. It's one of my favorite survival stories, though. I teach it in my lectures."

"I assume her survival is considered a one-of-a-kind miracle."

"Not just that. I teach it for the same purpose I want you to read to August."

"I see." Floyd grimaced.

"I know you're still skeptical, but Juliane survived her desolation and fear by remembering stories—or making some up."

"To keep the mind alive." Floyd chewed on the words.

"The mind and heart and body are connected, Mr. Floyd." Dr. Hope laughed at his stubbornness. "Did you read the second story in the book yet?"

"No. Is it as heroic as the first?"

"Not heroic. Miraculous."

"Another girl?"

"Joan Murray," she said.

"Tell me about her."

"Are you sure you want me to spoil it for you?"

"I don't mind. I intend to read the actual articles and facts later."

"If you say so. Joan Murray was on another plane. She was a seasoned parachutist." Dr. Hope smiled. "Her parachute gave up on her and she free-fell to the ground at eighty-one miles per hour."

"That's certain death." He tilted his head.

"She didn't die."

Floyd scoffed. "That's impossible."

"Impossible is not in the dictionary of miracles."

"I'm in the FBI, Dr. Hope. I've parachuted. My men parachute. I see brave men die all the time if their parachutes give up on them—the best they can hope for is a wheelchair and good insurance."

"It's in the book, and you can do your research. Joan and Juliane are real."

Floyd sighed. "What can I say? I will definitely check the authenticity of these stories. How did Joan survive, then?"

"Ants."

"Excuse me?"

"Fire ants."

"I'd prefer if you explain."

"Joan landed on a mound of over three thousand fire ants that stung her repeatedly."

"So?" Floyd squinted.

"You're an experienced man. What happens if thousands of ants sting you?"

"You die? Not to mention that she should have already been dead—"

"That's only one possibility," Dr. Hope interrupted. "The other possibility is that the ants' stings elevated Joan's adrenalin levels, enough to generate unmatched strength and resilience in her body."

"Is that what happened?"

Dr. Hope nodded. Proud again.

"That's unheard of, Dr. Hope. You're a scientist. You know better."

"I should, but part of my core still believes in the impossible. I accept the fact that science does not necessarily always shape the world's events when humans are involved."

"We're not a special species, Dr. Hope."

"Really?" She glanced at the TV set. "Then why are two of your young divers risking their lives to save one girl?

Floyd said nothing.

"The fear and adrenalin kept Joan's heart beating," Dr. Hope continued.

"Enough to keep her alive?"

"Enough to survive certain death..."

"How long was it before someone came to her rescue?"

"Six hours."

"Not as long as Juliane." He threw a glance at his silent mobile by the chair. Why hadn't Dixon called yet?

"Joan's battle with the fire ants is only part of her story."

"Meaning?"

"Her real battle came later."

"I assume she was badly injured."

"Terribly. Fractured bones. It's not like she survived this without a scratch, like in a superhero movie," Dr. Hope said. "But that, too, wasn't her real battle."

"What was it, then?"

"Joan's real battle was when she ended up in a coma."

Floyd looked into Dr. Hope's eyes, almost as if investigating her, trying to asses if this was a joke.

"Skeptical still?"

"Did Joan Murray wake up from the coma?"

"It took her three years, just like August."

"She actually woke up?"

"And raised two beautiful daughters," Dr. Hope said with hands in her pockets. Her eyes smiled at him.

Silence saturated the room for a while. Floyd wanted to look back at his wife, but preferred to keep his eyes on Dr. Hope, wondering if she would flinch. If she was telling lies. He wondered if her last name was actually Hope, not a scheme she used to help with her profession.

Dr. Hope didn't flinch. She seemed like a normal citizen. She was telling the truth.

Floyd swallowed hard. “Did someone read to Joan in her coma?”

“Yes.” Dr. Hope’s smiled broadened. “Her husband did. A favorite book of hers.”

Chapter 86

The shard of mirror drops to the ceramic floor and shatters into splinters, the same way lies scatter all over the place when the truth is revealed.

"I'm pregnant?" I say to Ryan. "Really?"

Instead of answering me, Ryan pushes me back into the bathroom and follows me inside.

I don't resist him, glimpsing two nurses entering the room as he closes the door behind him.

"Miss June, are you ready?" one of the nurses calls.

Ryan shushes me, whispering in my ear, "Tell her you need a minute."

I don't question him. I'm in enough of a trance to submit to whatever he suggests. I've been looking for my daughter for so long, and she is inside me. How is that even possible?

"Tell her," he repeats.

"I need a minute!" I shout back.

"One minute," the nurse says. "We're waiting. It's time."

I look at Ryan. "Time for what?"

"Get dressed." Ryan hands me my gown to put on. "Why is it so wet?"

"That's not it." I point at the spare gown hanging on the wall. "That's the one."

It's strange how I don't shy away from him seeing me naked. Stranger still is how I feel normal about it. I put on the gown. "You have to tell me more. How am I pregnant? Why do they want my baby?"

"We've got no time," Ryan says, glancing at the door. "Take this." He shoves the Kindle into my hands.

"Why is this important now?"

"I'll come to that," he says. "There is so much I can't explain. I don't have all the answers. I can only help you and your daughter."

"How long have I been pregnant?" I demand. "Will they take my child and burn me in the Furnace?"

"Shut up and listen to me," he says, glancing at the door again. "Just think about saving yourself and your daughter now."

I also glance at the door. How much of a minute has passed already? "How?"

"You have to get to the submarine by the shore."

"The submarine? It's real? Ashlyn is real?"

"You've been near it before, so you should find your way. I can't help you with that." He catches his breath. "There is fissure. A big fissure in the ground. It's next to the main road where the Jeeps drive."

"What about it?"

"It's big. Be careful not to fall in. The fissure is a landmark for the exact location of the submarine. You walk around it and head to the shore. Someone will be waiting for you. They will help you escape this island."

"In this weather?"

"That's why it's a submarine. Get to the dock. Save yourself and your daughter."

The nurse calls from outside, "June. It's time."

"How am I going to leave with the nurses outside?"

"I thought you'd never ask." Ryan points at the broken mirror.

I try not to shriek or wonder or question the possibility of what I'm looking at. I wonder how I didn't see it earlier. There is an open groove inside the wall behind the mirror, big enough to crawl through.

"All I needed was to break the mirror earlier?" I mumble.

"It's not a long crawl," Ryan says. "It gets you straight to the road leading to the forest by the shore. Good luck."

I head to it without thinking, pulling out the pieces of the mirror left hanging to the frame. "What about you, Ryan?"

"I'll keep them busy for a while. It will buy you time."

"Why are you doing this?"

Ryan hesitates. "Because..."

The nurses begin rapping on the door.

"Because of?" I don't think I can leave without knowing.

Ryan looks downward and taps his foot like a shy kid. "I like you," he says softly.

"You..." I don't know what to say or feel. "...do?"

"I know you don't remember, but I always did," he says.

"June!" The nurse's tone changes. "Don't force us to break this door. What are you doing?"

In an awkward position, I hurriedly climb over the sink and look into the opening, trying to see a light at the end of the tunnel. Whatever Ryan just said will take too long to explain. Neither of us has the time. The light I'm looking for is absent in the tunnel, but the scene brings back memories of me underwater, looking at the orange light beyond the surface. It also reminds me of the gap atop the place I'm trapped inside my dreams. It puzzles me how all of this is connected.

"Here." Ryan shoves the Kindle in my hand. "Use it as a flashlight. It's not much, but it can help. I've disabled password protection, so it's good to go."

I take it and throw one last glance at Ryan. "Thank you."

"If you don't come out now, we'll break the door," a nurse yells.

"If your kid was a boy, I'd ask you to call it Ryan, but it's not," he says. "Pray for me."

"I will see you soon, Ryan," I say.

"I don't think so." He smiles bitterly.

He is about the throw the wet gown away when his hand comes across a piece of paper. He unfolds it and reads it: "*January, April, May, June, or August*?"

"I found it in the Crib," I say, twisting my head back. "I thought I imagined it."

Ryan's eyes moisten. He rubs the paper with the tip of his middle finger, as if caressing it.

"Do you know what it means?" I ask.

He nods with blinking eyes. I can't interpret the look on his face. It's as if he is saying goodbye but is so happy and sincere about it. I don't understand how.

The nurses rap on the door harder. I can hear the sound of heavy boots outside. The soldiers.

I find myself abruptly crawling into the tunnel, fearing for my daughter's life. The Kindle light is faint, but it'll do. Whatever is going on with Ryan, it's too late to discuss, though I'm dying to know what the months mean.

Farther in, I hear him shout into the tunnel behind me. He says, "It's either August or June. You choose."

Chapter 87

Somewhere in the Atlantic Ocean

Jack feared for his future wife in the ocean below. Instead of actually searching for the last girl, he swam after Irene everywhere. Irene was fierce and relentless. She would not give up. He could not stand to lose her, so he ended up being her guardian angel.

They'd been diving too deep, especially in these weather conditions. The water was cold and murky. They'd come across too many plane parts. Wreckage from the fall. More seats. No girl.

Irene took a deeper dive. Jack followed.

They'd been told the last girl is in her late twenties but hadn't been given a picture of her. Dixon was a dick about it, challenging them, because he didn't want them to do it. He wanted everyone to go home.

Even Jack had doubts, but he was not going to abandon the love of his life. He'd never met a braver girl. He'd never felt so connected and real like he did with Irene. He wanted to be the father of her children.

Irene turned to face him and signaled her desire to go up. Finally, Jack thought, she must have given up on the girl. He willingly complied and paddled to the surface, as slow as possible in order to balance the pressure.

On the surface, he took off his mask, "Are we done?"

"Done with the ocean." She said.

"I don't understand."

"The ocean tides are taking the plane wreckage in one direction," she pointed behind her.

"The direction of the wind, yes I saw it." Jack shouted as a wave almost swallowed both of them.

"I have a theory."

"No theories, Irene. We have to leave. She could not have made it."

"Just hear me out," she spat water. "If she had the tiniest chance for survival, let's say she hung onto some of plane's wreckage, she must have drifted that way."

"Come on. She would have sunk. Most of the plane parts are underwater."

"Most, yes, but the rest is floating all around."

"That's a farfetched scenario."

"Miracles are farfetched stories, Jack," she said. "I'm going, with or without you."

"Going where? This isn't a park ride. We may end up with no oxygen in the tank. We don't have coordinates or GPS or maps for this part of the ocean. It's outside our permitted diameter of search."

“I know, but we might not need the oxygen tanks. I have a feeling she is on the surface, hanging onto something.”

“I have a feeling we’re going to die.”

“We won’t Jack,” she smiled like an enthusiastic child with a new toy.

“This is suicidal, Irene.”

“It’s not. Man up, hubby.” She winked.

“Did you just call me hubby.”

Her smile broadened. “If we save her, I might call you the father of my children. Come on.”

“All right.” He shouted. “Which direction again?”

“West, Jack. I think the last girl has drifted west.”

Chapter 88

My knees and elbows are on fire. I can barely tolerate the pain as I keep crawling. It's getting harder to breathe in this stink hole of a tunnel. I suspect it's getting narrower the farther I crawl.

"Breathe, just breathe," I say.

I try to breathe steadily with the least effort possible, which is a lot already in this claustrophobic tunnel. It feels like a long coffin.

I can't go back. I can't exit from the sides. There is only one way out: by reaching that light in the end. That, or I'll die here, eaten by the rats squealing next to me.

A faint shouting occurs in the distance. It's coming from the bathroom behind me. I'm too far in now, so I can't make out the words. Ryan must be battling with everyone else. How come he likes me? How long have I known him? What's his last name?

I inhale and cough dust but keep crawling ahead. My back is in pain, and I'm feeling colder. I suppose the cold means I'm nearing the end of the tunnel.

The shouting escalates. How many people are in the bathroom now? What are they saying? How is Ryan dealing with it? What is he telling them?

The light ahead dims. My heart pounds like a tribal drum in my ears. It's easy to hear the sound of your organs in this tiny space.

Ryan said the opening at the end leads to the forest, which is dark. I tell myself it won't be dark. I convince myself there is light at the end of the tunnel.

It's essential to lie to oneself when shit hits the fan. A small lie, big enough to overcome a terrible moment. I try not to go deep in the rabbit hole of my mind again. I'm crawling on all fours in a real-life rabbit hole already.

Is this rabbit hole the way out to save my daughter, or is it a way out of my addiction and induced insanity?

"Shut up," I tell myself.

I force my right arm into an awkward movement and pat my stomach. The love of my life is inside me. I'd do anything for her.

"Mommy is going to survive this," I tell her, wondering what I should name her.

The sound of a bullet echoes behind me. Someone just fired a gun.

Pray for me, I remember him saying. I hope I will not have to. I hope he is still alive.

I stop crawling, frozen by the feeling of guilt. Did they kill him? Who did? Maybe Ryan shot at them to escape.

Reality cracks in and proves me wrong. Someone roars behind me. A man. Not Ryan. His voice faintly echoes in the tunnel. Goosebumps spring on my arms. It's Major Red.

"Come back!"

I don't know why I can't move. That beast calling behind me. The killer of pregnant women.

Why the fuck can't I move?

"Come back, Brooklyn!"

My limbs are cemented to the ground. I'm so pissed off at myself. What the fuck?

Crawl, June, crawl! You're so close. So fucking close to the opening.

It baffles me why he calls me Brooklyn when he knows my name is June.

Shit, June. Why does it matter? Keep crawling. What's stopping you?

Another shot sounds behind me. It's inside the tunnel. Major Red is shooting at me.

It's fight or flight now. My limbs move like a skidding rat's. My breathing is all over the place. The tunnel's opening is so near. I have to reach it before they reach me. Of course, they'll be coming for me from the other side. But if I don't reach it soon enough, I will die inside this rabbit hole.

My mind races. I'm unable to see the tunnel's opening. Did I imagine it? I tell myself no. This is real. My daughter inside me is real.

I remember Brooklyn now. It's the name I gave to Mindy the nurse when I was with Ashlyn.

"Come back, or I'll kill your sweetheart."

Another shot sounds. It doesn't echo inside the tunnel this time. I hear a faint scream. It's Ryan.

My brain tells me I can't do anything about it. Whether Ryan did like me—or love me—or not, he is never going to be a priority over my daughter.

I'll pray for you, Ryan, just like you asked. I wish I knew your full name, but I will never forget you, even if I'm never going to remember my true past.

Right now, I have to crawl, if not for my life, then for the life inside me.

Chapter 89

I reach the tunnel's opening and crawl out without scanning my surroundings. My body hits the ground like a sack then rolls down a hill. It's too dark to see. Too fast to adjust or hang on to something. The only thing slowing me down is the muddy ground.

My eyes haven't adjusted yet. A scream escapes my lungs as I plow into a horizontal tree branch on the ground. The pain doesn't faze me. I reach for my stomach and twist my body to rest on my back and protect my daughter.

How long have I been pregnant? My stomach isn't showing. I don't feel like I'm pregnant. Was I impregnated sometime in the last two days? Up in Ward Nine?

Though I should be moving, I need a moment to catch my breath. It's only seconds before the soldiers will come for me. They must know where the tunnel leads, and even if they don't, it's not going to be hard to find me.

A couple of stars twinkle in the murky sky above. It's not raining anymore, but everything around me is wet. My left arm still hurts. An irritating feeling crawls through my body, from inside out. It's not pain. It's something else. It's as if I can't stand being in my own skin. Dr. Suffolk said it was time for my dose. I guess I'm in withdrawal now. My cocaine head needs a fix.

I pat my stomach again. "Don't worry. I won't let anything bad happen to you."

It occurs to me to wonder who her father is, but I skip the thought. I think I know the answer but won't—

A faint light flashes on the ground. I prop myself up and crawl back instantly, only to realize it's my Kindle. I should leave it behind and start running, but I'm worried it won't turn off and will lead the soldiers to my location. Crawling back, I pick it up. I'm right. The button was broken in the fall.

I can't run with it this way. It will constantly give away my location. Best to bury it, but then I'm suddenly curious, and start scrolling through my books. It will only take a minute. What if it has answers?

The list of books is infinite. I'm apparently an avid reader. It explains how I make up stories and mix fact with fiction. The Kindle is extensively organized. Categories, collections, and folders. The collections are labeled Romance, Thriller, Erotica, and Bestsellers.

My eyes seek something that stands out.

There is a folder with authors' names. Stephen King. Dennis Lehane. Gillian Flynn, and Yann Martel.

I don't remember any of them, but their names seem familiar. Curious I scroll through, looking for something that stands out.

Gillian Flynn's folder has one book, Sharp Objects.

Dennis Leanne's folder has one book, Shutter Island.

Yann Martel's has one book, Life of Pi.

Stephen King's folder has one novella, the Breathing Method.

None of the titles mean anything to me, but why is there one book in each folder? Those writers must have written more.

Time is scant, but I look for more folders. I come across one that sends shiver down my spine.

What the fuck?

The author's name just can't be true.

A beam of light infiltrates the night. Shit, I wasted time. I have to keep on going. Stupid. Stupid. Stupid.

Still my hands resist my wish to bury the Kindle. I have to reread that last author's name. How is this possible? It makes no sense.

The soldiers call my name in the distance. Soon the light will spot me. I have no choice but to bury the Kindle. I wish I could take it with me.

After burying it, I decide I have to let myself free-roll down the hill to buy myself distance from the soldiers.

My body is hit by every stone and bump during the fall. I can't feel any of it. All I'm thinking about is the author folder labeled *Ashlyn Ward*.

Suddenly something stops me from rolling down. It's not a log. It's someone's boots. Stinky sweat attacks my nostrils. Above me stands a soldier, sneering at me.

"Oh, hello, blondie." Hecker grins. "Where do you think you're going?"

Chapter 90

Mercy Medical Center, New York

"What happened to Ashlyn Ward?" Floyd said.

"I prefer if you sit down," Dr. Hope said. "This one is stranger than fiction."

Floyd picked his phone up and sat in the chair. "All ears."

"Ashlyn lived in a small town near Long Island," Dr. Hope began.

"That's here." He pointed at the window.

"Yeah, but I bet you've never heard of her town. A small island. One of those remote places, scattered in between bigger cities, barely a dot on the map that no one cares about. Electricity wasn't always available, nor was water in certain times of the year. It's hard to believe such places exist in America."

"It's not. I've seen them. It's a disgrace they're not talked about."

"So you get my point," she adjusted her glasses. "Ashlyn lived there with her sister and later with a stepbrother. Their father left when they were kids. A drug dealer. Their mother, a cocaine addict."

"I see."

"The mother worked double shifts. She was a nurse, but also worked in an asylum were Ashlyn's grandmother spent some time. Eventually, her addiction pulled her down the drain. She ended up in a mental hospital, the same time the grandmother ironically left."

"How old was Ashlyn?"

"Fourteen years old."

"Go on."

"Before entering the asylum, their mother re-married another man. A stranger who'd mysteriously appeared in town a few months before the wedding."

"Drug dealer?"

"On the contrary. A strong man in exceptionally good health. He claimed he was a doctor once but lost his license because of an abortion he gave to a young girl, out of empathy."

"Suspicious story."

"It also seemed strange he was in possession of big amounts of money."

"Why would a rich man come to such a small town?"

"Even stranger was the fact that he didn't oppose their mother's addiction, but paid for it."

"He was hiding from the law in an off-the-grid town."

Dr. Hope nodded.

“Usual story,” Floyd said. “I come across it every day. Small towns, let alone a small island, like you said, attract outlaws all the time.”

“It wouldn’t have been much of a story if he was just an outlaw, but I will get to that,” she said. “Remember the stepbrother I mentioned?”

“Uh-huh.”

“That was his son,” she said. “Father and son were part of some secret sect whose members hid on the island.”

“What kind of sect?”

“In the book, Ashlyn describes them as lunatics. They never had a name, but they had their own guns.”

“Custom-made?”

“Yes, but nothing heavy duty. Silver guns. I don’t remember the brand, but they had their insignia stamped on it.”

“Insignia?” Floyd had begun to dislike this story.

“A red sign they stamped on the side of the gun.” Dr. Hope’s voice weakened a little.

“What sign?”

“A swastika. A red swastika.”

“Fuck.” Floyd let out a sigh.

“Ashlyn could never explain who they were. Either neo-Nazis or just followers who hid among us.”

“Were they Germans or Americans?”

"American passports. She believed their fathers and mothers escaped Germany, pretending they were Jews."

"A plausible assumption. America is full of them. I'm shocked I've never heard of this story. I've led a few cases, catching such evil men."

"That was one of Ashlyn's remarks. That the evil that I'm about to tell you has never been documented or investigated."

Floyd lowered his head. "We're not God in the FBI. A lot of shit escapes us. Sometimes we overlook cases in favor of others." He raised his head to meet her eyes. "I've been guilty of that in the past, when I underestimated the severity of Flight TWA 800 in 1996."

"We all have our demons."

"What did those men do to Ashlyn?"

Dr. Hope adjusted her glasses again. Words seemed heavy on her tongue. Her firm jaw line lost its strength. "They raped her."

Floyd shrugged. The way Dr. Hope said it suggested this was only the beginning. He had nothing to contribute.

"Over and over again."

"All of them?"

"Well, she mentioned her stepbrother was first," she said. "She never mentioned his full name, but the boys called him Hecker."

Chapter 91

Hecker grips my ankles and pulls me across the mud. I wriggle and kick, but it has no effect on him. His heavy boots thud on the ground as I try to grab on to anything on along the way.

"Let go of me." I spit at his back.

"Shut up, whore!"

"Where are you taking me?"

"You know where."

I have no idea what he is talking about. My gown folds under me. I'm half-naked. My right hand reaches for the boulders on the ground, but Hecker is too fast. It's too dark to see where he is taking me, but he's dragging me upward, in the opposite direction from the submarine.

"Please, Hecker," I plead. "Let me go."

"I will, once I'm done with you."

"Why are you doing this?"

He stops without answering me, and momentarily drops my feet. I watch him reach for his zipper. I roll over and jump to my feet.

"Don't even think about it!"

I'm already running down the hill again.

"Stop it, or I'll shoot."

The cocking sound of the gun stops me in my tracks.

"Hands up, bitch."

Slowly, I turn around, both hands in the air. Hecker is pointing a silver gun, the one I carried on my way here.

"Remember it?" He waves the gun. His head tilts downward, but his eyes are up, piercing into my soul. "You thought you could turn things around."

"What do you mean? I don't know what you're talking about."

"I'm talking about Daddy's gun."

"Daddy?"

"Take off your clothes."

I take a step back, hands still up. I flirt with the thought of running away but he isn't bluffing about shooting me.

"There's nowhere to go," he says. "You're all mine tonight."

"The other soldiers will soon be here."

"You think they will stop me?" He cranes his head up and laughs. "They'll watch, and take their turns."

I take advantage of that fraction of a second during his egotistical mistake and run while he is looking up. I duck while escaping, in case he shoots.

"Fucking whore!"

A shot sounds near my ears. I stumble and fall, thinking I'm shot. I'm not. I pick myself up again and keep running aimlessly. His footsteps speed up behind me.

"Come back or I'll shoot."

"You're a coward!" I scream, taking a sharp left without thinking. I find myself digging deeper into the forest again, not sure where the shore is. I keep running, unable to form a coherent thought. The withdrawals in my body weaken me. It's not only dark, but I doubt I have the strength to keep running. I need my dose now.

In a blink of an eye, I'm hit with Hecker's gun on my back. It's puzzling how he found me. Maybe he knows the forest by heart. I drop to my knees and then fall on my stomach. The pain and shock tear me apart. My daughter. Did I just kill her?

Hecker pants like a hungry dog behind me. My head is flooded with dark scenarios. I don't care about what happens to me. It's all about the life inside of me. A surge of adrenalin gives me strength to roll on my back and instantly kick him in the balls.

He screams like a little girl, dropping the gun. It gleams in the dark. I pick it up.

He stumbles backward, holding his crotch in his hands. The gun feels so good in my hand. It feels like an old friend. I don't know why, but it's a much better feeling than when I first gripped it.

"How do I get to the submarine?" I stand over Hecker.

"Go to hell."

Instead of shooting him, I kick him in the balls again. He groans in pain and calls me bitch, whore, and slut. I wait for him to catch his breath.

"I'll keep kicking you until you bleed from your mouth."

Though in pain, he sneers at me. "I guess I'm not good enough for you, eh?"

My eye twitches when he says that. "What?"

"You want Daddy." He grins.

A Jeep screeches nearby. Soldiers shout at each other. Torches slice through the night. I can't stay here any longer.

I kneel down and point the gun to Hecker's balls. "I will shoot your nuts if you don't tell me how to get to the submarine."

"You'll never save your daughter." He chokes on a laugh. "You're a lowlife, white-trash, cocaine addict. A worthless slut. Never a mother."

It's crazy how words can hurt. The pain seeps to my forefinger. I don't hesitate and pull the trigger.

Hecker doesn't moan or scream. The bullet puts him into an eternal sleep. The shot comes out muffled, but it will still attract the soldiers.

I hear Ashlyn's dead voice in my head now. *Run!*

Chapter 92

Mercy Medical Center, New York

Floyd glanced at August, wondering why such a dark story was her favorite. He didn't mind Juliane and Joan's stories, but Ashlyn's was heading south.

"So some Nazi fanatics hide in a small town, have their leader marry a woman, and gangbang her daughters," Floyd recited, "It reminds of *Colonia*, the small town in South America. It's always been operated by Nazis who tortured its people."

"Ashlyn mentions the comparison in the book."

"Terrible things happen in the absence of law."

"You mean in the absence of humanity," Dr. Hope said. "None of the town members ever complained or talked to the press."

"I imagine we're talking about a town with one thousand or so inhabitants?"

"Give or take, but that wasn't just it. The father had other town citizens either bribed or killed."

"Why go this far?"

"Because Ashlyn wasn't the only one. They gang-raped so many other girls in town."

Floyd's face crumpled. "How many?"

"How many dead or how many burned?"

"Burned?"

"Ashlyn's mother owned the town's one and only gas station. The father and his friends raped teenage girls in an abandoned garage in the back of the station, among dirt, old tires, and mechanic's tools."

"What does this have to do with burning girls?"

"One time, a girl died during their acts. With plenty of gas and oil around, and being Nazis, they came up with the idea of a 'furnace.'"

Floyd closed his eyes. Not only to block the morbid images in his mind's eye, but to prevent tears from falling. "The girls, were they Jews?"

"That would be a clichéd fictional story," Dr. Hope said. "No, they weren't. The Nazi sect simply defiled races other than theirs. They built their own fantasy concentration camp in a small island on American ground."

"Just like that."

"Just like that. Pure evil. No big conspiracy behind it."

"I've always tried to reason why evil was committed in this world. The sad truth is that most of the times there is no explanation. People did horrible shit. As simple as that," Floyd still kept his eyes shut. "Please tell me there is a light at the end of this dark tunnel of a story."

"Not yet," Dr. Hope said. "I haven't told you about the cocaine yet."

“You did. The mother was an addict. The absent father was a drug dealer. The stepfather supplied the mother with her fixes.”

“True, but I didn’t tell about the role the cocaine played in the acts.”

“Don’t.”

“You know?”

“I’ve looked the devil in the eye, Dr. Hope,” Floyd said. “I assume they used the cocaine to lure the girls in.”

“Every teenager in the town was an addict.” Dr. Hope said. “They turned the girls into crackheads so they’d be their sluts.”

Chapter 93

I'm running in circles, escaping the lights from the Jeeps. They can't drive into the forest, so they've arranged the vehicles to surround it. Now the light hunts me in every possible direction. The only way out is to occasionally hide behind a tree or crouch beneath a few bushes.

The gun in my hand is useless at the moment. I need an invisibility cloak to escape. I duck again and start to crawl. The light can't reach the lower parts behind the bushes. My attempt to follow the breeze from the ocean is futile. The pain from my withdrawals is killing me. My sense of smell is weakening.

I keep crawling on all fours, promising my daughter a lie. There is no way I can make it, but I won't give in, not yet.

"June!" Dr. Suffolk calls for me.

I hear him clearly. He is nearby.

"I'm not here to hurt you."

I used to trust him, but not after he betrayed me. He tried to convince me I don't have a daughter. I struggle to stay quiet.

"Listen to me," he says. "I'm alone."

Another lie.

“The soldiers don’t know I’m here,” he says. “They can’t hear me, but not for long. Soon they’ll walk into the forest, looking for you.”

I keep crawling. A light hue in the distant sky seems like a reflection from the ocean.

“You shouldn’t have killed Hecker.”

I stop and hide behind a tree, waiting for a beam of light to pass.

“I’m not with them,” Dr. Suffolk says. “I can explain the things I told you.”

How can you explain telling me I’ve never left my room?

“I’m not here for what you did. I’m here for your dose.”

His words pull my legs to a stop. My heart tries to oppose me, but my body needs the fix. If I get my hands on this syringe, it’ll help me reach the submarine. How long do I have before I collapse?

“You need it,” he says. “I’m a doctor. All I care about is my patient’s health.”

I rub my shoulders. The nasty withdrawals feel like electricity pulsing from inside out. I want to tear off my own flesh to make it stop.

“Think about it,” Dr. Suffolk says. “Your daughter will not survive if you don’t take the shot.”

“You said my daughter is dead.” Words spurt out of my mouth.

"I'm sorry," he says. "Just show me where you are, and I'll give you the dose."

"I have a gun. I will kill you if you trick me."

"Deal. Raise a hand and I'll throw the syringe your way. You know how to shoot it. You've done it a million times before."

"I won't see it in the dark. Keep walking. I'll find you."

"Okay."

He crosses my line of vision. I tell him to stop. I'm behind him, crouched on the ground. "Give it to me. Don't dare look behind you."

"As you wish." He stretches out his hand behind his back.

I snatch it, finger on the trigger. I'm not quite sure how to inject myself. I just dip the needle into my left arm. I moan then begin to push...

Dr. Suffolk sighs, sounding exceptionally relieved.

I stop myself from pushing the syringe. "You little piece of shit." I pull it out. "That's not my dose. You were going to sedate me."

"Of course not. Please take it."

"Turn around!" I regret shouting and risking the soldiers hearing me.

He does.

"Hands on your head."

He complies, but looks disappointed. His plan didn't work.

"Why are you doing this to me?"

"I'm not doing anything," he says irritably.

"What did you mean when you said I'm famous?" I point the gun at him, still on all fours, ready to escape.

"Did I say that?"

"You asked me in the clinic. I asked you why think that. You said you couldn't remember. I thought you were being nice."

"You think so?" He lets his guard down. The son of a bitch smirks..

"When you convinced me I've been a prisoner in my room for three years, I thought you were trying to make me remember."

"And now?" He attempts to step forward.

"Back off," I'm about to pull the trigger. "I have a feeling you knew me from long ago."

He rubs a boulder on the ground with his foot. "You really don't remember me, do you?"

"Don't try to stall until the soldiers come."

"You can't escape. Can't you understand?"

"Just fucking tell me or I will kill you like Hecker."

"I was twenty-six when we first met," his eyes meet mine. "You were fourteen."

A chill shivers through my left arm. I close my eyes. "Motherfucker. You did my abortion?"

His response comes with a kick in my face. My eyes flip open. I've dropped the gun, and he is going for it. What I did with Hecker is happening to me now.

I crawl like a maniac after him and climb like a monkey on his back. He straightens up with the gun in his hand.

"Let go of me." He grunts.

I repeatedly slap him on the back of his head and knee his sides, not letting go of him. He swings sideways but keeps his balance, trying to plow his elbow into my face. My slaps ram down on his ears. It pains him the most. I don't stop slapping the son of bitch over and over again. I chain his waist with my legs. He eventually decides to run backward into a tree. If I let him, I will be squeezed to death.

The slaps on his ears keep coming until we almost reach the tree. Finally, he loses balance and wobbles on one leg. I grip his free hand and try to snatch the gun, but he holds on to it.

Still dizzy, he manages to balance on two legs again, but I don't let go of him.

"Stop it!" a soldier shouts.

"Kill her!" Dr. Suffolk orders him.

I bite his ear, wishing I could get the gun before the soldier arrives.

Too late.

The soldier aims his machine gun at me while I'm gripping Dr. Suffolk's hand. I freeze, and so does Dr. Suffolk.

"Kill her," Dr. Suffolk demands.

"I'll do it if you get out of the way, doctor."

"Is that it?" Dr. Suffolk slams his elbow back into my jaw in an attempt to get rid of me.

Blood spatters my lips. Before I fall backward, I manage to tighten my grip on his hand, reaching for his forefinger, and then... I pull.

The shot fires right at the soldier, who reflexively shoots back.

Dr. Suffolk screams. I fall back and roll to my side before he drops down on me. He is dead, so is the soldier, a few feet away.

Chapter 94

Somewhere in the Atlantic Ocean

Dixon grew impatient in the passenger seat inside the chopper. No amount of technology would help seeing through the weather outside. Most of his men below had left. He couldn't. Floyd's orders were to find Jack and Irene, as they must have had a reason to dive farther away.

"I bet they're dead by now," he told his pilot.

"Even if they aren't," the pilot said, holding tight, "this weather will kill us."

"I can't," Dixon mumbled. "He'll report it. I have bills to pay. My ex-wife is grabbing me by the balls."

"But we're going to die up here."

Dixon rubbed his forehead. "Are you sure we can't contact the foolish couple?"

"They're out of reach. Last signal showed they dove west, which is outside of our perimeter."

Dixon checked the map. "What were they thinking? The last girl could not have made it this far."

"Permission to fly back, sir," the pilot said. "It's now or never. I have children, too."

"Give me a few minutes. No one wants to leave this place as much as I do." Dixon sighed. "Floyd, is going to crush me if I leave like that." He tongued his cheek from inside, "I have an idea."

Chapter 95

I stumble on my way down the hill, following that light in the horizon. I hope I'm not chasing illusions.

Rolling down, I reflect on having killed three men in the last few minutes. It makes me wonder: did I kill more people in the past? I feel no remorse whatsoever.

A few consecutive bumps in the road slow me down. I didn't have time to pick up the gun after Dr. Suffolk and the soldier died. I ball myself into a fetal position, trying to protect my child. How long have I been pregnant?

The lights zigzag in the sky all around me, but I'm not stopping. The gravity of the slope downward slope helps. It's like I'm running down, mostly pulled by gravity. The light from the soldiers is actually a plus. I can see ahead of me.

Every few steps I spasm in wicked ways. It's as if I'm momentarily possessed or have no control over my limbs. Withdrawals. So little time before I collapse.

"June!" A loudspeaker calls behind me.

I pretend I don't hear it and keep running. No need to listen to their threats, or worse, their seductive reasoning to bring me back. My head has been fucked with, too many times.

The light in the distance shows a glittery surface. It's the ocean. Moonlight reflects on water. I'm not chasing illusions.

My legs speed up. Once I reach the shore, I'll look for the submarine.

Suddenly the world darkens all around. It's as if someone pulled the plug. I stop in my tracks, or I'll bump into a tree or a rock. The moonlight in the distance is much fainter now. I need a few seconds for my eyes to adjust. Is there a power outage? I can't hear the speakers anymore.

I don't like this. Something is wrong. Slowly, I step forward, not as fast as I wish though. There's hardly much to guide me in the dark.

My breath is loud. My chest is chugging like a locomotive. I better not listen to it and pretend I'm all fine. I hear someone moving in the dark. Footsteps. Soldiers. All over the place.

Shit, I have to run now. It doesn't matter what I bump into.

The glare of a flashlight stops me. I shield my eyes with the back of my hand.

"Oh, hello," a soldiers says.

Other soldiers laugh. At least ten of them. They fooled me.

"You."

The soldiers laugh again. The one in front says, "We want you."

If I can only find an escape route to my left or right. There is no way I can kill all of them, not without a gun. The soldiers approach me, slowly. Some of them rub their hands. Others rub their chins and laugh again. A few in the back clap their hands to a slow, sickening tempo of fear.

I try to breathe as slow as I can, which is incredibly fast already. Footsteps come in every direction, even from behind me.

This is it. There is no way out of this. I won't die without a fight though. I pat my stomach and say, "I'm sorry."

Chapter 96

Mercy Medical Center, New York

Floyd's phone rang. It was the call he'd been waiting for. Probably Dixon had news about the last girl. Still, Floyd couldn't pick up. He needed a moment. Ashlyn Ward's story rendered him physically immobile for a moment.

"Your phone, Floyd," Dr. Hope said.

"I know," he swallowed, picking it up without looking. "Yes."

"Are you watching the news?" Dixon said.

"TV's on mute," Floyd glanced at it. "Why?"

"Someone leaked the list of passengers to a news channel. The world knows the passengers are dead except one."

Floyd pressed the remote and changed the channel. "I see it now."

"It wasn't me, Floyd. I swear to God."

Floyd knew Dixon was behind it. An attempt to pressure him to get busy. Now he'd have to drive to the city and make a statement in a few hours. "It's okay, Dixon," Floyd smiled unexpectedly. "Whoever it was, we have to thank him."

"What?"

"I see the families have accepted their loved ones are dead, and now they're praying for the last girl to survive."

"Really?"

"It's called hope, Dixon. If one passenger survives, not necessarily their own, it still means something." Floyd smiled at Dr. Hope listening to his side of the conversation.

"What's gotten into you?" Dixon said.

Floyd knew Dixon would be upset. The fact that the public wanted the last girl saved meant he still had to stay in the field. "I'm only trying to see the bright side of everything."

"Bring your bright FBI ass here and then talk to me about optimism."

"Rescuing the last girl is an international request now, Dixon."

"Fuck international requests, Floyd. Three of my men died, one is missing."

"They'll be remembered, Dixon."

"Fuck Commemoration Day. I want to go back to my kids, man."

"*You* will be remembered, Dixon."

"I don't want to be remembered dead."

"You won't die. Your wife and kids will be proud of you."

"She won't," Dixon said. "She divorced me *because* I was a hero in the field. I thought she'd be proud of me then, but she ended up proud of the neighbor's dick, Floyd. What I have done in the field meant nothing to her. I want to go home and see my kids, whom I haven't seen for the past two weeks."

Floyd wanted to please Dixon and say, *fuck custody,* but it seemed an inappropriate time for witty remarks. He glanced back at August. They've been married for so many years. Happily, though she could not have children.

"What about the two divers?" Floyd said. "I received a message earlier. It's all over the news. Jack and Irene?"

"A young, naive couple who think they can change the world." Dixon said. "Fucking millennials."

"Did they find anything?"

"They're on their own now."

"How so?"

"They're outside the search perimeter. I told you they were naive."

"They must have a reason."

"Yeah, recklessness, and thinking they're young and beautiful and will never age."

"Enough with the bullshit, Dixon," Floyd said. "See why they've gone so far. They must have found evidence leading to the last girl."

"Old, optimistic you, Floyd," Dixon said. "I will look into it, but hey, I'm not afraid of you."

Floyd said nothing. Rescuers were under enough pressure in times like these. It was understandable. One of Floyd's pluses was his ability to drop his ego in such situations. Nothing here was personal. It was a job.

“You shouldn’t be afraid of me, Dixon,” Floyd said. “You’re a brave man.”

“And you’re a coward, Floyd,” Dixon spat. “You don’t care about any of us. Just about your public image and your medals. If you could’ve saved anyone, why haven’t you saved your wife?”

Floyd’s knuckles whitened, gripped the phone.

“She told you she felt sick. She told you she had been passing out,” Dixon said. “The day of the accident in the car, you pissed her off because—”

“Please stop.”

Dixon wouldn’t. Floyd knew it was a perfect moment for revenge. The man had always hated Floyd because of an earlier report on the TWA flight, when Floyd put the blame on him, and denied him a raise and a better house—and gave him a divorce. That was how Dixon saw it. Floyd was only doing his job.

“Because you slept with another woman, Floyd,” Dixon said, adding the last straw to the camel’s back. “To give you a child. August is in a coma because of your doing, James Madison fucking Floyd.”

Chapter 97

The approaching footsteps stop.

My fists are balled and my legs are twitching with tension. I'm ready to fight back.

"Stop playing games," I say. "Let's get this over with."

The soldiers still laugh and clap. It's as if it's a ceremonial act. As if they've done this so many times before.

Then all sounds stop again.

"We think you don't like us," one of the soldiers says, his hands gripping his buckle. He sounds familiar. I remember him. He is the one I met in the elevator on my way to Meredith.

I spit at him.

"See?" He says. "You don't like us, blondie."

"Why does everyone keep calling me blondie?"

"Because you are," the soldier cranes his head closer and winks. "Would you prefer bitch?"

I see him wearing the same grey outfit. Only this time the insignia is there. A swastika.

A long, unsettling silence veils the forest. None of them speak. I have nothing to say.

I wait. It's hard to predict their next move.

"Okay," the soldier waves his hands in the air. "She isn't into us, boys."

The soldiers *boo* with disappointment.

"Who does she want, then?" One soldier asks.

"Who else," the soldier facing me, smirks. "She wants him."

"Him who?" I ask, my eyes darting left and right.

The soldiers slowly withdraw, walking away.

"Where are you going?" I should be running but I'm so scared. "Him who?"

They keep walking further then split in two teams, left and right at a lower point down the hill. I watch them pull out their flashlights and point at the road in between, as if showing me the way to escape.

I shrug and I take a step forward then stop again. This must be another trap.

"I'd be running, if I were you," a soldier advises me.

What the fuck is going on?

"He is coming for you," he says.

"Who?"

"Daddy."

Behind me, footsteps stroll down the hill.

"Run," the soldiers say.

The footsteps behind me scare the shit out of me. I dash down the hill, barely breathing. I think I glimpsed a silhouette in the dark behind me.

Run. Run. Fucking run like hell.

The soldiers start clapping again, repeating one word, as if in some ritual or ceremony.

"Toot."

Clap.

"Toot."

Clap.

"Toot."

Chapter 98

Somewhere in the Atlantic Ocean

Jack took off the mask and inhaled all the air he could. He'd just broken through the surface after losing Irene in the abyss below. He still had enough oxygen for another dive. So did Irene, but he could not find her.

"Irene!" He shouted in a feeble tone, his voice sucked away by the wind.

Panic wasn't a strong enough word to describe his feelings. He should not have let her go on this mission. He hated how stubborn she could be. They'd been side by side in their search, all until she decided to follow her instinct and a hunch. When he turned after her, she was gone.

"Irene! Answer me!"

It was stupid calling for her up there. She was probably still underwater, but he could not find her, nor did her GPS work. He could not think of a worse feeling, being alone in the middle of the ocean, knowing he'd lost the love of his life.

He controlled his breath for a few counts, and reminded himself how good she was. She couldn't be gone, though the ocean was cruel and never befriended a diver, he couldn't imagine it. She saw something and soon she'll surface again. All he had to do was wait.

“Why the hell are we doing this?” He asked himself. “I should accept that job as a gym instructor when we go home. I want to be a father. I’m done with this shit.”

“Hey!” Irene called.

He turned around, hysterically searching for her.

“Here!” She waved.

He saw her and swam to her right away. “Where were you?”

“You have to come with me.” She said.

“Where?”

She pointed behind her. There was nothing to see but water.

“There is an island.” She said.

“What? There can’t be.”

“I saw it. Trust me.”

“Okay, but why should we go there?”

“I think she’s there, the last girl.”

“Come on, Irene. That’s not possible.”

“You saw we found nothing underwater,” she panted. “The island makes perfect sense.”

“No it doesn’t, Irene,” he reached for her arms. “Listen to me, we should go back. We’re tired.”

“I have a feeling she is on the island.”

“It’s not possible, baby. Can’t you see how far we are from the crash? We shouldn’t be here.”

“If we made it, then she could have.”

"I doubt she is a professional diver, or even a swimmer. Plus she would probably be injured from the plane crash."

"It could be a miracle."

"No, baby. It can't be."

"You love me, right?" she said as the water grew colder.

"I do, but this is suicide."

"Till death do us apart, remember?"

He could not oppose this sentence. He wanted to tell her it wasn't till naive stupidity and suicide do us part, but he said something else instead, "Baby, look at me," he tried to be as gentle as possible. "This will not bring him back."

"This isn't about him."

"No, it is. This is about your dad, honey."

"I'm telling you I have a feeling she is alive. How are we going to sleep at night if we realize we could have saved her tomorrow morning?"

A tide threw Jack off. He doubted they'd see a tomorrow if they didn't swim back now. "Your father was a brave man, Irene. A great diver. He went to save someone and he didn't make it back. You should be proud of him. You became a rescue diver like him. He would be proud of you. Let's go back."

Irene pushed him away. "I'm telling you it's not because of him. I'm going to save her."

"There is no last girl! She probably didn't make it. Listen to me. They gave up on your father. His teammates should've gone to rescue him. He spent a whole day alive on a shore. No one knew. It's not your fault. He is dead and this isn't going to bring him back."

"I thought you were a different man, Jack. I'm going to the island." She put the mask on and dove away.

Chapter 99

Toot is after me. Manfred Toot, the impregnator of women. The beast with no face. The man whose name I have carved on my gun and kindle.

My horrid past. He is after me.

I've passed the area lit with the flashlights, running like a maniac toward the shore. It's so far away. I thought it was closer.

I flirt with the idea of looking behind me. I need to see his face. What if I confront him? Maybe I'll remember. What if I kill him like I should have? This is what it's all about, right? Kill Manfred Schmidt, known as Toot, and save my daughter.

My legs are heavy. My footsteps weaken and drag. The pain in my arms surges to unbearable heights. Withdrawal symptoms are eating me alive. So many thoughts whirl inside my skull.

If Toot is a metaphor for *toots of cocaine*, how come he is an actual man? Is this happening or not?

I trip on some stone and fall flat on my face. Spitting mud, I stand up again. Nothing is going to stop me from reaching the shore. Hell, when I glance ahead, I can see the dock.

Ryan was right. It's far, but all I have to do is get there.

"June!"

The hair on my arms prickles when I hear him call my name. A gruff and dark voice that I recognize immediately.

"You're mine, June!"

No, I'm not. Nothing is going to stop me from reaching the submarine.

"Don't you love your daddy anymore?"

His last sentence kills me. I can't connect the dots, but I don't want to imagine this. I understand that Manfred Toot impregnated those women. I can live with him being the father of my child. The thing that I can't swallow is him being... my dad?

Chapter 100

Mercy Medical Center, New York

"I apologize for the call," Floyd told Dr. Hope.

"It's all right. I didn't hear much." She said, checking her watch.

"Am I keeping you from something. I thought you had to be somewhere."

"True, but it's not work, really. I was hoping I could meet someone. It's a story you will like, actually. I was hoping I can meet with—"

"If you're staying, I need to know the rest of Ashlyn's story." He said.

"I was hoping you read the rest. I just realized how dark the story is."

"Please," he said. "I'm not much of a reader, and I can't stand not knowing."

"Uhm..."

"I know the stepbrother's name was Hecker," he offered. "Tell me about the Nazi stepfather."

"He was a big man. Tough and feared. He liked to dress in an SS uniform, the Schutzstaffel, while he... you know."

"Where did he get the uniform?"

"He forced a few women to sew it for him and the other men," she said. "Actually it was Ashlyn's grandmother who supervised it."

"Wasn't she in a mental hospital?"

"For a while, but they couldn't pay the bills when her daughter checked in. She went home, though not fully recovered. Ashlyn mentions in the book that her stepfather bribed the hospital so he'd have a woman who'd take care of the girl issues."

"God help me. I don't want to even picture the hell they've been through. What was the grandmother's name?"

"Meredith," Dr. Hope said. "She lived in the attic, talking to herself most of the time. She knew all the secrets. She'd seen all the rapes, the killings, and the burning. She cleaned after them, and provided as much emotional support to the girls as she could."

Floyd felt dizzy. It showed on him.

"You wanted to know," Dr. Hope remarked.

"Yes, please, in hopes for a bright ending," He said. "What about that Nazi stepfather, you didn't tell me his name."

"Manfred Schmidt," she said.

"I've come across some Schmidt's but never heard of him. A typical German name. It makes me wonder how he slid under the authorities' radar."

"It could be because no one called him by his real name."

"What did they call him?"

"Major Red," she said. "His men, dressed as soldiers, called him Major. R.E.D., the last three letters of Manfred. They were also a metaphor for the blood on his hands."

Chapter 101

Major Red can't be my father. A girl should have some genetic or emotional connection to her father. This doesn't ring true. I hated this man from the gutter of my heart since meeting him. It just can't be.

Knowing his size and heavy weight, I feel I have an advantage of escaping him—if my withdrawals don't worsen.

My weary feet feel like they're about to give up on me. I try not to think about it. I keep my head up, looking at the dock in the distance, hanging onto hope.

"You'll be all right," I tell my daughter. "Whatever this is, even if I'm insane, or the worst mother in the world, I won't give up on you."

"You shouldn't have cut my face!" He roars behind me. "I will make you pay."

It occurs to me that his anger will not play in his favor. Somehow I pissed him off, and, like me, he is not in his right mind. I can outrun him. I can do it.

"You shouldn't have killed Ryan!" I spit back.

"I didn't," he says.

"I heard the bullet," I jump over a log and land on a weak foot, but balance myself again and continue down the slope.

"You killed him, not me."

"Nonsense!"

"You're so delusional."

"I don't mind it. But you won't have my baby. You will not burn me in the Furnace."

"I will burn you twice. Once for slashing my face. Twice for killing Hecker."

The conversation doesn't mean anything to me. Whatever he says, I will make it to the dock. I'm just using it to trace his voice and assess his distance behind me.

Looking ahead, I realize I've had a good head start. It's not that far anymore. All I ask for is my legs not buckling underneath me. My lungs can take it. My brain is fried anyways. As for my will, it's ten million men strong.

Soon I'll be—

Shit.

What just happened?

Did my legs buckle underneath me?

What's going on?

I'm...

I'm free falling?

I feel my heart is stuck up in my neck, as I'm falling. I thud and splash into something below. The pain is too sharp. I feel nothing. The words I try to speak don't come out, and my eyelids drape against my will.

Fuck.

Ryan told me to avoid the fissure in the ground. I didn't, and now I'm gone.

Chapter 102

"Now, is there a light at the end of this story?" Floyd said

"Depends how you look at it?" She checked her watch again. "Actually there is great light and optimism in the end." She smiles for some reason.

"I doubt it."

She tapped her watch. "Hmm. Time will tell very soon, but let me tell you the rest first."

"There is still more?"

"Ashlyn got pregnant."

"This story only gets darker."

"Bear with me," she said. "Major Red was going to send her to the Furnace."

"Apparently, he didn't."

"That's because a fourteen-year old girl had a plan."

"What plan?"

"To tell the truth to the world, but she didn't know how or when she could escape, so she had to wait."

"How wasn't she sent to the Furnace? Abortion?"

"Major Red didn't abort girls he planned to send to the Furnace, but he granted Ashlyn an abortion, and kept her alive." Dr. Hope. "Ashlyn played daddy's girl, and became his favorite bitch."

Chapter 103

I wake up in the fissure to the loud blare again. It's not a dream anymore. I know because I just fell in. I think I'm starting to remember.

My legs have weakened so much I can't move them. My back is in eternal pain. My left arm hurts and reminds me of my withdrawal symptoms. I can hardly move it. My right arm is squeezed under someone's body and I can't pull it from under them.

Water surrounds me everywhere at the bottom of the fissure. The smell of oil attacks me again.

Above, the opening of the fissure shows little light from the moonlight, and a few stars. In the distance, I can hear waves crashing onto the shore.

This is so real. I wonder if all my dreams were some kind of premonition. Did I see the future beforehand?

I'm about to cry for help when I remember Major Red is out there somewhere. I shut up.

One significant difference is that no one calls me mommy. Hell, I can't reach for my stomach to feel my daughter. If I've been only a few days or so pregnant, how did Ryan know she was a girl?

When I crane my neck to look at my stomach, it sends fire down my back. All I see is a car's tire leaning against the wall. A little to the right I see another tire. This one is still rolling out of a...

I'm in a car?

Half of my body is protruding out of some car. This is why I can't quite see the fissures opening above. Most of the car's body blocks the view. How did I fall into a car?

"Let's make babies," Major Red roars outside. "I'm coming for you."

I'm stuck here, unable to move. Soon he'll climb down this fissure or shoot me from above. I need to find a way out. A drop of water splashes on my face from high above. It smells like shit. It's not water. It's Major Red's sweat.

Chapter 104

Mercy Medical Center, New York

"Gosh." Floyd said. "She was only fourteen."

"She tolerated the addiction, the rape, and seduced Major Red to be his favorite girl, while planning her escape."

"How did she tolerate the..."

"This is when we come to the crux of my believing in miracles and hope."

"How so?"

"Soldiers used to honk the cars in the garage when Major Red had his fun. In a small forsaken town, they were celebrating in a ritualistic way."

"I'm not following you here."

"The honk sounded like a toot to her. That, and Major Red offering her toots of cocaine, she used the loud blare to block her memory every time she was raped. It's as if he used the sound of the car's honk as hypnosis."

"That's the strangest thing I have ever heard. She blocked her mind with the *toot*, and that helped her forget she's been abused over and over again. This doesn't make any fucking sense."

"Not forget," Dr. Hope said. "She used the sound, and the fact that she was high, to live in another fantasy and tell herself stories."

Floyd said nothing.

"That's what she wrote in her book," Dr. Hope said. "Ashlyn wrote tons of stories in her mind to keep her occupied. It didn't matter whether they were beautiful or dark stories. What mattered was that..."

"She kept her mind alert enough to survive," Floyd nodded. "Just like Joan Murray and Juliane Koepcke did," he sat down, watching August, and almost talking to himself. "Instead of feeling the darkness and hopelessness in her brain, she lied to it by making up stories."

Dr. Hope didn't expect him to understand. "I've once read that creativity only comes from pain," she elaborated. "Some artist's work is so touching because it's a result of them escaping a trauma. Call it a defense mechanism. Call it whatever you want. It helped her survive three years before she finally escaped."

"So she did escape." Floyd smiled.

"Yes, though none of the authorities believed her since Manfred had left town and burned most of the evidence."

"The fucker is still alive?" Floyd imagined catching him already.

"Who knows. Manfred Toot is a myth to the police. They've never caught him, and no one knew where he, or his men, went."

"She ended up writing this book, using stories of survival of women she admired, plus her own hell of a story in the end," Floyd said. "That's why it's called the last girl. The third story."

"Or the last girl who made it out of the Furnace," Dr. Hope said. "Like I said, no one believed the story, so much that the publishers preferred to keep it vague, whether it was true or fiction."

Floyd held his wife's hand closer. "I wonder what Ashlyn Ward told you, darling," he told her. "What did you two talk about?"

"I wouldn't address her as Ashlyn Ward when talking to August." Dr. Hope said.

Floyd squinted. "What do you mean? I remember August telling me she met Ashlyn Ward, the author. I actually remember clearly now."

"That's because she must have not wanted to expose Ashlyn's real name?"

"Ashlyn's real name?"

"Last year Ashlyn confessed her true identity on a TV show," Dr. Hope said. "She explained the reason why she used a pen name as an author. It's also called a pseudonym. Many authors do it."

Floyd picked up the book again. He looked at Ashlyn's face on the back cover. "That's not her, then?"

"It *is* her," Dr. Hope. "Though she now dyes her hair black and wears piercings and has a lot of tattoos that are not showing in the picture."

"I'm a bit confused here. Why did she use Ashlyn as a pen name then? Was she afraid Major Red would find her?"

"Major Red disappeared years ago, remember?"

"Then why use the name Ashlyn Ward."

"Because Ashlyn Ward is her sister," she said.

"What happened to her sister?"

"Major Red burned her in the Furnace. That's why she used her sister's name as her author name. An epitaph, if you like. Out of respect and love, and to immortalize her sister's short-lived life. She was," Dr. Hope swallowed hard. "Four years old."

"Fuck me," Floyd said. "Then what is the author's real name?"

"Brooklyn," Dr. Hope said. "She is known as Brooklyn Ward. Mostly known as Brook Ward"

Chapter 105

"Brooklyn!" Major Red calls from outside. This time I know why he uses the name. My real name. I am Brooklyn Ward.

Tears roll down my eyes, remembering my dead sister. Remembering my dark past, and what happened in my little town. Flashes of memories attack me one after the other. How I wish I'd never remembered.

"What are you trying to do, Brooklyn?" Major Red stands by the edge of the fissure. "You will never make it."

"I will not give you what you want." I say.

"I've had it once. I will have it again." He is climbing down.

All my effort to free myself is in vain. My left arm and legs aren't helping. I have one last hope. To free my other arm from under the corpse next to me. Who the hell is it?

I force my neck to twist. I think it cracks. I feel like choking, but I have to. The corpse is partially inside the car. I realize half of my body is outside because the door is broken. I must have had some kind of accident. I can't remember this part. It puzzles me how this is related to the plane crash.

Pulling my arm only increases the pain. I think I have to push instead of pull the corpse. If it only rolls over a bit, I can free myself.

Since I've twisted my neck, I want to see who it is next to me.

"Don't look west, darling," Major Red mocks me on his way down.

I crane my neck a little more. Intolerable pain almost puts me back to sleep. My body is in internal flames. I feel like I'm going to combust from inside out. But I manage to see the person next to me.

"Are you sure you want to look west?"

Then I see who is next me. A man. He is dead. The sight of him forces me into a loud cry.

I can't believe I'm looking at Ryan.

Pray for me.

I remember now. Ryan is my husband. Sergeant Ryan. The love of my life. What is his last name? Of course...

His name is Ryan West.

Chapter 106

Somewhere on the island

"Irene!" Jack called for his future wife, as he reached the shores of the island.

He took off his mask and the oxygen tank. He coughed a few times while resting on all fours. The island was too dark. He couldn't locate Irene anywhere. All he could hear was a loud siren-like sound in the distance.

He should have accompanied her earlier, but he was also glad he didn't, because he'd discovered something, diving before he arrived.

"Irene," he called out to the night. "There is no girl on the island."

Irene didn't respond.

"Trust me. I know."

Jack saw Irene's oxygen tank at the bottom of a hill leading deeper into the island. He wondered if she'd be near the faint sound in the distance.

"Irene," he called once more. "Please come back."

Irene still didn't reply. He worried something happened to her. This place oozed with creepiness.

“Listen,” he said. “She’s not there.” Jack began walking. “I’ve found her. I found her corpse on my dive minutes ago. The last girl is dead. No one made it out alive.”

Chapter 107

Mercy Medical Center, New York

Floyd patted his wife while Dr. Hope checked her watch again.

"The person you wanted to meet. They've not arrived?" He said.

"Actually I'm waiting for Brooklyn Ward." Dr. Hope said.

"Really? Why didn't you tell me?"

"I wanted it to be a surprise."

"How so?"

"You will understand once she arrives," Dr. Hope smiled. "It's the optimistic part of the story you've been asking about."

"Is she coming to see August?"

"I wish, but she doesn't know August is here."

"So she's here to meet you?"

A nurse burst into the room suddenly, "Dr, Hope," she panted. "There's been an accident."

"What accident?"

The nurse caught her breath and said, "You have to come to Ward Nine."

Chapter 108

"Get away from me!" I spit out words mixed with mucus and blood.

Major Red is still climbing down. His big frame blocking the light from above. A swarm of memories attack me. My childhood. My town. My sister. The rapes. Over and over again.

I remember the escape. I remember the price I paid for three years to make it out of this town. Damaged with PTSD and insomnia. I could not be with a man for years after. I had jobs like nursing and caring for dying people in hospices. I waited tables when jobs weren't available. I lived and ate alone. I couldn't even get a pet, fearing I'd disappoint it like I disappointed my sister. The worst part was my addiction. I stopped many times. Returned more times than I stopped.

At some point I could not pay the rent, and was offered a job as a prostitute. I'm not going to lie. I did it for a week. To my shame, I didn't stop because I hated it. Sex meant nothing to me anymore. I left the job because I couldn't let other men have me while I was playing fantasies in my mind anymore. Not because I'd lost the talent to escape the harsh reality into a made-up story in my mind. I couldn't do it because there was no *toot*. I couldn't do it without the honk of the car. My psychiatrist called it an anchor. The sound or word or circumstance associated with a certain act to recall a memory or a feeling.

"June," Major Red drools on his way down. "Come to daddy."

A few years later, I met Ryan. He was younger than me. He'd been molested as a child and had a calm demeanor about him. He didn't want sex. He wanted to be loved. More even, he wanted someone he could love and take care of. I fell in love with him.

Ryan helped me turn my crackhead stories into books. I uploaded them online. Dark books that people resonated with. I never told them about my past, but it showed through in my writing. Finally, I made a living, not by selling books, but by sharing my pain with thousands of people in pain.

"Here I come, little bitch," Major Red is so close. I can see his face. The diagonal cut I'd given him once when I was fourteen. That was before I became his little bitch.

Ryan was deployed most of the time. That was a bonus. As much as I loved him, as much as I needed him, I was hard to live with. The time spent away helped me. I needed my space, though that was usually when I sank into the cocaine world again. That's when Ryan had to help me pick up the ashes all over again.

He'd been with me since I was twenty-one. Had I not made money from my pain I sold online, I'd have not survived financially.

Ryan wanted a child. He always did. We still didn't have sex. I couldn't do it. Guilt of having aborted a child in my youth haunted me. How could I have a child? What kind of mother was I going to be? What was I going to tell my child about my past?

That's when I started dying my hair, wearing piercings, and getting more tattoos. I was under the impression that Brooklyn Ward had to die. And to resurrect her, I adopted the identity of my lovely sister. I wrote under the Pen name Ashlyn Ward, the girl who'd never been, and could have been so much.

Major Red's heavy boots splash onto the ground. He is standing right before me. "I'll get what I want now," he smirked.

I can't move, chained in every way possible. I stare at him, wanting to beg him to not hurt my child. Especially now that I remember it's not his. It's Ryan's. At some point, I finally had the guts to do it and bring a child into the world.

Only we seem to have had an accident.

Major Red kneels down to touch me, and I spit out all the curses I know at him. I'm hysterical. Going mad. I just remembered the rest. Ryan was driving. He insisted he would, as I was not in a position to do so. I remember where we were going.

Chapter 109

Somewhere on the island

Jack heard Irene call for him. She seemed to have been calling for a while, but he couldn't hear her because of the loud siren.

"I'm here!" She called. "Come here. You have to see this."

Jack climbed up the hill. "Did you hear what I just told you. I found the last girl underwater. She is dead."

"It doesn't matter," Irene shouted back. "Just come over."

Jack saw her stand a few feet up, staring downward. He climbed further and she reached out for him.

"I think you didn't hear me," he said. "There is no last girl."

"Really?" She wasn't looking at him, but downward.

"I'm sorry, baby. She didn't make it. I saw her underwater. You were right about her drifting that far."

"That's okay!" She knelt down, looking at something.

"There is no one to save, baby." He stepped up and saw she stood at the edge of a huge fissure in the ground. He could not believe what he was looking at, though he now realized the source of the loud blare.

"Can you see it?" She said.

"What the—" he shouted. "Yes, I can."

"She needs help."

“Of course,” Jack said. “Let’s climb down.”

Chapter 110

Mercy Medical Center, New York

"Ward Nine?" Dr. Hope asked the nurse. "That's not my ward. That's the emergency room."

"We'll be needing you. I was told to get all the help I can."

"What's going on?"

"Brooklyn Ward," the nurse said.

Floyd almost flinched, holding August's hand. Did she just spasm a little? He didn't want to think what August just did was real, and continued listening to the conversation.

"What about her?" Dr. Hope said. "Did she arrive? Wait. What does she have to do with the emergency room?"

"She hasn't arrived, but we're preparing for her arrival," the nurse said. "She had an accident."

Floyd could not dismiss the twitching in August's hand now. What was going on?

"Accident?" Dr. Hope tensed.

"She and her husband were driving to the hospital when their car's axel broke."

"And?" Dr. Hope held her hands up.

"They fell into a fissure," the nurse said. "Right by the road leading out of Suffolk County."

“Suffolk County?” Floyd said, gripping his wife’s hand as hard as he could. “That’s right here.”

“She was coming to check in,” Dr. Hope explained.

“Check in?” Floyd said. “In Ward Four? Neurology?”

“No,” the nurse answered him. “Ward Six. Gynecology. We call it the Crib.”

Suddenly, August’s twitches turned into spasms.

“Baby,” Floyd shrieked. “What’s wrong?”

“Let me see,” Dr. Hope rushed to the bed.

August spasmed as if electricity ran through her body. Floyd stood helpless, “What’s wrong? What’s happening to her?”

Chapter 111

Fissure, Suffolk Country, Long Island

"Is she alive?" Jack said, climbing down after Irene who'd already jumped her way down.

"She is," Irene said. "The man next to her is dead."

Jack made it down. He knelt next to Irene. "What the hell happened here?"

"A car accident," Irene said. "They fell in the fissure for some reason."

"Was she drunk?" Jack said, looking upward. "Could the plane crash have something to do with it? Maybe it flew too low before crashing and the driver panicked."

"It's possible, but look," Irene said, pointing at the track marks on the woman's arm.

"Shit," Jack said. "She looks like she had a recent injection." He pointed at a needle nearby.

"I don't know," Irene said. "All I know is that we're here for a reason."

"Reason?"

"Think of it? We're looking for a last girl and find this woman. We have to save her."

"Okay, baby. I'll go get help." Jack said, about to climb up again, but stopped at Irene's tense grip. "What?"

Irene pointed at Brooklyn's stomach. "We don't have time."

Jack squinted in the dark. "Is she pregnant?"

The woman snapped, opening her eyes and crying in tears. "Get away from me!"

"It's all right. I can help," Irene tried to touch her face.

The woman spat back. "Get away from my child!"

"It's okay," Irene said again. "I can help. Trust me, I can help."

"Help with what, Irene?" Jack said.

"We have to deliver this baby, Jack," Irene said. "We have to."

"I'm not sure, Irene. Let me get help."

"There is no time. This is destiny. I'm here to do this. We're here to save lives. My father would have done the same."

Jack glanced back at the panicking woman. "I doubt we can save hers," he remarked.

"Even so," Irene said, sliding out of her diving suit. "This woman has been brave enough to hang on, trying to bring this baby into the world. I can't imagine how long she's been struggling down here. How long has she battled death to stay alive? She knows she could die, but the baby will not," she turns to face her. "*Breathe, just breathe.*"

Chapter 112

Somewhere in the Atlantic Ocean

Dixon was smoking a cigarette, happy this whole mess was over. He was finally going home.

"So you're going to see your children?" The pilot asked.

"Nah," Dixon took a drag. "I'll go have a few beers with the boys."

The pilot frowned. "I thought this was all about going home and seeing the ones you loved."

"You're too young to understand. I do love my children and want to see them. But they hate me. I never feel myself when I'm with them. Let's go get that beer first. What about you?"

"I will go see my children, sir."

"Sure you're not in for a beer?"

"Not now, sir."

"Don't you want to celebrate this moment. We've just fooled the system," he elbowed him playfully.

"I'm happy with going home. You go have your beer."

"Shit!" Dixon growled suddenly. The chopper shook violently in midair. "What was that?"

"Hang on, sir," the pilot didn't look like he was in control.

"What the hell is going on?"

The pilot pushed a few buttons then his face went pale.

"What?" Dixon demanded, holding onto his seat's edge.

"I fucked up, sir," the pilot said. "I guess I miss-calculated the coordinates."

"Co-ordinates?"

"We're flying right into some dangerous weather conditions. I should have taken another route—"

There wasn't much more to say. The chopper took a dip sideways. Dixon knew he wasn't going to get that beer.

Chapter 113

Mercy Medical Center, New York

Dr. Hope called for help. The nurses held August by the arms to keep her from spasming.

"What's happening to her?" Floyd demanded.

"She is in shock, I guess." A nurse said.

"How so when she can't feel..." Floyd stopped his own words mid-sentence. He realized that August *did* feel. Did she hear their conversation? If so, why is she spasming now? "Dr. Hope, please answer me."

"I think..." she said while helping the nurses. "I think there is a chance we might lose her."

Chapter 114

The young girl and her friend are helping me give birth. There is no sign of Major Red nearby. I can't feel anything. I can't even crane my neck to look. If I should feel pain down there, I don't. I'm numb to my body and senses. All I have is my mind. That powerful engine that kept me alive all this time.

Though I can't tell what was true and what wasn't, I know I made up most of it, connecting stories to real life facts. My mind generated a story, accompanied by the honk of the car produced by Ryan's hand bound to the wheel. He'd cut a piece of his shirt before dying and wrapped around his hand to guarantee it keeps pressing the horn. He knew me more than I knew myself. He knew I needed the anchor.

"Hold on!" The girl tells me. I think her name is Irene. Such a brave soul. "Your baby is on the way."

I want to smile but have no facial strength to do it. Smiling with my eyes doesn't work either, not with all the blood on my eyelids. I smile with my heart. With my mind. With that nameless power inside me that defies the rules of the world we live in.

"We're almost done," Irene says. "But I need your help. Push with me."

Whether I'm pushing or not, I have no idea. I tell my mind to push and help my baby come out, but I have no evidence of it happening. It makes sense that I'd die after giving birth. I'm in such a low place. All I want is for my daughter to arrive.

"That's better!" Irene says.

The memory of my escape when I was seventeen comes back to me. I can't quite remember what happened to Major Red and his son. I only remember running with a jar in my hand, escaping this God forsaken, nameless town. The jar had Ashlyn's ashes in it. I had picked them up from the Furnace.

"Push!"

All I want is my daughter to come into this world. All I want is that she gets a chance I never had. None of the girls in the Furnace had. This has to work. Ryan sacrificed himself for her. I did my best. And the universe sends those two people. This should work.

My head feels so heavy, but then I hear the sweetest cry I've heard in my life.

"There she is," Irene greeted me. "You've made it!"

Though I can't feel physical happiness, it doesn't matter. I've done it. I am ready to go. It's been a struggle, this life. I think I've done good.

Irene asks me an important question, "Do you have a name for your daughter?"

Chapter 115

Mercy Medical Center, New York

Floyd stood back, watching his wife wither away. All this talk about people coming back from comas wasn't going to help now. If he just knew what pissed his wife off so much?

"I need you to come closer," Dr. Hope said.

Floyd did, almost hypnotized.

"Hold her hand," Dr. Hope said. "This isn't science by a stretch. As a doctor I have nothing to offer her. Hold her hand, Floyd."

Floyd sat next to August and did as he was told. August began to calm down. He looked back in awe at Dr. Hope. "But I was holding her hand before."

"I know," Dr. Hope said. "I have no explanation, but look," she pointed at August.

Floyd saw a slight hint of a smile on August's face. He wasn't sure though. "Is she smiling?"

"I'm not sure," Dr. Hope said. "But that's not what I'm pointing at."

Floyd looked again. It wasn't August's face, but her forefinger. It was pointing somewhere.

"She is pointing to the book," Dr. Hope said.

Floyd rushed to pick it up again, flipping frantically through the pages.

"What are you looking for?" Dr. Hope said.

"I have no idea," Floyd said. "But there must be something. Maybe Ashlyn's signature? Maybe a dedication."

"So?"

Floyd found nothing. He looked disappointed. August began spasming again.

"Check out this page," Dr. Hope pointed to a dog-eared page. The only dog-eared page in the book.

Floyd flipped to it, and opened it. There was a scribbling in blue ink at the top of the page.

He read, "January, February, May, June, or August."

"What does it mean?" Dr. Hope asked.

Chapter 116

Irene's question reminds me of an old woman I met every year. A big fan of my work. Time and time again, I felt she was a mother to me. She couldn't have children, and convinced me to have one of my own, explaining how lost she felt without experiencing motherhood. Next to Ryan, year after year, she'd managed to persuade me.

"What do you want to call her?" Irene laughs with tears in her eyes, holding my daughter in her arms.

It's sad that I can't hold my own daughter, now that none of my limbs are functioning. She is so beautiful. She brings hope to the darkness we're in.

"Do you want me to choose a name for you?" Irene says.

"No," I manage to say.

I remember the woman, my biggest fan. Her name was August. I wanted to call my daughter Ashlyn, but she suggested I name her after her: August. She laughingly claimed girls named after months were the strongest of all. I said I can't give my daughter the same name, as I intended to keep August in my life for a long time

"That's okay," she'd said. "Still, you can choose: *January, February, May, June, or August.*" She winked.

I remember now. I'd chosen one of them. The month I was going to give birth to her. The month with the most sunlight. Ryan had a necklace made with her name. I've been wearing it for seven months.

I crane my neck as much as I can and take one last look at my daughter. Things come full circle. I tell Irene, "June."

Epilogue

Chapter 117

Six Years Later

The lecture is full of students, young authors and critics. I stand with the blackboard behind me, giving my seminar as a multiple New York Times bestselling author. Everyone is nice and acts as if listening. In truth they're watching me, thinking about my black hair, piercings and tattoos under a neat business woman's dress.

They're thinking about daddy's girl.

This isn't my first lecture in the past six years. It's almost the fiftieth. I'm used to the looks, to the skepticism, to the confusion in my audience's eyes.

Some never consider it a true story. They think it has to be part fiction. Life is neither so brutal nor do people overcome such adversities. What kind of fourteen-year-old girl submits to becoming a daddy's girl to survive and eventually escape? Is it even possible to tolerate the shit I've been through?

The FBI never backed up my story. They admitted the occurrences of some rape events, and evidence of the existence of a furnace in my small, nameless town—it's not even on the map, as are a few towns in America. They've also found substantial evidence for baby killings. Still, they never admitted my story for lack of conclusive evidence.

The only man working on it until this day is James Madison Floyd.

Other members of the audience have another theory about me. It shows in their looks when they size me up from top to bottom. They're not looking at me as Brooklyn Ward. They're looking at the teenage bitch. Well, now the thirty-four-year-old bitch who sold her pussy's story for a mere seven million dollars advance payment for her book—and movie rights in the making.

I imagine they're thinking about the multiple men raping me, wondering if I liked it. They're not here to applause or listen. They're here to judge. It makes them feel better about their lives.

As for the few FBI members other than Floyd, they're here looking for evidence. Though not admitting to the truth of my story, they're investigating the disappearance of Manfred Schmidt and his son.

The irony.

In the end, I address those who have the capacity to believe, or hope—and certainly forgive. I tell them about the power of our brain, the power of imagination and to tell stories. Why we tell stories, and why we love them.

I tell them about our unique weapon only humans possess: imagination. It may not be the best of weapons, as it can lead to delusion sometimes. But if done right, it can save our lives. Stories can save our lives. It's said that it's imagination that helped us humans to surpass Neanderthals, apes, and every other species.

In the past few years, I had the honor of helping so many girls who had stories no one wanted to listen to, or even consider. Those are the ones who make my life the most meaningful.

Of course, my number one reason for living is the girl climbing down the stairs of the lecture hall, running into my arms, calling me 'Mommy!'

Chapter 118

June West, my daughter, is a blondie. She has Ashlyn's eyes and Ryan's hair and smile. But deep inside she is a six-year-old tough cookie like her mother.

"Where are we going now?" She asks, sitting in the passenger seat next to me.

"We're off to meet aunt Ashlyn," I say, turning the wheel.

"Ash!" She pronounces proudly. "I didn't bring her gifts this time."

"She'll be happy to hear from you. That's what matters."

"She will be surprised to know I decided to become a pilot."

"Is that so?" I raise an eyebrow.

"I saw this plane in the sky today, and remembered the story you told me about when I was born, mommy."

I had told her how I'm a hell of a good writer. How stories helped me survive. How my mind reeled, connecting unrelated incidents into semi-coherent plots, like when I saw the plane crash in the Atlantic, moments before Ryan lost control of the wheel the day she was born.

"Pilots can fly like birds," June says.

"You want to be a bird, you little monkey?" I tickle her, driving with my left arm.

She giggles and laughs, reminding me of the four-year-old Ashlyn. "And I want tattoos like yours, mommy."

I'm not sure what to say. My left arm is covered in tattoos now. A feeble attempt to overwrite my past and hide the needle marks. It's better not to encourage her, not at this age. On the bright side, my tattoos are meaningful. I had an artist write the names of the two hundred and thirty passengers on my left arm. In memorial and respect for the deceased on the plane.

I wish I could remember the names of the girls from my childhood, but I seem to have blocked this part of my memory into a grave in my skull.

I stop the car. We've arrived.

In the cemetery we pay our respects to aunt Ashlyn Ward. I've buried her ashes inside an urn that I had placed in a coffin. Ashlyn deserves to be remembered, not just as my pen name author, but as a human being. It's also nice to see June pray on her knees with laced hands. She seems so serious about it.

I wait as she tells Aunt Ashlyn about her flying plans and tattoos. June claims she can hear Ashlyn talk back to her. I never comment or ask about the things Ashlyn tells her. I'd like to think it's true, not that my daughter has an imaginary friend who is her aunt. Besides, if I know what Ashlyn tells June, I think I will break down in tears.

Chapter 119

Back at home, we wave at our Argentinian neighbor, Adriana. Pregnant with her fourth girl, she never ceases to get enough of children. I met her years ago in a clinic. We both battled addiction.

In the evening, June and I are preparing dinner in the kitchen. I live in a big upscale house in Manhattan. Not that I like it, but when you have a child, you want the best for them. More than the best. Besides, I imagine there is little chance she'd face the shit I have where we live now.

I've never tried to marry and don't think I will. I'm not comfortable with having sex, still. I experienced it a few times with Ryan. It was different from what I've experienced in the past, but I will always remember Ryan's gentle thrusts. He was so shy.

We don't go visit Ryan's grave in a cemetery. He'd always told me he'd prefer being remembered inside the house, so he is basically living with us. Right now June is preparing his plate for dinner. It's a bit strange but she likes it.

"Who's coming for dinner?" She asks.

"A lot of friends," I say.

"Do I know them?"

"Some."

The doorbell rings. She runs toward it and pulls the heavy door with all her might.

"Uncle Jack!" She squeals.

Jack and Irene enter the house, but without their three-year-old. They'd probably left her with Irene's grandmother. They'd taken some time to have children, since Irene wanted to save more lives before she became a mother.

"Did you kiss your mom on the cheek today?" Irene asks June. "She's been through a lot to bring you into this world."

I smile and hug Jack, then squeeze Irene in my arms.

"Irene is the one who helped bring you into this world, little princess." I tell June.

"Again?" She rolls her eyes. "I've heard this story a thousand times. I'm hungry. Let's eat."

"Not before our last guests arrive."

Chapter 120

Until our next guests arrive, I leave June with Irene and Jack and climb up the stairs to my private bathroom. Inside I look in the mirror and massage my forehead. I take a deep breath then open a drawer with a secret key. Looking at the substances inside, I feel a bit guilty.

Just like every time.

I set things up and snort a line of coke.

Surprised?

I've tried to stop for years, but couldn't. It's this or I go crazy. June needs me. It's my dirty little secret. My vice. My PTSD boogeyman. Maybe I can stop one day. I'm only using a little now. Not abusing. It's not an excuse. It's real life. A professional doctor supervises me.

I wish I could tell a better story. A hundred percent clean sheet and new start. A miracle of unchained proportions. A happily ever after with no stains from the past.

But I'd be lying.

It's possible to rise back from the ashes against all the odds in the world, but not without some burns and scars here and there. Those burns make us who we are.

How else can I forget killing Manfred Toot and his son, Hecker. Not in my made-up story that kept me alive and awake, but in real life, twenty years ago.

I hadn't looked into the eyes of darkness for three years to only escape in the end. I had to avenge Ashlyn. And boy, I did it. With a mirror's shard across Manfred's face before I shot Hecker in the balls with his father's silver gun. I'd killed Dr. Suffolk, who'd kept their secret and participated occasionally, earlier that day. I sedated him and injected him with cocaine until he overdosed.

Then I pushed the semi-blinded Manfred into the Furnace in the back of my mother's garage.

It wasn't Major Red who'd burned the town to the ground. It was me. The perfect crime. The perfect justice.

In fact, I burned them all in the Furnace. Three years of torture were long enough to study their ticks and weaknesses. They were busy raping me and the girls. I was busy killing them.

The doorbell rings again. I wipe under my nose. A smile forms on my face.

Chapter 121

Climbing down, Irene is wide-eyed, staring at me. "When did this happen?" She points at my guests.

June and Jack welcome them.

Irene is still smiling, so much that tears trickle down her face. I pat her then go to meet my guests.

James Madison Floyd is tall enough not to be missed. He stands behind a wheelchair where August sits. She had awoken a few weeks ago, arguably after Floyd read to her every day for six years. I've never seen someone as happy as him today.

I kneel down in front of her and kiss her hand. Her speech hasn't been good. She hands me a paper with a few words: June & August.

I hold back the tears and give way to June. August reaches out to hug her. June never met her before, but for some reason she broadly smiles and buries herself in August's arms.

Later that night, we gather around the dining table, eating. There is nothing better than the good company of friends. It has taken me years to find them. A few, not many are all I need, preferably with something in common. Be it catastrophe or hope. It doesn't matter. What matters is the helping hand that pats the wound, not necessarily heals it. The sweet mouths that entertain with a story, not necessarily true. All the things that keep me going forward and never looking back.

We're laughing at the table.

When I look at Jack, Irene, Floyd, & August, I realize that each of us has their own version of *Toot*, the bogeyman in the closet, the demon from the past. We beat him, one way or the other. It doesn't mean he is not coming back, but hey, next time we'll be even stronger.

THE END

Read on for a preview for Thirteen Years of Snow, my upcoming next psychological thriller.

Afterword

A big, heartfelt thank you for choosing to read my book.

Joan Murray, Juliane Koepcke, Vesna Vulovic, & Poon Lim are real people. Some dates and events have been altered to fit the storyline. Their stories come across as unbelievable, but they're a hundred percent true, and tremendously admired and inspiring.

If you enjoyed The Last Girl, please take a moment to leave me a four or five-star review; I would be very grateful. It doesn't need to be more than a couple of words, and it makes a huge difference.

This is your link: http://bit.ly/LGirlReview

Also join my mailing list to receive special offers, exclusive bonus content, and news about upcoming new releases. OR if you are interested in reading samples from my next novel **Thirteen Years of Snow.**

About the Author

My name is Nick Twist. I'm an ordinary guy next door who loves to write. I have written a few fantasy bestsellers under the name Cameron Jace. I have an insatiable interest in the origins of folktales and urban legends, not as fantasy but as real life facts. Then when I've recently became interested in psychology, I've realized what my real interest is: childhood. Be it a thriller or a fantasy, usually based on real facts, I want to visit my protagonist's childhood or adolescence and see how much it shaped the adult they have become.

The Last Girl is my first attempt into writing thrillers. I hope I did well and that you enjoyed it. Brook Ward is a dear character to me. You and I may not have not met in real life but hey we met in the pages of this book.

If you'd like to write to me, please use the following email:

camjace@hotmail.com

Or one of the social networks below (you will find them listed under Cameron Jace.) Just click the link.

COPYRIGHT

This is a work of fiction. Names, characters, organizations, places, events, and incidents are either products of the author's imagination or are used fictitiously. Any resemblance to actual persons, living or dead, or actual events is purely coincidental.